Dead S

"Another wild adventure . . . Check out the highly entertaining *Dead Sexy* for a walk on the wild side."
—*Romance Reviews Today*

"The second Garnet gem is a delightful whodunit fantasy [with an] offbeat chick-lit style. Tate Hallaway combines romance, paranormal, and mystery into a fun read."
—*Midwest Book Review*

Tall, Dark & Dead

"What's not to adore . . . Tate Hallaway has a wonderful gift, Garnet is a gem of a heroine, and *Tall, Dark & Dead* is enthralling from the first page."
—MaryJanice Davidson,
New York Times bestselling author of *Dead Over Heels*

"Tate Hallaway kept me on the edge of my seat . . . A thoroughly enjoyable read!"
—Julie Kenner, *USA Today*
bestselling author of *Good Ghouls Do*

"Curl up on the couch and settle in—*Tall, Dark & Dead* is a great way to pass an evening."
—Lynsay Sands,
USA Today bestselling author of *Vampire, Interrupted*

"Will appeal to readers of Charlaine Harris's Sookie Stackhouse series."
—*Booklist*

"I'm looking forward to more from this author."
—SFRevu.com

continued...

"Unique, intriguing, and a sexy read . . . lively and fresh . . . and the ending will leave you clamoring for more."
—*Midwest Muse*

"Funny and captivating . . . in the style of the Sookie Stackhouse series [with] an intrepid and expressive heroine . . . Look out, fans of the paranormal, there's a new supernatural heroine in town sure to become an instant favorite . . . Tate Hallaway is an author to watch!"
—*Romance Reviews Today*

"I love how Garnet handled everything that came her way with grit, humor, and attitude as she kicked some serious butt! . . . Hallaway keeps you glued to the pages."
—*Romance Junkies*

"[Hallaway's] concise writing style, vivid descriptions, and innovative plot all blend together to provide the reader with a great new look into the love life of Witches, vampires, and the undead." —ArmchairInterviews.com

Titles by Tate Hallaway

Romancing the Dead

TATE HALLAWAY

BERKLEY BOOKS, NEW YORK

THE BERKLEY PUBLISHING GROUP
Published by the Penguin Group
Penguin Group (USA) Inc.
375 Hudson Street, New York, New York 10014, USA
Penguin Group (Canada), 90 Eglinton Avenue East, Suite 700, Toronto, Ontario M4P 2Y3, Canada
(a division of Pearson Penguin Canada Inc.)
Penguin Books Ltd., 80 Strand, London WC2R 0RL, England
Penguin Group Ireland, 25 St. Stephen's Green, Dublin 2, Ireland (a division of Penguin Books Ltd.)
Penguin Group (Australia), 250 Camberwell Road, Camberwell, Victoria 3124, Australia
(a division of Pearson Australia Group Pty. Ltd.)
Penguin Books India Pvt. Ltd., 11 Community Centre, Panchsheel Park, New Delhi—110 017, India
Penguin Group (NZ), 67 Apollo Drive, Rosedale, North Shore 0632, New Zealand
(a division of Pearson New Zealand Ltd.)
Penguin Books (South Africa) (Pty.) Ltd., 24 Sturdee Avenue, Rosebank, Johannesburg 2196,
South Africa

Penguin Books Ltd., Registered Offices: 80 Strand, London WC2R 0RL, England

This book is an original publication of The Berkley Publishing Group.

Copyright © 2008 by Lyda Morehouse.
Cover design by Monica Benalcazar.
Interior text design by Kristin del Rosario.

PRINTING HISTORY
Berkley trade paperback edition / May 2008

Library of Congress Cataloging-in-Publication Data

Hallaway, Tate.
    Romancing the dead / Tate Hallaway.—Berkley trade pbk. ed.
      p. cm.
    ISBN 978-0-425-22133-4
    1. Witches—Fiction. 2. Vampires—Fiction. 3. Goddesses—Fiction. 4. Booksellers and book-selling—Fiction. I. Title.

PS3608.A54825R66 2008
813'.6—dc22

                    2007046040

PRINTED IN THE UNITED STATES OF AMERICA

10 9 8 7 6 5 4 3 2 1

For Shawn,
twenty-two years together and still going strong

Acknowledgments

As always I must thank those who believe in what I do and continue to support it. A big thanks goes to Anne Sowards, my insightful editor, who always knows better, even when I initially doubt her, and Martha Millard, my agent, the best advocate a writer could hope for. Also, my writers' group, Wyrdsmiths, deserves my deepest gratitude for, well, putting up with me (and my diva tendencies) and their guidance and support throughout the novel-writing process: Eleanor Arnason, Bill Henry, Doug Hulick, Naomi Kritzer, Kelly McCullough, Rosalind Nelson, and the ever fabulous Sean M. Murphy—extra special thanks to Naomi and Sean for reading the beta version of this book in the midnight hour. Shawn and Mason Rounds also get my love and appreciation for understanding that ima's job is, in point of fact, writing.

1.

Sun

❦

**The masculine principle, husband,
or men in general**

Could I really see myself married to a...vampire?

The diamond ring on my finger sparkled in the early morning light. My bicycle nearly ended up in the ditch more than once as my eyes kept straying to the golden band. Married? Me?

It wasn't that I didn't love Sebastian. It had been easy to say yes, and I'd meant it. But Sebastian *was* a vampire, and, well, neither of our lives was terribly conducive to marriage. I had a tendency to pick up and run in the middle of the night, although usually that was because I was being chased by Vatican assassins or the FBI or Voodoo Queens or because the Goddess I harbored in my belly had gone all destructo-wacko on somebody.

Things had been calm for a few months now. In fact, I'd started negotiations with the owner of the occult bookstore I manage, Mercury Crossing, to buy him out with whatever loans and spare change I could patch together. I guess that must have gotten Sebastian thinking about settling. Settling!

Did I mention he's a vampire?

My mind continued to try to wrap itself around the idea of the white dress when some kind of wild dog jumped out of the ditch. Okay, actually, it was just sitting there on the side of the road, munching on the road-killed remains of Bambi's mom, but seeing it made me nearly fall off the seat of my bike.

At first I thought it had to be a wolf, except the animal was too mangy and too leggy. As it hunched over the deer carcass, its chin dripped with blood. Our eyes met and I had that freakish feeling of a keen intelligence behind the glittering alien, inhuman gaze.

So I did what any Witch who harbored the dark Goddess Lilith within her would do; I shrieked like a girl.

"Argh! Go away, you big, scary thing! Run! Scat!" I pedaled like a maniac, waved my arms, and tried to think bigger, threatening animal thoughts, instead of I-could-totally-be-eaten ones.

The wolf, or whatever it was, cocked its head at me as though it thought I was the biggest dork in central Wisconsin. Then it padded into the cornfield.

At least my close encounter with the wild kingdom got me thinking about something other than Sebastian for at least two or three minutes. But once my heart rate had settled to normal, it shot back up again.

Are there wolves in Wisconsin? Maybe, but was I really ready for marriage?

* * *

The sun beat down on the concrete mercilessly, and it wasn't even eight a.m. yet. Sweat slicked my arms and my legs. Hopping off my bike, I leaned it against the cast-iron fencing around a scrub oak, not bothering to lock it.

I'm sure there are plenty of bike thieves in Madison, Wisconsin, but State Street, where my bookstore Mercury Crossing is located, has a kind of hippy sensibility. I'd actually had my bike stolen once . . . and returned. I only knew it had been taken because the lock was broken and very carefully replaced.

Having my bike "borrowed" was one of the reasons I loved Madison. That and the fact that no one even gave me more than a cursory glance in my bright bloodred mini and black, sparkling halter top. I wore spiderweb tights and black Converse high-tops. My hair was a mess of short, dyed-black spikes. I passed a guy in a suit, maybe even a politician, on his way up to the capitol building, and he gave me "the nod" of stranger-small-town greeting.

I loved this town.

Could I see myself living here as a married woman? I chewed on my lip. I'd think about that later. Right now I had a shop to run.

"Hey," William said with a bright smile. "Raise your right hand!"

I slowly raised my hand, confused. I'd been shelving the discounted remaindered Wiccan books in the used section when William bounded up.

William had been my friend since I started work at Mercury Crossing. He'd recovered nicely from having been possessed by his former girlfriend, the Voodoo Queen. You'd think William might have considered giving up on his constant search for "true" religion, given that several of the ones he'd found jumped up and bit him in the butt. But, like our friendship, William was remarkably resilient. In fact, our friendship hardly faltered despite the fact that he had tried to kill me; and William went on to try an online UFO cult the very next day.

Speaking of which, I couldn't tell what religion William was into today; he looked fairly normal. His mouse-brown hair hung in lanky curls to his shoulders and his round John Lennon glasses perched on the end of his nose. He wore a basic brown shirt, slacks . . . I noticed the red string on his wrist. Aha! Kabala!

"Oh," William said after studying my upraised palm for a moment. "You've got your right-hand ring on the wrong finger."

"My what?"

"Right-hand ring?" William sounded less sure. "I've seen the ads in the *New York Times Magazine*. You know, treat yourself to a ring instead of waiting for a man. Oh." I watched the realization slowly dawn in William's eyes. "But you've got a . . . well, a significant other of the male variety, er, species, or former human, or ex-human. Uhm."

I thought I'd better put him out of his misery. "Yes, Sebastian asked me to marry him."

"And you said yes? Are you insane?"

It was a question I'd been asking myself. But before I could reply, he went on. "It's going to be all *Highlander*, Blossom. Think about it, in a dozen years it's going to start looking like Ashton Kutcher and Demi Moore around your place. After that? Hello, Michael Douglas and Catherine Zeta-Jones. Well, except gender reversed. You know what I mean. Anyway, yikes! When you're eighty, people are going to think he's your grandson. How awkward is that going to be?"

I should never have gotten William a subscription to *In Touch* for his birthday, yet I had to concede that he brought up a rather salient point. If Sebastian never aged and I did, how would we explain our apparent age difference to other people? Then, there was all the physical stuff. I'd have the advantage of always having a hot, young body next to me in bed, but Sebastian, well . . .

I shook my head; I didn't want to consider fifty-six years from now when we hadn't even set a date for the wedding yet. "We'll cross that bridge and all that," I said to William, who was still clucking his tongue at me.

"Yeah, sure," he said, unconvinced.

"Anyway, didn't that dude in *Highlander* love his wife forever, even when she was a hundred years old?"

William frowned as though trying to remember. He sounded disappointed to have to admit, "Yeah, I guess he did." He tapped a finger against his cheek a few times, then pointed it at me. "What about the ghouls? Are they going to be bridesmaids?"

"Come on, that's hardly fair," I said sharply. "Now you're just looking for a reason not to be happy for me, William." Truth of the matter was that I *sincerely* didn't want to think about the ghouls right now. The whole needing-other-people-for-sustenance thing was an issue Sebastian and I had yet to tackle.

"Sorry," William said curtly. "Congratulations."

I opened my mouth to say something, anything, to break

the increasingly awkward silence, when he said, "Oh, and that lady from Bear Claw Press is here."

His abrupt switch of subject startled a laugh out of me. Pretty soon William smiled too. I flashed him a fond look as I made my way to the counter where the publisher's rep waited. What did I say? Resilient. William and I were cool again.

I spent the rest of the morning listening to pitches about the newest books on aromatherapy, holistic living, and acupuncture for your pets.

The afternoon was so slow that I let William go home early. Then, wouldn't you know it? About a half hour to close everyone and their dog decided today was the day to buy candles, tarot decks, and smudge sticks. I was ringing up items and answering phone calls, while trying to direct people to the section on Rolfing.

In the middle of all this chaos, a woman came up to the counter and introduced herself as Marge. Marge had a broad, smiling face, long graying curls, and a loud Hawaiian shirt on. "I saw your poster about the open audition for the coven."

I'd warded the poster so that only people with magical talent could read it. I squinted at Marge, giving her my aura test. She had an earthy green aura, held tightly against her body, but very strong. I'd guess she was a green Witch or a kitchen Witch with that kind of energy. There was something else that caught my magical eye momentarily. A bright glow emanated from a dog-shaped charm that hung around her neck on a silver chain.

I was about to ask Marge about the necklace when business interrupted. A long line of customers formed behind Marge. "Are you buying anything?" I asked her. She smiled and shook her head.

I expected that she'd move to the side, but she didn't. Thus, I had to reach around Marge to take an amber necklace a customer offered. Marge, meanwhile, seemed completely oblivious to the fact that she was blocking the flow of paying customers. "I'm looking forward to the meeting tonight," Marge said.

"Uhm, oh yeah, me too," I said, suddenly remembering I had been hoping to slip out early myself to go grab munchies and lemonade for the meeting tonight. Sebastian and I had decided it was time to start our own coven. It was a big step for me, committing again.

My last coven had been murdered by the Order of Eustace, a rogue paramilitary organization bent on destroying practitioners of true magic, who take very literally the line in Exodus about not suffering a Witch to live. I'd only survived because I was late to the meeting, and because I had the presence of mind to call the Goddess Lilith into me when the agents attacked. The whole event had left me scarred, both mentally and physically. My eyes changed color that night in Minneapolis, and so did my whole world. I hadn't dared form a coven since.

But I'd put a lot of demons to rest since then. The order wouldn't be bothering to look for me anymore. Thanks to a powerful spell that comingled my blood and Sebastian's, their agents think I'm dead.

My name had even been cleared with the FBI, which had been led to my doorstep by following an investigation into the death of the Vatican agents Lilith killed in Minnesota.

Parrish, my vampire ex-lover, had taken the fall for me, actually. In fact, Parrish sacrificed his life—or unlife, given that he's also a vampire—so the case could be closed.

I wondered where he was and if he was okay.

A customer standing behind Marge cleared his throat noisily. "Oh, sorry. Miles away," I muttered as I rang up the customer, took his money, and made change—all the while maneuvering around the immovable Marge. "Do you need directions or something?" I asked her.

"No." She rocked back on her heels, smiling. "Nice wind chimes."

I glanced over my head at the crystal chimes hanging on hooks from the ceiling. We had all sorts. There were jade beads strung with gold chain for prosperity; heavy, wire-wrapped amethyst crystals supported by silver wire for psychic clarity; and jangly glass bells that, well, just annoyed me. "Did you want to buy one?"

"No, just admiring them."

I gave the next person in line an I'm-sorry-about-this-oddball-standing-in-your-way smile. She pursed her lips into a thin, disapproving line and glared at Marge. For a second, I thought she might give Marge a shove, but instead she thrust the book around her with an exaggerated sigh.

Glancing at the title I suppressed a snarky smirk and explained to the lady that it would cost her $24.99 plus tax to find *Inner Peace: The Tibetan Way*.

Marge said, without preamble, "My grandmother was a Witch."

"Really?" I murmured politely.

"Yes," Marge said, apparently feeling emboldened by the merest hint of interest. "I'm FamTrad."

FamTrad was short for Family Tradition, which meant that she was a hereditary Witch and may have come from a long line of women who secretly kept the Old Religion alive after the Inquisition, or Burning Times. I had no problem with the first claim, but the second always raised my eyebrows a little. There is a lot of contention in the witchy community about the origin of our religion and whether it was made up in the twentieth century or if it has been practiced as is since some prehistoric matriarchy. I'd be happy with either answer, honestly, because it's my firm belief that all religions were made up at one time or another and just because something is new doesn't make it any less real or true.

I had no doubts that the power itself was old. I had Lilith in my belly, after all. It didn't matter to me, however, if She came to me because there was an unbroken method of practice since time immemorial or if the first modern Witch just happened to stumble on the key through meditation and good fortune. For me, what mattered was that it was real. It worked.

However, that breezy attitude can get me in a lot of trouble with hard-liners. So I just smiled and nodded at Marge.

Another customer frowned at Marge's back. This one must have been from out of town, because, without the customary midwestern hesitation, he actually said, "I've got a lot of stuff here, lady, can you move out of the way?"

Marge startled and took a step to one side. She mumbled an apology and gave me a sheepish look. I smiled kindly back. I knew she didn't mean any harm. Marge just seemed like one of those oblivious people who never seem to get the hint that it's time to go. I was about to be blunt with her about it, when she said, "I think in my past life I was Mata Hari."

O-kay.

It wasn't that I discounted the idea of past lives. I was more than certain that, like perennials in the spring, souls passed this way again. However, a little red flag always went up when people mentioned having lived the life of a famous, or infamous, person. The majority of us weren't kings or queens. If souls did recycle, then a vast percentage had spent their previous lives much as they do now: toiling through an unremarkable existence. Again, personally, I think that's perfectly wonderful. Even as a middle manager in the 1930s, a life lived is a worthy one, lessons can be learned, and wisdom gained. You don't have to be Cleopatra to have been blessed.

Between this and the FamTrad stuff, all these outlandish declarations made me wonder what Marge felt she had to prove to me. I already knew she had power. Not only had she seen the poster I'd bespelled, but I'd sensed it flowing from her aura.

It was now about five minutes to close and there were still three people waiting to be helped. So I put on my kindest, most charming smile, looked Marge directly in the eyes, and said, "Listen, I'm sorry. I've really got to ask you to leave right now, but I'd *love* to hear all about it tonight, Marge."

And that was my fatal mistake.

Six hours later, I was cornered—literally pushed up between my bookshelf and the window—by Marge, who was, in point of fact, telling me all of her past-life sexual exploits in excruciating detail.

I eyed the pewter statue of Kali that sat within arm's

reach on the second shelf. If Marge didn't stop talking soon, I planned to use it to bludgeon my way back into the middle of the room. Thing was, I hadn't had a chance to talk to anyone else tonight, and, worse, we were running out of lemonade.

The sun had gone down several hours ago, but it was still eighty-seven degrees. At least the breeze coming in off the lake through the open windows brought a little relief. My apartment was the upper floor of a creaky, old Victorian with wiring nearly as ancient as the plaster-and-lath walls, which meant no AC. Every time I tried to plug in an air conditioner, the breakers blew.

Strategically placed fans shifted the hot air around, and I had provided lots of pitchers of ice-cold lemonade to mitigate the heat—except now we were running precariously low.

"Hmm, mm-hmm," I muttered as Marge continued to regale me with her former prowess in bed. I had tuned Marge out the first time she mentioned cunnilingus, because while it might be nice to experience, it was not a word I found palatable when bandied about with impunity.

I tried to catch Sebastian's eye, but he was completely focused on a leggy, blond foreign exchange student named Blythe. She was a comparative religions major and a Londoner. Neither of them noticed me frantically trying to get their attention.

Marge seemed to notice my focus drifting. Her eyes darted to Blythe and Sebastian furtively, and then she'd blurt out something awkwardly embarrassing about sex and espionage. All the while, she twiddled with that dog pendant of hers.

Marge started explaining some Kama Sutra position the

Mata Hari had found particularly useful, and I broke in, "I've been admiring your necklace. Where'd you get it?"

She stopped midsentence and looked down at the pendant between her fingers like she'd never seen it before in her life. "Uh, this?"

Marge at a loss for words—this was interesting. "Yeah. Is it Anubis? Is it magical?" I asked, knowing full well it was from my earlier aura scan. Still, I thought maybe I'd seen one on someone else here tonight and I wondered if it was associated with some local coven I didn't know about. "Do you think I should carry it in the store?"

"Oh no, you couldn't do that," she said quickly, as if I had suggested doing something rude to her grandmother. Her eyes flashed to Sebastian and Blythe and then to the floor. "It's just something silly and personal. It doesn't mean anything."

Marge had just lied to me. I looked at Sebastian, who still only had eyes for Blythe. Why had Marge glanced at them? Was the dog some kind of symbol that involved Sebastian? Legend would have you believe that vampires can transform into wolves, but Sebastian always flatly denied he had the ability to change shape. He always started getting all nerdy whenever I brought it up, quoting laws of physics and the conservation of mass, whatever that was.

Could the pendant be another vampire's symbol? Was Marge a ghoul? "So," I said, trying to act like I was changing the subject when I really wasn't, "how'd you get interested in magic?"

"Uh, well, my family, you know," she stammered, taking a step backward.

What was going on here? Most Witches loved talking

about when they "came out of the broom closet" and how they discovered, or rediscovered, the Craft. Actually, the analogy with the gay and lesbian community was a good one. We often lived in a kind of secrecy in a world dominated by a religion not only very different from our own but which actively despised and misunderstood us. In safe places like a coven gathering, people tended to like to bond over "war stories" of growing up in a hostile environment.

"So you've always been a Witch," I prompted. Stepping forward, so Marge would have to move back. "What kind?"

William inserted himself smoothly into my advance, like that rescue I'd wanted ten minutes ago. "Hey, Garnet, you're out of lemonade. Do you have more you can make? Maybe in the fridge?"

"In a second," I said, but Marge had already fled into the crowd. "Damn."

William frowned. "Oh. Did I interrupt something?"

I shook my head. "No, it's fine. I'll talk to her about it later."

So, with William in tow, I refilled the lemonade and chips, and then went to check in on Sebastian. Or, at least, I tried to.

"Hey," I said, coming up to where Sebastian stood. Sebastian looked good despite the heat. Sebastian was cool and collected with his Old World–style long hair tied back at the nape of his decidedly unsweaty neck.

Looking at him, I could hardly believe this amazing man had asked me to marry him only yesterday. He was wickedly handsome—long, straight, black hair; sharp aquiline nose; and the sculpted, graceful body of a dancer . . . or, more accurately, a predator.

Okay, so that last part shouldn't have been sexy, but it was. Sebastian had intense gold-brown eyes, not unlike that wolf I'd met on the road. It had been the first thing I'd noticed about him. I'd never met a real person who had an honest-to-Goddess "penetrating gaze," but Sebastian did. It was captivating.

Thrilling, even.

That is, when he was looking at me—which he wasn't right now.

Not at all.

Sebastian had murmured a quick hello, but he and Blythe were deep into a conversation about some obscure British television show I didn't even know he watched. I listened to them for a few minutes and realized I had nothing of substance to add.

Blythe's chuckle cut above the ambient noise. Sebastian's broad smile showed off the tips of his canines.

His fangs had dropped! They only did that when he was excited, if you know what I mean. Sebastian was totally into Blythe.

Lilith roiled in my stomach.

I had the urge to interrupt Sebastian and Blythe's nostalgia fest to point out that *I* harbored the dark Goddess Lilith in my body and so could crush any newcomers like a bug, but, well, that would just be petty.

Lilith clenched my stomach again as if to say: petty, yes, but satisfying.

I didn't like to think of myself as jealous, but being engaged to a vampire would make the most laissez-faire person a bit twitchy. The problem was blood, of course. Sebastian needed a lot of it, more than one person could physically provide. There *have* to be others.

Add to this the fact that while I found the whole biting thing to be an absolute rush, I hesitated to become my boyfriend's main supply. Sexual politics were complicated enough without adding one's place in the food chain into the mix. I wanted Sebastian to desire me for me, not for my fabulously salty and iron-rich O-positiveness.

Which was why my nerves prickled around Blythe—who knew what interest Sebastian was showing? In a weird way, I'd be happier if he was just into her. However, as a potential meal, things got complicated fast. If she was a rival girlfriend, I had legs to stand on when I told him I'd rather he stayed focused on me especially given the ring on my hand. But a ghoulfriend? What could I say? Pick something else off the menu, I don't like who you're having for lunch?

Lilith rattled uneasily against my ribs.

That's when I realized the room had hushed, as if everyone were suddenly holding their breath. People were staring. At me. Or rather, they were gaping in wonderment and horror at the fraction of Lilith that had slipped up into me.

Even Sebastian stopped talking, and he and Blythe turned slowly in my direction as if expecting to see a monster lying in wait for them. Which, I suppose I was, except the slow burn I'd had on evaporated under the intense scrutiny of a room full of Witches.

I decided to use this opportunity to turn the situation around. I cleared my throat. "Uh, we should probably get this meeting started, eh, Sebastian?"

"Ah, right," he said, though I knew he could sense that

something ugly had nearly erupted a moment ago. He and I shared custody of Lilith, kind of. Thanks to a spell that had involved comingling of our blood, Sebastian was sensitive to Lilith's moods. At least, he used to be. Over time, I'd noticed that our connection had been fading. Because Sebastian had regular blood transfusions, our empathetic bond grew weaker with each new ghoul.

Humph. Another reason to hate them.

Blythe gave Sebastian a possessive glance, and put a hand in the pocket of her loose-fitting cotton capris. She looked great, standing there. Her hips were full, her stomach, which I could see plainly thanks to the tan belly shirt, was flat and toned like a rock star's.

"So, uh," I said, feeling suddenly kind of foolish to be caught with Lilith hanging out. "I guess everyone noticed the Goddess, eh?"

There were nods around the room.

"Is that what that was? A Goddess? It felt more malevolent to me," said a character I'd mentally dubbed "broody warlock guy" in my head. His T-shirt glorified some death-metal band and silver skulls on his knuckles advertised his general badass-itude. He had long, blond Viking hair and wore a Thor's hammer necklace.

"Well, yeah," I admitted. I looked over at Sebastian for support. Taking my hand, he smiled and nodded encouragingly. I squared my shoulders. I knew this part was going to be tough. I had a hard time talking about Lilith, especially with new people. Worse, fellow Witches might take umbrage with the fact that I had pulled down such an awesome power and unleashed it on anyone, even if they *had* just murdered my coven. I'd used magic to kill. No matter how you sliced it, that was black magic.

"That's the first order of business," I said. "I kind of harbor the dark Goddess Lilith."

"Kinda? Isn't that like saying you're sort of pregnant?" a woman who'd introduced herself to me as Xylia said. Xylia perched on the windowsill, gnawing on a carrot (the only thing I'd provided that a strict vegan could eat). Rail-thin with a super-butch buzz cut and a muscle shirt from the Michigan Womyn's Festival, she stood up now and narrowed her eyes at me.

"Okay," I confessed. "Lilith *is* a part of me, and I'm not just talking about when I call down the Goddess as part of a ritual. I mean, all the time." I surprised myself by bringing up the central aspect of seasonal gatherings—the moment when the High Priestess symbolically becomes the Goddess. I hadn't really celebrated the usual Wiccan holidays since merging with Lilith, partly because I didn't know how to deal with the fact that I now was a Goddess full time, and partly, I realized for the first time, because I missed having a group.

"Lilith?" Marge said in a small voice, as though she had just now absorbed the information I'd laid out earlier. She stood in the archway between my living room and dining room, gripping a sweating glass of lemonade with whitening knuckles. "You mean, like *the* Lilith."

I nodded.

"Isn't Lilith primarily a Christian goddess?" Blythe asked no one in particular.

"Judeo-Christian," Marge added. "She's a succubus and baby killer in Jewish folklore."

"Excuse me! Baby killer . . . ?" I sputtered in protest, "Now wait just a minute—" But the conversation continued right over me.

"Like with a lot of the vilified 'demons' of the Judeo-Christian myths, I believe there's a root Goddess much older—Assyrian, maybe?" William added.

"She's associated with screech owls, I think," someone I hadn't been introduced to yet added. I was pretty sure he'd come with Marge. He was short and doughy in a pleasant I-love-cooking sort of way. I thought maybe his name was Max, but I couldn't remember. He had long, straight, brown hair that he wore pinned back from his face. Large, thick glasses balanced on a pug nose.

"Lilith kicks ass." Broody Warlock nodded his approval.

And so the debate began. Well, as far as reactions to my admission of harboring a Goddess known as the Mother of Demons went, it wasn't necessarily a bad one. At least no one had run screaming for the door. Of course, we still hadn't gotten around to mentioning Sebastian was one of the living dead, as it were.

One major hurdle at a time.

I gave Sebastian a return squeeze to let him know I was okay and let go of his hand. Since everyone was talking around me, anyway, I moved over a step in order to slump down into an empty spot on my bright orange couch. Sebastian perched on the arm, which creaked dangerously under his weight.

The breeze coming in from the windows behind us finally brought a little relief. As darkness deepened, the buzzsaw hiss of cicadas gave way to the soft chirp of crickets.

Barney, my cat, sneezed delicately from somewhere

under the couch. She'd been hiding out since the first potential coven member arrived. Usually she was fond of company because it meant more attention for her, but she was allergic to magic—or, at least, she wanted me to believe she was.

"How'd it happen?" Trust Broody Warlock to turn the conversation back to me. "Isn't trapping a demon major dark-arts type stuff?"

"Not demon, Griffin," William said to broody warlock guy, having apparently learned his name at some point. "Goddess."

"Whatever," Griffin said dismissively. "The point is you don't control something that powerful by accident, do you?"

Griffin's question bothered me because I didn't have a good answer for him. I shifted my seat, feeling the rough upholstery stick to my exposed, sweaty skin. Shrugging, I said, "I didn't trap Lilith."

He squinted at me like he didn't quite buy it. "Yeah, sure," he said. "But why? What makes you so special?"

There was the million-dollar question. Thing is, I never did know exactly why Lilith didn't just return to the ether afterward. Why was she trapped with me? Or was it that she chose to say? I mean, I'd known other Witches who'd summoned the strength of Gods and Goddesses during times of crisis. None of them ever reported having gotten "stuck" with one on a permanent basis. Perhaps, part of the problem was that I didn't just call on the strength of a Goddess, but on the Goddess herself.

Actually, when I admitted it to myself, what I'd asked the universe for that night was much more visceral than just naming some Goddess for protection. I'd wanted vengeance.

I didn't care who or what aided me as long as they served up an eye for an eye.

Uh. That was so not cool. I tried not to think about that or about the fact that Lilith might have been attracted to just that kind of thinking.

"Back off, dude," William said in my defense. "Garnet didn't ask Lilith to stay, okay. It just happened."

"Yes," Sebastian said, his voice smooth with just a hint of threat. "You sound jealous, boy."

Griffin took a step forward at Sebastian's words, and I thought there might be a fight, so I stood up. "Look," I said, "I really don't know why Lilith stays with me," I admitted. "It's something I'd love to know the answer to. Maybe that's something we could find out as a group."

I saw a few wan smiles that were beginning to warm to me.

Griffin and Sebastian still eyed each other threateningly, so I thought maybe this was a good time to nudge Sebastian about item number two on our agenda. "So, Sebastian," I said. "Should I tell them or do you want to?"

"I will," he said, with a particularly hostile look at Griffin. Then, he let his steely gaze sweep the room. "The other thing you should know is that I'm a vampire."

Nobody said anything for several minutes.

The problem was Hollywood. Everyone in the room was scrutinizing Sebastian trying to decide if he fit their image of a vampire. Other than the long black hair and sharp, handsome features, he probably didn't. He did have a penchant for wearing black, but not exclusively. Tonight, in deference to the heat, he wore a UW-Madison T-shirt. He had faded, scuffed jeans he usually wore to work in his garden and tennis shoes. If I didn't know him, I might guess he was some kind of hippie, the kind to grow his own herb, if you know what I mean.

No leather coats, no slow-mo high-kickin' ninja moves. I'd been telling him for months that he should invest in a lot more leather or at least some cool, blue-tinted sunglasses or something. The more people looked at him, the more incredulous they seemed.

My eyes strayed to the spider plant hanging on the remaining bit of longbow arrow shaft still stuck in my wall. The Vatican witch hunters had transfixed Sebastian to the wall there. They'd "staked" him through the heart, but to everyone's surprise—other than Sebastian's, of course—it hadn't killed him. That's when I realized that everything I thought I knew about vampires from the movies was suspect.

"So you're like a psychic vampire or something?" Max asked, clearly voicing the question on everyone's mind.

Sebastian glanced at me because he'd just lost our bet. Now he owed me a dinner out at Portabello's. I'd told him that the group would much more easily swallow my Goddess than his vampirism.

He sighed. "No," he said.

"So . . . you're a bloodsucker?"

William cringed about the same time I did.

Having been on the receiving end of the glare that pinioned poor Max right now, I pitied him. "That's not the word I'd use," Sebastian said.

"Okay. You're a blood drinker," said Blythe. "That's cool. I mean, it's your thing, but what does it have to do with the coven?"

It took me a few seconds to figure out what Blythe was talking about. Then I suddenly remembered that there were regular humans who called themselves vampires who got turned on by cutting or biting people and drinking their blood.

"He's a *real* vampire," William said. "Not just someone into blood."

"Vampire," Xylia said. "You seriously expect us to believe the whole coffin, risen-dead thing?"

Sebastian opened his mouth to reply when Marge said, "To rise from the dead, you'd have to be really old, like from before the Civil War."

Everyone looked to Marge askance.

She blinked a little under the scrutiny, but continued. "Embalming," she said. "It's not required here in Wisconsin, but it's really unusual for someone not to be unless they're Amish. Although embalming is kind of a stupid practice. Doesn't really preserve the body, not long-term anyway, and then you have all the pollutants that leach into the ground water. But, the thing is, even if you managed to not be embalmed, you'd still have to bust through the coffin, plus the sheer amount of concrete you'd have to break through in the vault." She counted each point off on her fingers. "Nope. You get buried, you're staying put, I say. Plus, most people are cremated these days, anyway. It's a real problem for monument manufacturers. Although cemeteries prefer it. Saves space, you know."

Some people were looking a little green in the gills. William asked, "And why do you know all this?"

"Oh," she said, her hand fluttering to that pendant of hers. "I'm the secretary at Sunset Memory Gardens."

"You work at a cemetery?" I couldn't tell who'd said that, but they sounded pretty ooged out by the idea.

"I answer phones," she said a bit defensively.

"Well, okay then," I said, steering the conversation back on track as best I could. "I know this is a lot for everyone to take in. I also figure you have some decisions to make now that you know our secrets. Some of you may choose not to come back. That's cool. I only ask that you respect our need to keep secret what you've learned here."

"Like anyone'd believe me, anyway," someone muttered.

"Someone would," I said sharply. "The Order of Eustace has come here once before. If they caught wind of us . . ." The Order considered themselves a modern offshoot of the Inquisition, and they used any means necessary to destroy practitioners of true magic. For them to find us? It didn't bear thinking of. I didn't want to go through all that again. My voice broke a little, despite myself. "I'm just asking you to be careful."

"We're meeting at my place next time," William said. "Interested parties can talk to me about getting directions and stuff before you leave."

"That's great, William," I said with a smile. "So, everyone should feel free to 'eat, drink, and be merry.'" I said, quoting a bit of the Charge of the Goddess.

People instantly started talking among themselves. I noticed Marge eyeing Sebastian from the archway. Her gaze was steady and measuring. I'd been surprised how accurate she was about vampires. Parrish had explained to me that the practice of embalming pretty much wiped out vampirism post–Civil War. I guess embalming had been put into common practice at that time because so many dead soldiers needed to be transported long distances. Given that part of the process involved exsanguination, no turned vampires survived it. Burial, it seemed, was a necessary part of the magic of transformation. You could still do it, of course, you just had to make sure that no one else took care of the body. Harder to do in this modern era.

Her knowledge made me suspect she was someone's ghoul. I turned to Sebastian. "Are you eating Marge?"

"Sorry, what?" Though he tried not to show it, I could tell by the way he slumped against the back of the couch that he'd been pouting.

Poor baby. Sebastian wasn't used to being regarded as a loony. Most days he passed for normal.

Not like me. I didn't even dress normal. Tonight, I'd chosen a black, sparkly, spaghetti-strap tank top and a black mini covered in red bats. My hair was spiky and dyed jet-black, like the eyeliner I used to ring my eyes. Plus, every time I opened my mouth to comment on someone's aura or the alignment of the stars people looked at me like they furtively eyed Sebastian right now. I patted his thigh. "Marge," I said. "Is she one of your ghouls?"

"None of my ghouls are here. In fact, I'd be surprised if anyone's were. Ghouls are discouraged from practicing magic," Sebastian said.

I snorted. "There are rules about this?"

"Certainly. Think about it for a second, darling. What would happen if all the cows in the world could cast spells?"

Should I be offended he was talking about people as cows? Still, I got the picture. "There'd suddenly be a lot more vegetarians."

"Right," he said.

"You said the ghouls were 'discouraged,'" I repeated. "But how do you enforce it?"

"There are ways," he said cryptically.

I raised my eyebrows. There was a lot I didn't understand about ghouls, mostly because I didn't really want to know. I tried not to have any contact with them, and honestly, this was about the most Sebastian or I had ever talked about ghouls or ghoul culture. Given my jealousy issues, I was okay with that, so I let it go.

Anyway, the lemonade needed refreshing again.

Sometime after midnight, everyone, even Blythe, who hung on until the last possible moment, went home. Sebastian and I were alone at last.

"So," he said as he closed the downstairs door. "What do you think? Anyone worth having?"

Having? That was an interesting way of putting it. Was he thinking about *having* Blythe or just being inscrutably British? Instead of asking him that, I decided to swallow my jealous impulse. "I don't know. Who did you like?"

We started up the stairs. My bare feet slapped noisily on the hardwood. We were in the foyer, which was the public space between my apartment and the downstairs neighbors. The foyer had vaulted ceilings covered in pressed tin. The wainscoting was worn in places and the plaster was cracked, but you could still see the ghost of its former glory in the oak trim and the tulip bulb chandelier. I stepped past the blue recycling bins heaped with the neighbors' cheap brown glass on my way to my apartment door.

"Blythe seems promising," Sebastian commented casually.

I'll bet. "You think?"

"She's studied a great deal. That sort of knowledge can be very useful."

Sebastian would be turned on by smarts. It was kind of his thing, being an alchemist himself. He approached a lot of things with an Age of Enlightenment kind of scientific approach. Me, I'm like Barbie; math is hard.

Sebastian held the door to my apartment for me like a gentleman, and I slipped through under his arm. As I passed, I caught the scent of him—a strangely compelling combination of axle grease and cinnamon.

"Yeah, but book smarts will only take you so far in real practice," I said.

"I'd like to give her the benefit of the doubt."

Hmmm, there was so much I could say to that, but I couldn't seem to formulate any response other than pursed lips.

"What about you?" Sebastian asked as he flopped himself down on to the couch. "Anyone you liked?"

"Griffin," I said just to be argumentative.

Half-filled plastic cups and potato-chip crumbs littered my apartment. Despite the postparty/postapocalyptic décor, I couldn't summon the energy required to tidy up. Just looking at the clock on the wall made my eyes gritty and my throat scratchy with a desire for sleep. Cleanup would have to wait until morning.

"You liked the metalhead?"

I settled into the oversized beanbag on the floor opposite Sebastian. It smelled a little like nacho dip and someone else's aftershave. I made a mental note to spray down the vinyl with Lysol later. "You just don't like him because he gave you grief." Plus, despite the death-metal look, he was kind of cute.

"Well," Sebastian said, sitting forward to rest his elbows on his knees. "It does present some problems if he remains resistant to me."

Resistant to him? Did he want to have everyone in Thrall so he could have them for lunch? My lips twisted up before I could stop them.

"What's that look for?" he demanded.

"I think it's good to have someone in the group who pushes a bit, someone who doesn't take everything on faith. I think it makes the coven more honest."

Sebastian's eyes roamed over me for a long moment before he spoke. "I get it," he said. "He's like you used to be."

"Hardly," I laughed. "I was the earth-mother sort. Birkenstocks and hemp skirts."

"Yeah, but you were the one who riled things up, weren't you? Who asked the questions no one else would."

I gave in to a smile. "Yeah, I guess I was."

"All right then. You can have Griffin if I can have Blythe."

Again with the "having." "Okay," I grudgingly agreed, hoping we were only talking about coven membership and not anything more.

"Anyone else?" Sebastian asked. His eyes glittered with excitement. Despite being able to wander about in the daylight, nighttime energized Sebastian. I could tell he was ready and willing to spend all hours debriefing and comparing notes. It wasn't that I didn't want to, but I didn't have his superhuman stamina.

"Can we talk about it in bed?" I said around a yawn.

His eyes twinkled. "Absolutely."

I smiled, but my shoulders sagged. I wasn't really in the mood for sex, but I also didn't have a good reason to turn down the offer. For once, I had the day off work tomorrow, so I could sleep in. The hour was late, but once things got under way I'd certainly forget all my sleepiness. Still . . . I couldn't help but wonder what prompted this sudden interest. Was it really me or was he still thinking about Blythe?

Of course, if I said no, she'd seem ten times more attractive.

"You're not up for it, are you?" Sebastian asked. "Too worn out, love?"

"I'm never too tired for you," I said. Smiling, I held out my hand. I was tired, but I was going to be damned if I was going to let that other woman occupy his mind. He wanted sex? I was going to take that boy and show him why he came home to me every night despite all the other ghouls.

His grin widened as I led him to the bedroom.

2.

Moon

❧

KEYWORDS:

Instincts, Moods, Habits

Sebastian flipped me over and went for my throat.

We'd been playing kind of rough from the start. A little tease here, a little taunt there. I'd pulled at his clothes and he'd torn my underwear a bit. In the morning, I was going to have cloth burns in odd spots.

Now I found myself holding on to the headboard and feeling his breath hot on my neck. His hands roamed the contours of my breasts. I shivered. He was going to bite me, I was sure of it.

I arched my back, driving us together, harder. I needed him to know I wanted it. His lips touched my neck soft, fluttering. I pushed us deeper and was rewarded with a deep moan from him. Teeth nipped at my shoulders, pricking skin, but not sinking deeply. I rocked faster.

The headboard banged against the wall, and I felt a twinge of embarrassment thinking of my downstairs neighbors.

The flush of my cheeks was lost in the general heat of passion. Sweat trailed down my body, slicking the spaces between us.

Sebastian groaned. I was certain his vocalization was a prelude to biting me, so I steeled myself to surrender to it. Thrusting myself toward him, I found myself vaguely disappointed when it was lips, not teeth, that met my shoulder. Sebastian came a moment later and, thankfully, didn't seem to notice that my own passion flagged.

We disentangled and lay on the bed panting.

The heat of the room was stifling. Even so, Sebastian reached out and entwined his hand with mine. His thumb caressed the back of my hand where our fingers curled together. We lay there holding hands, and I could sense his breath evening out. My own eyes started to feel heavy, but I rolled onto my side and gave Sebastian a heartfelt peck on the cheek.

"I love you," I whispered in his ear.

He chuckled. "I always thought that when you said that after sex, it didn't count."

"Only for a guy," I teased, stroking his hair with my free hand. Unlike mine, his was silky and completely devoid of sweat. "How is it," I asked him, "that you're impervious to the temperature, but you're not cold as a corpse?"

I felt the mattress bounce as he shrugged. "Magic?"

Unlike a traditional vampire, Sebastian had been "turned" by his own alchemical formula. As he was fond of saying, he had no blood sire but science. Though, when his formula ran out after a thousand years, we discovered that there was also a strong element of magic that he hadn't been able to reproduce until he met me—well, me and Lilith, anyway.

"Do you think we should tell Lilith about our engagement?" I asked, flopping back to stare at the ceiling.

"How are you proposing we do that, exactly? I mean, doesn't She already know?"

It was my turn to shrug. "I suppose," I said, "But I get the sense She'd love to see you on your knees."

Sebastian hadn't actually gotten down on one knee for me, but he had been awfully romantic. He'd sent me a formal invitation to high tea at his place. On our first day together, he'd made me cucumber sandwiches and the whole traditional thing. So, I'd dug out a nice sundress, some white gloves, a big straw hat, and sandals. I imagine I must have looked a bit like a Goth Mary Poppins tooling up to his farm on my bike. He'd had the whole thing laid out under the maple tree in his backyard. Of course, this time his herb garden was in its full glory. William Baffin roses climbed on the rail fence. Sunflowers and daisies nodded in the hay-scented breeze.

Sebastian had put fresh mint spears in the iced tea and treated me to smoked salmon spread, cream cheese puffs, and a curried mushroom-filled pastry I could still taste melting on my tongue. He'd dressed for the occasion, too. A white cotton shirt with the sleeves rolled up, black jeans, and barefoot. Okay, so it wasn't an Armani suit, but the gentleman farmer look suited him better. Then, after a pleasant hour of food and conversation, Sebastian informed me that it was only proper we have a cup of hot tea as well. I protested that it was too warm outside, but he insisted. Plus, he'd said, I could read his fortune in the tea leaves. Even though I said I didn't do that kind of magic, I found myself staring at the dregs anyway. A ring was there at the bottom. *Your future,* he'd said, *is with me.*

Goddess, I love this man.

I looked over at Sebastian. His hair had come unbound and it hung loosely around his face in dark waves—sexy bed head—but he was frowning so hard creases appeared between his eyebrows. It wasn't the expression I was expecting. I was about to ask him about it when he said: "I'm not getting on my knees for Lilith. No way."

I gave a little wicked laugh. "Why not, darling? It could be fun. There are plenty of worshipful things you could do while you were down there."

"Garnet!" Sebastian said.

I rolled my eyes at him, even though I wasn't sure he could see me in the dark. "Are you seriously shocked, Sebastian? Aren't you older than the Victorians?"

"Significantly," he sniffed.

"Then get over yourself," I teased. "In fact," I added, jumping up to straddle him. "I think maybe you ought to practice. Lilith might demand all sorts of demeaning positions from you."

He chuckled, low and hungrily.

I wasn't going to get any sleep.

Yet at some point I must have nodded off because the insistent chirping of house sparrows woke me from a pleasantly wicked dream. Blearily, I glanced at the bird feeder that hung just inches from my bedroom window. I was fishing around on the floor for a slipper to toss at the screen to discourage the noisy birds when Barney came to my rescue. She lumbered along at top speed and threw herself so hard against the screen, I thought for a second she might tear through it and plunge to her doom one story below. The birds scattered. My cat sat down, dignified, as if she'd intended all along not to catch and eat one, and primly cleaned a paw.

Sebastian groaned and buried his head under a pillow.

The very best thing about having a vampire lover who wasn't allergic to the sun was waking up next to him. I'm a firm believer that people show more of their true selves first thing in the morning before they have time to compose the masks they put on for other people. Sebastian, I'd discovered, was a lot like a lion. When he didn't have anywhere to be, which was often, he luxuriated.

Today, for once, I didn't have to go into the store. I flopped back down and closed my eyes, ready to oversleep to the point of waking up mildly grumpy because half the day was already gone.

Of course, I couldn't.

I made a valiant effort. I probably lay in bed for six or seven extra minutes before giving up and making my way to the bathroom. After my usual morning routine—a quick shower, dental hygiene, and several vitamins—I decided that I'd tackle some of my friends' natal charts. I'd finished about a half a dozen before I heard Sebastian getting out of bed.

Barney hopped up on the kitchen table where I'd spread out my books and lay down on the chart I was working on. Absently, I scratched her belly. She snapped at my fingers, reminding me that I'd neglected to fill her food bowl. I was in the middle of shaking the last of the kibbles from the box when Sebastian came in searching for coffee.

"Morning," Sebastian murmured. He detoured slightly from his trajectory to give me a peck on the cheek. The sunlight did nice things to his half-naked body, highlighting lines and angles. He looked like a rumpled Adonis in need of a shave. Yummy. I let my hands, which had automatically reached around to encircle his waist, slowly caress his rib cage and flat, hard stomach.

As my hand rested against his taut belly, I flashed to what William had said. How weird would sex be when I was all wrinkles and gray and he was still hard and lean? How impotent would I feel when he went off to feed on his twentysomething ghouls then?

Sebastian's fingertips brushed my hair. "What are you thinking?"

Just then Barney sneezed wetly on Sebastian's bare feet. She started to hack dryly as if she planned to toss a hairball onto his toes. I gently nudged her with my foot until she got the hint and padded off to sun herself in the tower room.

Barney especially disliked Sebastian because, unlike other vampires, he had been made by alchemical sorcery. She rather liked my ex, Parrish, and I always figured that, because he was dead, he smelled like something a cat would drag in. Sebastian's magic flowed continually through his veins, and, well, it apparently made Barney gag.

"She's not going to like living at my house, is she?"

His house? I hadn't really considered it, but I supposed it didn't make sense for Sebastian to move into my tiny little apartment. No, no, of course I'd move into his place, I practically lived there now.

Before I could reply, a soft munching sound came from the tower room where I kept all my plants. "Barney," I yelled, grabbing the squirt bottle from its place next to the bread maker. "Stop eating the lucky bamboo!"

"Maybe she could live in the barn," Sebastian murmured, leaning against the counter, cup of coffee cradled in both hands.

I aimed the nozzle at Barney. Her face was buried in my tattered bamboo. Seeing the bottle armed and ready in my hands, she bolted. The force of her leap set the plant stand rocking, but I was able to grab it before it toppled.

"Barney is an indoor cat," I yelled over my shoulder as I straightened the pot and checked on the violas and pansies. The tower room had windows on all sides, and they were all open to let in the morning air. The heat had broken and I could hear seagulls crying in the distance.

Sebastian shook his head with apparent bewilderment. "A barn would be perfect for her. Cats should live where they can catch mice and rats. It's their job. It's what they do."

"You still think dogs should be used only for hunting," I said with a fond smile as I came back into the kitchen. I reached around him to refill my own cup. What would I do with the coffeemaker? I'd bought it at an estate sale because it was teal. I'd never seen such a hideous plastic monstrosity in my life; it was love at first sight. I'd brought it home and lovingly decorated it with purple stick-on rhinestones.

In his kitchen Sebastian had one of those fancy espresso machines that I'd never learned how to operate. He made cold press for his "everyday" coffee. Damn good coffee; weird machine. I'd have to learn how to use it if I was going to live there every day for the rest of my life.

The rest of my life.

Sebastian smiled at me. "You still have that curious dread on your face. What's on your mind?"

I shrugged and looked around my tiny kitchen. Chipped

cheap veneer covered the cabinets. Maroon and black carpeting speckled with a multitude of stains shrouded the floor. I never quite understood why my landlord had carpeting in the kitchen. The rest of the place had gorgeous, polished hardwood—except the one room in the house where food was most likely to be dropped.

"It's going to be weird to leave here," I said.

Sebastian leaned against me so our arms touched. I let my head rest against his shoulder. "I know," he said, stroking my hair. "We could always buy a house in town. Something that would be ours."

Tilt.

I knew the whole buying-a-house-together thing was what was expected, and that was the problem. This whole domestic discussion felt very Ward and June Cleaver, and I'd never wanted to be those people. What was next? Me in an apron, while Sebastian complained about how hard it was to find a good AB-negative ghoul? "Um, I need to get cat food," I announced, putting my full cup of coffee in the sink with the other dirty dishes. "I'll be back in five minutes."

Then, I fled.

Summer was in full bloom. Deep violet clematis climbed over fences, monarch and viceroy butterflies sipped from pink milkweed flowers, and every time I paused for even a second for a stoplight, mosquitoes buzzed in my ears and nipped at my exposed skin. Despite the bugs, I was considering going for a ride around the lake before heading home when I heard a strange, tiny, distorted version of the 1812 Overture. A distant car stereo? A radio station coming in on my fillings? An especially complicated squeaky wheel? D'oh! My cell phone!

I fumbled at the pack at my waist until I found the phone. Then I randomly jabbed at buttons until the ringing stopped. Jamming it under my helmet in the vicinity of my right ear, I said a cautious, "Hello?"

I was what could be considered a late adopter when it came to cell phones. They went against my attempts to be Zen. Plus, even though I was embarrassed to admit it, I was a bit of a fuddy-duddy when it came to technology. I knew how to use a computer well enough for work, but I didn't have a laptop or an iPod or a BlackBerry or even a thumb drive. I wouldn't even know what those things were, except Sebastian loved gadgets. After a run-in with some killer zombies a few months ago, Sebastian insisted I carry a cell phone. *Garnet,* I could hear him saying, *next time you're surrounded by the powers of Darkness, dial 911.*

"Hello?" I said again into the phone, wondering if the ringing had stopped because I'd hung up or if Sebastian was just being coy.

"Are you coming back or did I scare you off for good?" It *was* Sebastian. He sounded grumpy.

"There was a long line at the pet store," I lied.

"I'm not sure I'll be here when you get back," he said. "I have things to do."

I shifted the phone to the other ear. It was hard to keep my balance on my bike while talking on the cell phone. "I'm sorry," I said. "This whole marriage thing is going to take some getting used to."

" 'Marriage thing'? If I didn't know any better, Garnet, I'd say you were afraid to commit."

"You only proposed the day before yesterday. Give me a chance."

There was a long pause. I shifted the phone again so I could make a wobbly right turn. If this conversation was going to go on any longer, I'd have to stop, only I wasn't sure if I could brake with just one hand. "All right," Sebastian said at last. "But I'm going in to Jensen's. Hal told me they got a 1966 Mustang convertible I need to look at."

Sebastian would probably do more than look. Jensen's was the garage he sort-of-mostly worked at. Somehow Sebastian had convinced his boss, Hal, to let him work only when he wanted to and only on the cars he liked. I chalked it up to vampire glamour. "Okay," I said. "No hard feelings?"

"Don't forget I'm at the Horticultural Society tonight."

Sebastian was an herbalist and he'd been invited to lecture on the occult properties of certain common weeds.

"I'll be there with bells on," I said trying to sound peppy. I wasn't convinced we'd smoothed over our rough patch yet. "I love you," I said.

"I love you too." I could hear the "even though you vex me" in the sigh Sebastian uttered before disconnecting.

At that moment a big dog dashed out from between two parked cars, and I fumbled for my brakes. Still clutching my cell in one hand, I instinctively squeezed the other hard. The bike flipped.

I slammed into the asphalt, going head over teakettle. The bike came over next and tangled me in wheels and frame. I scraped on my palms and bruised my knees. Thank Goddess I always wore a helmet, I thought as I picked myself up.

As I righted the bike and inspected myself and the cat

food bag for serious damage, I saw something in the corner of my eye. On the opposite side of the street sat the dog, only it wasn't a dog at all. Its eyes were too yellow and its nose too thin.

A husky? No, more like a wolf or a coyote? In town? Then, just a second after I registered what it was, it trotted off. It disappeared into overgrown hedges separating two houses.

I hauled my battered body back onto the bike and shakily started up the street only to stop ten feet later in front of the remains of my cell phone. Picking it up, I discovered that the hinge had snapped and the battery pack was missing. I looked everywhere for the battery. My best guess was that it bounced along the curb until it slid into the open grate of the sewer. Great. I'd probably just contributed to the pollution of the lakes. Dumping the bits and pieces into my fanny pack, I headed home.

I limped up to my apartment with bloody knees and scraped palms, grateful there wasn't an unsatisfied vampire waiting for me. After filling Barney's food bowl and changing her water, I belly flopped onto my bed. Facedown, I tried to relax, tried not to focus on the throbbing of scrapes and bruises or the fact that it was terribly, terribly convenient that Jensen's needed Sebastian when he hadn't taken blood from me last night.

Stop it, Garnet. Just because he was gone, it didn't automatically mean Sebastian was out biting some other girl's neck. It was, after all, very likely that Sebastian needed to run away from our complicated relationship the same way I had this morning.

I shut my eyes and attempted to center. Flipping myself over onto my back, I rolled my shoulders to try to relax. Instead I was distracted by the feel of sweat sliding underneath my breasts. The bike ride had been a workout, and the temperature—and worse, the humidity—was on the rise again.

I wondered, what was up with all the dogs? Maybe I should meditate on it and see if the Goddess would send me a sign. I closed my eyes and slowly began relaxing my body, starting at my toes. But before I got to my head, I was asleep.

Apparently, the Goddess wanted me to date Orlando Bloom because that was the only dream I had during my three-hour nap. I woke up with that hot, exhausted feeling of having overslept. Making my way to the bathroom, I brushed the slime off my teeth and drew myself a cold bath.

Cold baths are a treat in the heat of summer. Once my body got over the initial shock of settling into the water, I found it as refreshing as dipping into a lake. It took a little courage to splash my head all the way under, but when I did I could feel my body temperature dropping pleasantly. In less than ten minutes the water stopped feeling freakishly chilled and now seemed almost warmish.

I washed my hair and then relaxed in the tub for a few more minutes. I kept an ear cocked for the sounds of Sebastian coming back. Thinking I heard a footstep on the stair, I rushed out of the tub. I shrugged into my robe, shouting, "I'm in here, Sebastian!"

When I didn't hear a reply, I went out to investigate. A

quick glance revealed no one there. All I'd heard was the old house creaking and settling.

I stared at the door for a moment, still hopeful. Then, with a frustrated sigh, I gave up and wandered into the kitchen to hunt up lunch. I heated up a bowl of tofu stir-fry from a Vietnamese take-out container. The veggies were wilted and the rice gummy, but it passed for sustenance. By the time I was finished, it was time to get dressed to meet Sebastian at the Horticultural Society.

Since I was the girlfriend—oops, strike that, fiancée—of the lecturer, I thought I should try to look respectable. From somewhere in the very back of my closet I found a brown tea-length skirt. In my chest of drawers I discovered a white button-down shirt, which I think I'd actually borrowed from Sebastian some time ago. Still, they went together reasonably well, and the shirt, miraculously, didn't need ironing. Much.

Shoes were a bigger problem. Even my most conservative pair had bat-wing buckles. Similarly, most of my hosiery involved glitter and/or spiderwebs.

Given the temperature and the state of my tan (which was dark for me, that is, not so pasty as to stand out), I decided I could go without nylons—besides, if my knees started bleeding again . . . well, pulling mesh from a scab was ugly, ugly business. Luckily, the skirt covered the scrapes.

I gelled my hair into its usual spikes, because flat hair just made me look like Eddie Munster. I noticed that there was a faint line of blond beginning to show at the roots. I was going to have to dye my hair again soon or I'd end up looking like a skunk.

Pulling at a bit of my hair, I looked at the blond. I didn't really need the Goth-girl disguise anymore. Not only had the Vatican witch hunters decided I was dead, but the FBI had closed their case on me as well. I wasn't running anymore. Hell, I was contemplating the big settle—marriage. Maybe I should go down the aisle as a blonde.

I swallowed hard. I watched my throat bob in the mirror in the classic image of fear. My eyes showed it too. No wonder Sebastian was cranky with me.

Well, when I saw him tonight I'd let him know how much I wanted to be with him. I'd missed him terribly all day; I couldn't wait to see him again.

I called Jensen's to see if Sebastian was planning on picking me up or if I should phone for a taxi.

"Haven't seen him all day," Hal said in his usual, disinterested way. Where other guys might have offered to take a message at this point, Hal simply let silence sit on the line almost like a challenge.

"What about the Mustang?" I asked.

"What about it?"

"There is a '66 convertible there, right?"

A moment of silence, and I held my breath. "It isn't yours, is it?"

"No," I said.

"Good. 'Cause I'm still waiting on parts."

After an exchange of awkward good-byes, I hung up.

I wanted to be more surprised that Hal hadn't seen Sebastian all day, but I wasn't. I called for a taxi and reminded myself that a vampire's wife was going to have to make peace with the idea of his ghouls.

* * *

My stiff upper lip lasted all the way to the University Club, but then I found myself surrounded by Volvo-driving baby boomers so into their gardens that they tended to sneer at me when I mispronounced the Latin name or, worse, called my plants by their common designation.

I managed to make small talk about roses and mullein and wild mustard with a few of the friendlier ladies while we all waited for Sebastian to arrive. About ten minutes before the lecture was to start, I thought I spotted him slipping in the side door. I rushed over, grateful to finally have someone decent to talk to.

About a foot away, I realized my mistake.

My warm, welcoming smile withered. It wasn't Sebastian who'd just walked in—it was his son, Mátyás.

3.

Mercury

KEYWORDS:

The Intellect, Volatile Action, and Children

Noticing my quickly crumpling smile, Mátyás's own expression brightened. That was the thing about Mátyás: you could always count on him taking a tiny bit of pleasure from other people's misfortunes, especially mine.

The last time I saw Mátyás, one of his cronies had put an arrow through my thigh. Just seeing that sarcastic smirk again made my leg twinge. Mátyás had Sebastian's aristocratic features, with irises a shade paler, almost golden. His black hair fell just long enough to be perpetually in front of his eyes. Truth was, Mátyás could have been handsome, if he wasn't always so bitter and angry looking.

Of course, he *was* cursed to be a teenager forever, so it wasn't entirely his fault. I imagined it would be pretty miserable to be seventeen for the past hundred and fifty-some years. I would feel a bit more pity for him, if he didn't have the annoying tendency to refer to me as his daddy's "chew toy."

"Darling Garnet, it's so very nice to see you alive and well," he drawled in a way that implied the exact opposite. "Where is dear old papa?"

"What are you doing here? This isn't really your kind of scene, is it?"

Mátyás shrugged, while looking around me for Sebastian. "I stopped by the farm to drop off my things. I noticed the calendar on the fridge. Where is he? We need to talk."

"You're staying at Sebastian's? For how long?" And, then, as it occurred to me, I added, "You have a key?"

His smile was toothy as he pulled a ring out of his pocket and jangled it in front of my face.

I scratched my chin with the middle finger of my left hand. Yes, juvenile, but something about Mátyás brought out the worst in me. Besides, this way I had the opportunity to both give him the finger and flash the engagement ring.

He stared at my ring finger with a look that I could only describe as stricken. "So it *is* true. Dear God. I think I'm going to be sick."

"Nice," I said.

Mátyás opened his mouth, no doubt to shoot off another insult, when one of the gardening matrons cleared her throat, surprising us both.

"Excuse me, Ms. Lacey?" the lady asked, peering at the name badge I'd been given when I first came in. "You're Mr. Von Traum's guest tonight, right?" I nodded. "Is there a problem?" she asked. "Is Mr. Von Traum expected to be late?"

I reached for my cell phone only to remember that I'd smashed it when I tumbled over my bike. "I'm afraid I don't know," I told the lady. "The last time I talked to him, he was planning to be here." In fact, he'd been the one to remind me not to be late. "Mátyás, do you have a phone? Mine's broken."

Without a word, Mátyás pulled a cell out of his suit coat pocket and handed it to me. I dialed Sebastian's number and got his voice mail. I left him a message reminding him that he was supposed to be here in—I checked the wall clock—three minutes. "This isn't like him," I told the gardening lady, as I handed Mátyás's phone back. "Something must be really wrong."

"People have paid for their tickets. The food has been catered," she said, her voice starting to sound a bit shrill. "There's nearly a hundred and fifty people here. It's the best attendance we've ever had."

My own nerves were starting to jangle. "Sebastian isn't the sort to just blow this off. Something terrible must have happened. He must have been in a car accident, or . . ."

"Or, he's off playing blood sports with another woman," Mátyás suggested casually.

The gardening lady, who had continued to sputter about arrangements that would have to be undone, stopped and stared gape-mouthed at Mátyás.

Mátyás locked eyes with me. "Or have you asked him to give all that up as part of your new life together? Say, how *is* that working out for you?"

"This is not the time, Mátyás. I'm seriously worried about Sebastian."

"Should I cancel? Or do you really think he's just held up?" The lady asked Mátyás, apparently hoping for a better answer from him than what she'd been getting from me.

"My father is fairly indestructible," Mátyás reminded me. "Very little keeps him from what he *wants*."

"Maybe you should try calling him again," the club president helpfully suggested.

When the door swung open, we all turned expectantly. The young woman who ducked in smiled apologetically when she noticed all the attention focused on her.

Sebastian hated being late. He thought tardiness was a social affront. When we went places together, we were often the first to arrive. I remembered when he'd miscalculated the time it would take to negotiate the traffic to Hal's house and we'd resolutely sat in the car so we wouldn't be twenty minutes early for the holiday party.

Even if Mátyás was right and Sebastian was with a ghoul, he'd still find a way to make it here on time. This wasn't like him.

Something was really wrong.

"He's not coming," I said, and somehow I knew it was true.

Despite my pronouncement, the club president fussed and fretted until almost thirty minutes past the hour before calling the engagement off. I stayed to help fold up chairs, still hopeful that Sebastian might show. Mátyás hung around to gloat, though I noticed him surreptitiously checking his cell a couple of times, so he might have been a bit worried himself.

"She must be something else," Mátyás said from where he leaned against the wall near the stack of folding chairs.

"Who?"

"The ghoul," Mátyás said, sounding a bit disappointed that I missed the point of his clever barb.

"Give me your phone," I said.

"I've already tried him. He's still not answering."

I raised an eyebrow, surprised he confessed to being worried. "I want to call a taxi. I'm going home. Maybe . . ." I was going to say that maybe I'd see him later, but I didn't like the implication that he might be gone for good. "He'd go there."

"I'll give you a ride."

I put my finger in my ear and wiggled it. I swore Mátyás just offered to take me home.

He rolled his eyes. "Seriously. Come on. My Jaguar has got to be more comfortable than a cab."

Go into a car with him? After he and his cronies tried to kill me? When he had left me for dead? I looked at him, his hair falling in front of his eyes and his tailored suit covering his teenage lanky fram. He looked like a kid. "Are you sure you're even legal to drive?"

"A hundred and fifty years plus," he said with a wry smile and a jingle of his keys.

After the cool of the University Club, outside felt like a sauna. Despite the setting sun, heat waves shimmered on the asphalt as we walked to Mátyás's brand-new, jet-black Jag. Despite having a boyfriend who was very into vehicles, I didn't normally understand the appeal of all that steel and such. This car, however, looked cool. It was low and predatory and dangerously fast. He caught me admiring his car and let slip an I-can-tell-you-think-it's-sexy grin. I grimaced in return, annoyed that he noticed me checking out his ride.

Mátyás beeped the doors open. My butt clenched when I slid onto the painfully hot leather seat. The air conditioner brought the smell of new car. I jiggled my legs until I stopped sticking to the seat. Mátyás watched me out of the corner of his eye as his did all the usual preparations to drive.

I said what I sensed he wanted to hear, but I gave it to him dry and uninterested. "Yeah, yeah. It's a cool car." It was true anyway. Even the dashboard looked spiffy and space-age. It must have cost a fortune. I wondered where Mátyás got the money for something this expensive. Then, the scrapes on my leg twitched and I remembered the Vatican agents. Had he gotten paid to betray his father? "Thirty silver pieces buys a lot these days, eh?"

Our uneasy truce shattered. He shot me a bitter look and flipped on the CD player with his knuckle. The thrash of speed-metal guitar filled the interior, killing any attempt at conversation. Suited me fine. I only wished I had my cell phone so I could check to see if there were any messages from Sebastian.

Where could he be?

Goddess, I prayed that he was okay.

I stared out the window, biting my fingernails to the quick with worry. At some point the sun set completely and the strobe of streetlights was replaced by long stretches of complete darkness. When the whiff of manure came in through the vents, I thought to ask, "Where are you taking me?"

He turned down the music a notch, and said, with what

appeared to be genuine confusion, "Home. Aren't you living at the farm?"

How was it that Mátyás always managed to stumble right into all the thorny issues in my life? "No," I muttered.

A smile twitched at the corner of his mouth. "Oh. My bad."

I snorted. If only he really meant that. "We might as well check to see if Sebastian stopped there."

Mátyás hummed happily along with the music the rest of the way.

I strained to see Sebastian's car in the driveway as we approached the farmhouse. My heart pounded at the emptiness. "He's not here," I said.

Mátyás's smile widened as he pulled in to the dirt drive. "She must be one hell of a ghoul."

"Shut up," I snapped. "I'm really starting to freak out. Aren't you worried?"

"He's a thousand-year-old vampire, Garnet," Mátyás said, switching the engine off. "He's got mad survival skills."

"Maybe," I said, struggling out of my seat belt.

"Where are you going? His car isn't here."

"I know," I said, opening the door. "But I still want to check things out. You know, see if there's any sign of a struggle."

He laughed. "Who are you, Miss Marple now?"

"Look, as you say, he's a thousand years old. You don't think he made any enemies in all that time?"

Mátyás unsnapped his own seat belt with an incredulous shake of his head. "Okay, Inspector Clouseau, lead on."

There's something inherently spooky about approaching a farmhouse at night. Sebastian's was no exception, especially given the fact that he normally had the house warded to appear abandoned. Where the porch naturally sagged a little with time, the shadows and Sebastian's spell made it seem in complete disrepair. The lights were off and the windows reflected only hollow blackness.

I had to rub my eyes to banish Sebastian's wards, but even then the place seemed dark and forbidding. The house was set quite a ways back from the highway, and my feet scrunched on the beige sandstone gravel of the drive. A highway light illuminated the country graveyard next door, with its lichen-stained, tilting headstones. The surrounding cornfields rustled with hushed whispers and bullfrogs bellowed lowly in the damp roadside ditches.

I scrambled to the unlit porch and put my hand on the doorknob.

"Honey, we're home!" Mátyás shouted from behind, making me jump. Noticing my reaction, he smiled broadly. With a jerk of his chin in the direction of the cemetery, he said, "Home, creepy home, eh? Perhaps I can understand your cold feet. I mean, especially given the place really is haunted."

I pursed my lips in response. A ghost had come with Sebastian's house. Sebastian always said that he figured that Benjamin was the reason he was able to get such a good deal on the mortgage, but I knew he enjoyed sharing his house with a poltergeist. I'd feel a lot more comfortable if we weren't pretty sure Benjamin had ax murdered his wife in the "guest" room upstairs. It was only a guest room in theory because no one had ever stayed there since the murder, and Benjamin wouldn't let anyone change a thing about it either.

Maybe I *would* take Sebastian up on that offer to move somewhere new. "Let's see if he's home, shall we?" I asked Mátyás, irritated that he'd somehow made me uncomfortable about a house I already spent more than half my time at.

I tried the knob. I was strangely relieved to find the door locked, and not, say, hanging off its hinges. Today's newspaper was tucked by the threshold. I grabbed it and the mail from his box. Using my key, I let myself in the front door. I flipped on the overhead light. The house was quiet, empty.

Being a hundred-year-old farm house, Sebastian's living room wasn't grand or spacious. He filled the rectangular space with modern, comfy suede couches and leather chairs. Books lined glass-fronted, built-in cases. An expensive Persian rug accented polished maple floors. Abstract art hung on the ivory-gold painted walls. Central air kept the place cool. A book rested on the arm of Sebastian's favorite high-back leather chair.

I sighed. His place was much more grown-up and classy than mine. My stuff was *so* going to get sent back to the rummage sale it came from when we combined households.

"So," Mátyás said, flopping down on to the couch. "No signs of a break-in?" he asked from where he peeked in over my shoulder. "Are you sure the bedroom's empty?"

"Sebastian?" I walked over to the open staircase and called up in concession to Mátyás's suggestion. "Hello? Anyone at home?"

A wind ruffled the lace curtains on the landing upstairs, even though the window was closed. Cold kissed my cheek. "I mean besides you, Benjamin."

When Mátyás put his boots up on the glass coffee table, I almost heard Benjamin's growl of dislike. With a sudden jerk, Mátyás's feet were shoved off. Mátyás sat up straighter, looking around for the culprit. He gave me a glare like I'd put Benjamin up to it. I shrugged as innocently as I could muster. It wasn't my fault Benjamin had good taste in people.

I checked Sebastian's answering machine to see if he'd called here thinking I might come back. There was a message from Jensen's telling him details about the Mustang and another from the Horticultural Society lady expressing her extreme disappointment that Sebastian was a no-show at tonight's event. I noticed she didn't offer a date for rescheduling. Ouch. Automatically, I scribbled down notes detailing the calls on the pad near the phone as was our routine.

Mátyás sat on the couch still glancing around a bit nervously, as though he expected Benjamin to make another move on him. I leaned against the railing of the open staircase and noted how Mátyás looked uncomfortable and out of place. The last time he'd been in this house, he'd secretly been allied with Vatican assassins that wanted his father's alchemical formula for vampirism. We'd nearly died to protect it. Mátyás had let us live, but not for a lack of trying.

"Have you and Sebastian reconciled?" I asked him as kindly as I could.

He didn't even turn to face me, he just chuckled darkly. "How likely is that?"

Well, it didn't seem impossible from where I stood. I knew that both men loved the other in their own way, despite all the twisted family history between them. I didn't say anything, though, because I didn't want to presume to comment on his relationship with his father.

"Yeah," he said to my silence. "Exactly."

"Then why are you here? Why come back?" I hoped my tone didn't imply what I was really thinking, which was wondering if he'd come back with another agenda again. Maybe Sebastian's disappearance wasn't really such a surprise to him, after all. Perhaps he was back to finish the job he'd started.

His eyes narrowed. "Oh, now I'm responsible for his disappearance?"

"I didn't say that," I said, then just as quickly asked, "So are you?"

"No." Mátyás said gruffly, though I thought I could sense a trace of hurt in his tone. "Disappointed?"

Unconvinced, maybe, I thought. "Why are you here again?"

"To torture you, of course."

With that, he stood up and walked to the kitchen door. I followed behind, turning on lights. It was freaky that he didn't seem to need the light to find his way around; it was almost as if he could see in the dark. But I might have been imagining things. He probably just knew the place well. I was never really sure how extra-human Mátyás was, being a dhampyr and all.

A dhampyr is what you get when you cross a vampire and a human. As far as I knew, Mátyás was the only one, ever. Traditional vampires like Parrish were dead. Their skin was cold, they didn't need to eat or breathe, their hair didn't grow much, and, well, let's just say a sperm bank would be uninterested in their deposit. Sebastian was, for the most part, *fully* human. Thus Mátyás.

Like I said, I never knew what, if any, superhuman

powers Mátyás possessed. Other than his longevity and his awesome powers of annoyance.

Sebastian's kitchen smelled like roasted chili peppers and stewed tomatoes. There were bottles and jars of all sorts around. Sebastian had just canned tomatoes and made several batches of salsa, which sat upside down on towels on the counter beside the stove. A few remaining fruits ripened on the windowsill.

Mátyás reached into the fridge and pulled out a bottle of beer. I watched him hunt through the drawers for a bottle cap opener.

Our eyes met as he shut the drawer by my hip. I leaned against the counter, arms crossed in front of my chest. "I'm not here to kill him," Mátyás said. "Or you."

"Really," I drawled. I was still unconvinced. "How convenient that Sebastian is missing when you show up."

"Actually, it isn't terribly convenient," Mátyás said with a snarl. He levered the opener and gave it a forceful shove. The top came off with an audible pop and fizz. "I think he's making a huge mistake and I was hoping to talk him out of it. Now I see it's too late." He tipped the bottle in the direction of my ring before taking a swig. "I shouldn't have wasted my time. I should have stayed in Rome."

"Italy? Still hanging out with the Order of Eustace then?" I tried to make it sound casual, but my voice sounded strained even to me.

Mátyás glared at me from where he leaned against the kitchen counter, bottle poised at his lips. He took a long, defiant swallow. His eyes never left mine. Finally, he said, "Do you really want to broach that particular topic with me?"

I sure as hell did if Sebastian was in danger.

"Depends," I said slowly. "Do you have any new tats you want to tell me about?"

For a supposedly secret organization, the Vatican assassins liked to advertise their membership with a red-lettered tattoo of the numbers 22:18, a reference to the biblical chapter Exodus's admonishment not to "suffer a witch to live." If Mátyás had joined, he'd have gotten the tattoo. It was required, even of their sensitives—the magically abled turncoats that helped them hunt down and destroy Witches and their covens.

The kitchen was so quiet that the ticktock of the wall clock measured the seconds before Mátyás answered. "No new ink," he said finally.

His answer was so cautious that I wondered what he'd left out. "What aren't you telling me, Mátyás? Are you working for them in some other way? Or . . . Oh!" Suddenly I remembered that the Vatican had promised to try to resurrect his mother, Teréza who Sebastian accidentally left in a state of suspended reanimation when he tried to pass on his vampirism in the traditional way. "Do they have your mother hostage? Are they asking for a trade?"

"Trade?" he repeated incredulously. "I already told you I'm not working for them."

"So sue me for being suspicious. It wouldn't be the first time you'd sell out your father for your mother's sake."

"That's unfair," he snapped.

"Is it? You left us for dead."

"I did, did I?" Mátyás took a long pull on his beer. I could smell the yeast from across the room. "Is that how you remember it?"

I had to break eye contact because I suddenly remembered

how Mátyás had, in fact, not entirely betrayed us. Though my spell had fooled the Vatican agents on the other side of our magical circle, Mátyás had stepped through and knew that Sebastian and I were alive, and, even though the order wanted us eliminated, he'd walked away without letting on that there was a chance we had survived the ordeal. It had been mercy so much as Mátyás was capable of it. "Fine," I said. "Are you planning on betraying us now?"

His eyes narrowed to slits. The fingers holding the beer bottle tightened. "No."

I stared at him trying to decide if I believed him.

Mátyás broke eye contact to look at the wall clock. "It's only been a couple of hours. Maybe we shouldn't be pointing fingers just yet. It's possible he'll come home any minute—blood on his lips and a spring in his step."

"Stop it," I said, though I knew it was a distinct possibility.

"If he's not back by morning, you can paint me as the villain then, okay?"

Not back by morning? My heart skipped in my throat. "Bright Goddess, Mátyás, you don't think . . . ? He'll be back by then, won't he?"

"Yes, of course, he will," Mátyás said, though his eyes didn't meet mine. Reaching for his cell phone, he said, "Look, maybe we should try Papa again."

I nodded and watched anxiously as he dialed. In the quiet of the kitchen, I could hear the phone ring. By the third tone, I knew there would be no answer. Mátyás stared at the ceiling as Sebastian's voice asked him to leave a message. He said something short and curt in a language I didn't recognize—not that I knew a lot of languages, but it wasn't Spanish, which I knew the sound of from spending some formative years with *Sesame Street*.

As he snapped the phone shut, it occurred to me that Sebastian might be ignoring any calls with Mátyás's caller ID. "We should try from here too," I said.

"You think he's avoiding my calls?"

Mátyás sounded genuinely hurt by the suggestion, so I was gentle when I said, "It's good to cover all our bases, don't you think?"

But I didn't have better luck. As I replaced the receiver in its cradle, it occurred to me that there was supposed to be a way for me to check my cell phone voice mail remotely. I started hunting for the cell phone manual. I was sure Sebastian had kept it here at his place because he always teased me that I'd lose track of it. Which was true, of course. Pushing papers aside in his junk drawer, I wished he were here to tell me which "safe place" he'd put the damn thing in.

I heard the bottle clink in the kitchen, which made me think of my neighbors' recycling bins. I picked up the phone again and called my answering machine at the apartment to retrieve its messages. William had called to let me know that he'd found a bunch of vegan pate recipes he planned on serving at the coven meeting at his place tomorrow. After that, there was a hang up. I tended to get a lot of those as my number was one digit off a hair styling salon, but this time it sounded ominous. I listened to the quick click-click three times, straining to hear the sound of Sebastian's breathing or any extraneous noises. Did that sound like how Sebastian usually hung up the phone? As

I finally gave up trying to decipher it, Mátyás came into the living room.

I could tell he was acting cool and distant again by the swagger in his hips. "Still no answer, eh? She's keeping him quite preoccupied."

I narrowed my eyes. "Am I really that much fun to poke at?"

"Yes." Mátyás smiled, leaning his hip against the backside of the couch. "You'll make an excellent wicked stepmother."

"I suppose that makes you Cinderella?"

"Prince Charming." He smiled.

"Oh, you're a *prince*, all right."

"Finally, we agree on something," Mátyás said, feigning exasperation, except a smile slipped out—one, much to my surprise, I found myself returning.

The rumble of a passing semi rattled the window slightly, and for a second I mistook the sound for a car coming up the drive. I rushed to the curtain and glanced outside, disappointed by the bright red glow of retreating taillights. Holding the muslin aside a little longer, I scanned the darkness. All I really saw was my own worried expression staring back at me.

Upstairs, Benjamin threw a pile of books on the floor.

Noticing Mátyás's startled jump and sheepish recovery, I said, "Even Benjamin's worried. That can't be good."

Perhaps in deference to our shared smile, Mátyás merely shrugged. "He's a vampire, Garnet."

"That doesn't mean he can't get in trouble," I said. "He could be hurt."

"Or he could just be off having the time of his life," Mátyás said. Then, holding up a hand to stop my hot retort, he added, "Even the police won't file a missing person's case until he's gone at least forty-eight hours. You saw him today?"

I nodded. "A couple of hours before the lecture."

"Had he fed recently?"

I pursed my lips and shook my head, not trusting my voice not to betray my frustration that I couldn't get Sebastian to take my blood the night before.

"How long had it been?"

How was I supposed to know? It wasn't like Sebastian shared his bloodletting calendar with me. "I don't know," I muttered.

Mátyás was smiling again, but it wasn't at all the kind I wanted to share. "If you're worried," he purred, "maybe you should call them."

"What?"

"I know he keeps his black book around here somewhere," he said, walking back into the kitchen.

I stomped after him, curious, despite myself. Mátyás must be putting on a show rifling through all those recipes and such on the top of the fridge; there was no way Sebastian's estranged son knew more about where he kept his most personal things than I did.

"Black book?" I repeated, even though I was afraid I knew exactly what could be found in this supposed book of Sebastian's.

"Ah, here we go." Mátyás held up a thin black planner. He started flipping through it. He stood close enough to me that I could smell the beer on his breath. I resolutely kept my eyes from looking down at the book.

"I'm not going to call those . . . ghouls," I told him.

"No worries, darling. I'll do it," Mátyás said.

I snatched the book from him. "No, you won't."

Mátyás put a hurt expression on his face. "I thought you were really worried about Sebastian. Perhaps if I called, you could put your mind at ease."

"You're not doing this. Nobody is doing this," I said. My hands shook just about as much as my voice. I really wanted to hurl the book out the window, into the trash, at Mátyás's smug face—anything to get the tangible evidence of the other women out of my hands.

Mátyás held up his hands in mock surrender. "I was just thinking of you."

"Liar," I snarled. Before I succumbed to the desire to pummel him, I turned on my heels and trudged up the stairs. After nearly tripping on Mátyás's suitcases in the hall, I threw myself on Sebastian's bed. Tears burned in my eyes as I caught the scent of Sebastian's shampoo on the pillows. In my hands, I still clutched the book. I threw the evil thing against the wall with a shriek of frustration.

I lay on the bed and stared at the corner where the black book fell. After several attempts to ignore it, I got to my feet and picked it back up. The book itself was thin and flimsy—cheaply made. The edges were worn and the spine broken. My fingers felt the roughly textured cover as though looking for some clue as to its contents without actually opening the thing. There were no identifying marks on the outside, nothing to indicate that it held anything earth-shattering. What was I afraid of? That I would find the name of someone I knew? So what if I did? Sebastian took their blood; he wasn't sleeping with them.

Was he?

This was the part of the whole ghoul situation that I was never entirely sure about. All my interactions involving Sebastian and biting happened during sex, but they didn't have to. The times I'd seen Sebastian sink his teeth into someone in a nonsexual way, it was always ultraviolent—with the intent to kill. But I imagined there could be a happy medium . . .

Right?

I shook my head. I never asked, so I didn't know the answer. Never more did I regret my resolute policy of ignorance than I did right now. If I did open up this book and called any of them, I wouldn't even know if I was talking to food or a fuck-buddy or whether there was a difference.

I set the book down on the bed—no, *our* bed. The bed where Sebastian and I made love, the bed we were going to share after our marriage. I couldn't go through with the wedding with this big secret hanging between us. Despite everything, I still didn't believe that Sebastian had just lost track of time. He'd always had ghouls, and he never missed an appointment before. Something else must have happened to him, and maybe one of these people had seen him last, knew what time he left—something that might help me figure out where he was and what kind of trouble he was in.

Besides, what did I have to say other than, "Is Sebastian there?" or "Have you seen him today?"

Closing my eyes, I tried to summon the courage to walk downstairs and pick up the phone. Instead of finding any extra mettle, I felt Lilith roiling just beneath the surface. Her presence reminded me that I *could* try magic first. Unfortunately, I didn't have a celestial GPS system, but I could tug the blood connection that was forged between us the night we joined forces to defeat the Vatican agents. At least then I would know if he was still alive. Maybe too I could tell if he was in any kind of trouble. It was worth a try.

And, as a bonus, I wouldn't have to talk to any ghouls.

I got off the bed and put Sebastian's black book on his dresser. I didn't want it in my hands because I was afraid it would become the focus of my energy. I needed to be thinking purely and openly about Sebastian's whereabouts, and the book would taint my visualizations, direct my search.

Since I was up, I locked the door. The last thing I wanted was for Mátyás to wander in hoping to taunt me. Then, I took my clothes off.

Normally, I wasn't a huge proponent of going "sky-clad," which is to say naked, in solitary rituals. It served a purpose in group work—by building trust and the vulnerability that could push a person outside of their comfort zone into the place where magic lives. That being said, I tended to find it distracting now that I was past that place in my life when I felt I needed to be open and raw and exposed for the Goddess to find me. After all, I now had a Goddess, quite literally, within.

But my skirt felt tight and restricting, and my shoes just plain hurt. It didn't make sense to be half naked, so I opted for full nudity. Besides, when trying to find my lover, it made sense.

In fact, I decided to lie down on his side of the bed.

Breathing deeply of the trace of his scent on the pillow and sheets, I centered myself. Of all the rooms in his house, Sebastian's bedroom was the one that I could almost imagine belonging to a storybook vampire. He had a four-poster bed with an honest-to-Goddess canopy, complete with drapes. It was sexy, romantic—a lot like him.

The room had a lot of windows, all of which were shut tight against the heat. Lace curtains obscured the light from the highway. An ornate oak dresser in a Louis XIV style sat against one wall, and a dresser with a triptych mirror occupied the other. The closet, large enough to walk into, overflowed with clothes from all aspects of Sebastian's life—oil-spattered coveralls, T-shirts, jeans, leather jackets, opera coats, Armani suits, and a tuxedo or two.

Framed botanical drawings of various herbs hung on the walls; some were even real, pressed leaves with notations in Sebastian's handwriting. On the surface of the dressers, silver frames held sepia-faded photos of people who were once important to Sebastian.

This was a very personal room.

Reaching deep inside, I unlocked the door that held back my magical sight. Suddenly, the room swirled with the black tendrils of Sebastian's residue energy. Darker spots hovered over places he'd lingered—one photo on the dresser was completely obscured. I resolved to look more closely at that picture once my work was done.

I relaxed deeper into a meditative state and felt myself floating just above my body. Looking down, I searched for the thin thread that bound Sebastian and me. It was silver, worked through with gold and badly frayed. I'd sensed that our empathic tie was growing weaker, and it was obvious in the astral plane. I gave the cord a tug, and felt the firmness of a connection. Sebastian was still alive, at least. If he wasn't, there would be no resistance, and the cord would have come back severed.

I was just about to pull myself along the cord when I started at the sight of a man standing in front of me. Tall and reedy, built like a farmer, he had mouse-brown hair and a day's worth of stubble on his chin. He looked as surprised to see me as I was to see him.

"Garnet?" Though I'd never heard him speak before, I recognized his voice instantly.

"Benjamin?"

It was Sebastian's house ghost.

He looked as solid as the bedpost he leaned against. I'd never seen him this way; it was like I'd suddenly switched to high-definition TV after years of rabbit ears and no cable.

"What are you doing here?" he asked. "Are you dead?"

"I hope not," I said, glancing down at my body. Other than the fact that every time I saw myself like this I couldn't help but think it was time to start getting serious about diet and exercise, I appeared to be breathing normally. "I'm looking for Sebastian."

"He's not here," Benjamin said. A scowl darkened his face. "But that boy of his is."

I smiled. "I don't like Mátyás much either."

He grunted. "Sebastian changed the wards last week. Told me I had to let the brat in."

Last week? Sebastian must have done it as part of his plan to ask me to marry him. "You could always go downstairs and throw some things around," I suggested mischievously. Benjamin was technically a poltergeist; he could knock pictures off the wall, flip light switches, and all that kind of annoyingly creepy stuff. "You know, rattle his cage."

"Gypsy boy might cast a hex on me," Benjamin said in the direction of the stairs, with a shake of his head, but he didn't sound really concerned. "Anyway, I promised Sebastian I wouldn't scare his boy too much."

Lucky Mátyás, I thought. I never got the special treatment.

"Heck, sure you do, ma'am. I'm under strict orders not to kill you."

Well, wasn't that nice? "Uh, thank you."

"My pleasure," he said kindly, though his eyes watched me darkly. His image flickered slightly, and I thought I caught the glimpse of a more sinister image beneath— something gaunt, empty-eyed, and hungry. Though it was gone so quickly, I wasn't sure I hadn't imagined it.

"So, how are you fixing to find Sebastian?"

"Oh," I said, lifting the thread in my hand to show him. "I thought I'd follow this."

Shielding his eyes, he peered into the distance in the direction the thread seemed to be leading. "I can't see the end of it. You sure it's still connected?"

I shrugged. "It's all I have."

"Is he in trouble?"

I was beginning to think so. I nodded.

"You'd better go," he said. "I'll watch over this end of you."

I wasn't entirely sure how comfortable I felt with that idea, especially given the way Benjamin stared at my naked body. On the bed, my body shifted as though in response to his predatory gaze. Quickly, I wove a protection spell triggered to wake me if Benjamin came within an inch of me.

Sebastian might have asked him not to kill me, but he might have forgotten to include a clause about maiming.

Sensing the magic, Benjamin's lips pursed as though he was affronted. I heard him mutter, "Offer to do someone a favor. Humph . . . women."

I expected him to turn heels, but he continued to lean against the bedpost with arms crossed.

The dark flashed behind his eyes again as he said, "You'd better get on your way, missy."

With a nod of good-bye, I pulled my astral self hand-over-hand along the thin wire. Space and time compressed in fits and starts. Despite pulling with the same strength, I seemed to speed along the county road, but slowed as I passed a spot near the side of the highway where someone had placed a handmade cross and a teddy bear. It was as though I progressed with more difficulty past places where spirits might linger, where someone else's grief might hold a ghost in place. I shivered. I moved my feet quicker, but it was like walking through mud, or like that dream where you're running but can't make any headway. The bear's button eyes flashed in the headlights of a passing car.

Once out of the pull of the memorial, I found myself in Madison proper in less than a second. On the lake, moonlight competed with streetlights to shine on the whitecaps. Wind brushed through the leaves in the treetops. The pungent scent of lake—a strange combination of dead fish and the heady scent of fresh water—clung to the dew-dappled grass. A man walking a dog approached me. At least, that's how my eyes first registered him. As they drew closer, I saw it was a man walking in the footprints of a coyote.

Sebastian's thread disappeared. Or, rather, it came undone in a chaotic burst. Suddenly, instead of a single cord, it diverged into hundreds of tinier ones, each leading in a different direction.

"What the hell?" Which one of these was I supposed to follow? When I tugged the microfibers, each held firm as though they *all* led to Sebastian. "This is impossible," I muttered.

The man and the wolf stopped and cocked their head in my direction. In the darkness, I had only the impression of sharp features and dark eyes. Even at a distance, the intensity of his gaze hit me. Instinct urged me to run. This was the stare of a true predator, and I got the sense he saw me much more clearly than I could see him.

He reached up a hand and . . .

Waved?

The absurdity of his gesture made a hysterical giggle rise in my throat. I waved back.

Then, fear got the better of me and I turned and fled for home. I could hear the galloping pad of paws behind me. At the highway marker, when I was forced into a slower pace, I heard a howl. I tried to push myself faster, uncertain that he would be held by the same energy. "Don't look back," I whispered to myself frantically, feeling like a child trying to escape a nightmare. I swore I could feel hot breath on my neck just as I snapped forward into my own body.

I sat up with a gasp. My skin felt cold and clammy. I glanced around the room for Benjamin, but, of course, could no longer see any trace of him. "Benjamin? Are you there?"

The light flicked once in response.

"Good," I said. "Listen, please don't let anyone in. I was followed."

Wind shrieked around the dormer.

"Thanks," I said. Shivering, I was grateful not only for Sebastian's guard ghost, but also that he kept his house heavily warded. I cautiously crept over to the window, half expecting to see a wolf under the cemetery's streetlight. All I saw was the white glow of the marble gravestones and the wind bending the tufts of tall grass that grew close to the bases where the lawnmower couldn't reach.

I got up and collected my clothes. On the dresser next to Sebastian's little black book sat the picture frame that had been so obscured by Sebastian's lingering touches. I picked it up, as I imagine he must have so many times. The worn black-and-white photo showed a group of smiling men in uniform posing jauntily against what looked to me like a World War II military plane. I strained to pick out Sebastian among them, but he didn't seem to be one of the men pictured. Curious.

Setting the picture back down, I glanced at the clock. It was ten thirty in the evening. Too late to call a stranger, at least so my mother had taught me. My hand hovered over the book anyway. At the last minute, I took it with me as I went to the bathroom to take a long, hot bath.

After ten minutes of soaking in scalding water, my skin finally warmed up. Had my body grown cold because I nearly killed myself on my little astral walkabout? Leaning back into the bubbles, I tried to banish that thought.

A knock made me shriek.

"I'm ordering pizza. What do you want on yours?" Mátyás asked through the door.

"Good luck with that," I said, sliding deeper into the bubbles.

There was a long pause on the other side of the door. "What do you mean?"

"Sebastian's wards," I said. "The pizza driver will never find this place."

"Oh, right," he muttered.

I couldn't tell if he was still there when I suggested, "There's always a pizza in the freezer. I'll take veggie."

I heard a grunt that sounded affirmative, then footsteps going away.

With a deep sigh, I picked up the little black book from where I balanced it on the edge of the sink. My fingers made wet marks on the cover. Steeling myself, I flipped it open. Alison. Andrea. Cindy. Margaret. Susan. Traci (with an "i", no less). Walter.

Walter?

He lived six blocks from my house. Walter? I couldn't get over it. Walter wasn't even a terribly sexy name. I mean, I guess I figured if there was going to be a man's name in this book it would be something hot or exotic-sounding like Valentine or Jean-Baptiste, but . . . Walter? Who was this guy?

Then, I noticed interspersed between the entries were people with addresses in other states, even other countries. Some names were crossed out. Others had updated information—changes in phone numbers, cell numbers, even e-mail.

I shut the book. The image of Sebastian e-mailing kinky notes to Walter down the block made my brain explode. I decided that what I needed was beer, food, and sleep, in that order.

By the time the pizzas came out of the oven, I was dressed in comfy sweats and on my third round. As someone who didn't drink a lot, I knew I was utterly and completely wasted. However, as a plus, I found everything Mátyás had to say intensely hilarious, which I could tell annoyed him and only made me laugh harder. I devoured two-thirds of the veggie pizza, drank another beer, and fell over on the couch, sound asleep.

Apparently, beer gives me nightmares.

I dreamt my astral self had gotten caught in the spirit sinkhole of Lakewood Cemetery in Minneapolis. *All around me stood giant marble slabs—some of them were ten-foot Celtic crosses, others had stone-faced angels perched on top, staring down at me with empty, blank-white eyes. Shades drifted just out of sight. Something chased me now, a big, black dog. I kept trying to find the front gate, but somehow ended up moving deeper and deeper into the necropolis. Grave images—upside down torches, cherubs, and crosses—flickered through my peripheral vision as I ran. Its snapping teeth as white as gravestones. "I come in peace," said a crow sitting on a mausoleum.*

"Yeah, right," I mumbled sleepily.

A thorn pricked my finger and I glanced at the gravestone: Sterling. Silver, yeah, that's what I needed, a sliver bullet.

"No, really, it's nine o'clock. You're late."

I blinked to see Mátyás smiling gleefully into my face, as though he anticipated my reaction: "Oh, shit," I said, jumping up and then grabbing my pounding head. "Oh, ow!"

With Mátyás's laughter chasing me, I stumbled up the

stairs to find a change of clothes. I went over to "my" drawer and pulled out a bloodred bra and a black halter top. Then I dug through my corner of his closet until I found a decent pair of jeans and my black-and-red Converses.

As I hunted up some socks and accessories, I glanced at the bed, which was still made. It looked empty and unused. I smoothed the places I'd wrinkled when I lay on it last night and, unconsciously, checked out the window for Sebastian's car.

Turning away, I pulled a comb through my hair. Then I retreated to the bathroom to brush my teeth and try to do something with my general appearances. Given how I felt inside, I thought I managed to look half decent by the time I emerged.

Mátyás stood just outside the door with a cup of coffee in one hand and Sebastian's darkest sunglasses in the other. "You might need these," he smirked. I narrowed my eyes at him, even though I took his offerings gratefully. "Dhampyrs are impervious to the aftereffects of alcohol, I take it?"

"Totally," he said.

Jamming the sunglasses on my face, I growled, "As if I needed another reason to despise you."

"You should be nicer to the boy who has the Jag."

My fuzzy brain couldn't track the logic of his statement. "I should?" I asked somewhat feebly.

"I'm giving you a ride."

"You are?"

"Yes, and you're bringing along the black book."

"I am?"

"Yes, you can call as I drive."

The pattern we'd been establishing came to a crashing halt. "The hell I am," I said, putting my hands on my hips. "Just so you can gloat."

"I guess you'd better call a taxi, then," Mátyás said in that tone that implied that he knew it was the last thing I wanted to have to do when I was already so late. It would take a taxi from town twenty minutes to get out here, and another twenty to get back. It would cost a fortune too, though I always kept taxi money in my purse.

I squinted fiercely at him and then realized the effect was lost behind the dark glasses. "Fine," I huffed and grabbed the book from where I'd left it in the bathroom on the back of the toilet.

I'd been hoping for a repeat of our drive out in which Mátyás listened to his CDs and we didn't speak. I should have known I wouldn't be so lucky a second time.

"You're a sloppy drunk," Mátyás observed as we pulled out of the driveway. Daisies and Queen Anne's lace growing in the ditches bobbed their heads in our wake. Though Mátyás cranked the AC, I cracked open the window. The stale, recycled air made me feel claustrophobic and nauseous.

"Hmmm," I said, since, as fuzzy as my head felt, I could neither confirm nor deny his assessment. The sky was a dazzling shade of blue and, despite the shades, I squinted. We passed a group of horses grazing on a steep hillside. Hawks glided overhead, riding the thermals.

"You didn't like what you found in that book, did you?"

I shot a warning glance at him.

"You're going to have to get used to them. You're not his only chew toy, just his current favorite."

"I'm not his chew toy at all, I'm his fiancée." I clumsily waved my ring finger at him. "Remember?"

He pointedly ignored me. The shadow of a white pine windbreak fell across the highway in a long stripe. I thought I might have shocked him into submission and that I would get to ride the rest of the way in relative peace and quiet until he said, "Yet my mother still wears his engagement ring."

My head whipped around to him so fast I almost barfed. "What?"

Mátyás shot me an oily smile. "I think you heard me, but I'm more than happy to repeat myself. Let me say it nice and slow: my mother wears Sebastian's ring. The heirloom."

Despite myself, I glanced at the ring on my finger. The diamond glittered and the gold shone, but . . . and, I hated myself for even entertaining this thought, damn Mátyás, but, it looked so much like the classic engagement ring that it was almost devoid of any personality. Parrish, a vampire ex of mine, had given me a ring once so that we could fool the FBI into thinking I was his fiancée. It was Black Hills gold— old and worn, but clearly loved. I knew when Parrish gave it to me that it meant something to him, that it had *history*.

I closed my fist when I noticed Mátyás watching me. "Yeah, well, Sebastian never did marry your mother, did he?" I was pleased to see Mátyás wince for once. "New ring, fresh start, you know?"

Yeah, that seemed plausible. In fact, I'd already convinced myself it was true. Mátyás must have bought it too, because he finally lapsed into blessed silence and we didn't speak again until he pulled up to the cross street closest to my store.

I hopped out and shut the door. Leaning in the window I'd cracked open, I said, "Hey, thanks for the ride." Even though he was still not looking at me, I lifted the little black book to show him. "I'll let you know if I find Sebastian."

Mátyás glanced at me through the curtain of his dark hair. The vulnerability that flashed through his eyes for a moment made him seem the age he looked. "Do," he said crisply. Then he powered up my window so fast he nearly nipped my fingers and then took off with a roar.

State Street is a pedestrian mall, and in the summer it could pass as a quiet street in New York. People bustled: going places, doing things. Maples and quaking aspen lined the streets. Pigeons and buskers loitered in every alcove, crooning softly. Every ten paces ragged homeless men begged for spare change. Punks and skateboarders sunned themselves and surfed the Internet on painted iron benches. The smells of Thai, Indian, and Afghani food mingled in the morning heat. Once in front of Mercury Crossing, the scent of sandalwood incense overwhelmed everything else, even the diesel of passing city buses.

I took a deep breath and squared my shoulders. William looked up from the register when the chimes jingled. "I'm sorry I'm late," I said as I rushed to stow my backpack under the counter. "I overslept."

"Overslept?" William sounded kind of disappointed.

"Yeah," I said, as I went though my getting oriented rituals. Using my swipe card on the computer, I punched myself in.

"Just overslept? Seriously? No ghosts or super-zombies or

anything like that? I mean, usually when you're late something supernatural is going down."

I had to laugh. I stopped fussing and leaned a hip on the counter and smiled at William. "Yeah, okay, Sebastian is missing and I can't find him on the astral plane, Mátyás is back, and I have to contact Sebastian's ghoulfriends. Oh, a wolf or some kind of dog has been stalking me."

"A werewolf? I thought you said there weren't werewolves."

Trust William to cut to the subtext of my wolf comment. "I didn't think there were."

"But you saw one?"

"I saw a wolf . . . or a big dog, in the city. During the day."

"Timber wolf? Gray wolf? You sure it wasn't a coyote? Actually, I just read a whole article about coyotes that said they're becoming a big problem in major metropolises. There was this amazing picture of a coyote that had gotten himself trapped in an elevator in San Francisco or somewhere like that."

I shook my head. I actually had no idea if I could tell the difference between any of those. "All I know is that it wasn't a dog."

"But it was a person?"

"In the astral plane I saw a man walking with the wolf, kind of on top of it. He didn't happen to call here, did he?"

"The werewolf?"

"Sebastian," I clarified. William shook his head. "I'll just check the answering machine to be sure."

"Yeah, no problem. The store's been quiet."

Summer usually was. The University of Wisconsin students were on break, and though we had some regular clientele, tourists tended to window-shop and not much more. I nodded and headed for the back room.

I sat down in the wooden swivel office chair and unearthed the answering machine. My heart skipped a beat when I saw the flashing light. The first message was from a local artist who wanted to come in to see if we might be interested in carrying her Goddess-themed pottery on commission. I jotted down her number. The other was from Slow Bob, who came in mostly on a substitute basis, asking if there were any hours available for him to work.

Nothing from Sebastian.

I sighed. Even though I hadn't really expected that he would call here, I still felt disappointed.

On impulse, I dialed Slow Bob. Bob had gotten his nickname because, even though he worked diligently, speed was not his forte. Despite being an excellent organizer, it was disastrous to put Slow Bob on the register during a rush, which, of course, was often when we needed help. I got Bob's voice mail and left a message that if he wanted, he could pick up a shift tomorrow afternoon.

I might need the time if I still hadn't heard from Sebastian.

Next, I called back the artist and told her to come in the following Tuesday with a few of her best pieces. She was thrilled, and I was happy to have made her day.

I set Sebastian's black book down on the blotter. Receiver in hand, my finger hovered over the first numbers. I checked the clock overhead. It was almost eleven. What were the chances any of them were even home? Most likely, they had day jobs. All I had to do was leave a message asking if they'd seen Sebastian in the last several hours.

I stared at the name: Alison.

My heartbeat ticked in my throat as the line rang. Her voice mail made her sound perky and half my age. Britney Spears sang a few notes before the beep. I stumbled through my request, left my numbers for both the store and home, babbled far too long, and hung up.

This was much harder than I expected it would be. It was weird enough having a list of names rattling around in my head, but now I had Britney Spears too? That gave me horrific images that combined Sebastian and some barely legal woman in schoolgirl uniform fetish wear. Did he like that sort of thing? What if, while we were making out, he was thinking about Alison in bobby socks and pom-poms?

It was too much.

Standing up, I started to clean. I organized, dusted, and filed. As I filled wastebaskets, I emptied my mind. I didn't want to think about Alison, so I kept myself busy. After the back room, I tackled the front. Despite the constant air-conditioning, sweat prickled under my arms.

When I next looked up, I saw a familiar face. I was still trying to place the doughy features and bright, shiny brown eyes, when she said, timidly pointing to herself, "Marge? From the new coven?"

"Oh, right," I said, putting down the paper towel and organic, nontoxic cleaner I'd been using to dust the bookshelves. "I'm sorry. Can I help you?"

"I was just . . . well, I was curious . . ."

I waited patiently for Marge to gather up the courage to ask her question. Maybe she was used to being interrupted because when I didn't snap impatiently or try to guess, she sighed.

"Lilith," she said. "Since I'm going to be working with Her, you know, I wondered if you, like, had any books."

"Of course," I said with a smile, and I showed her to the section. It was sort of sweet, if a little nerdy, to want to "study up" on my resident Goddess. I felt very flattered. "Let me know if you need anything else."

"Oh, I will," she said gratefully.

I went back to my furious cleaning, thinking and worrying. Stopping short, I went back to find Marge, who sat cross-legged on the floor with a book in her lap. "Hey," I said as quietly as I could, but she jumped anyway.

"You surprised me," she said breathlessly, slamming the book shut hard.

"Yeah, sorry about that, but can I ask you a question?"

She pointed to herself again, as if she couldn't believe she had anything of value to offer. "Anything!"

"Have you seen Sebastian by any chance?"

She looked confused and a little panicked. "You mean since the other night?"

I nodded. There was no reason to think she had, but I was starting to feel desperate. "I know it's a long shot, but . . ." I shrugged. "He missed an important gig last night. I'm a little worried about him." Goddess, why did I tell Marge that? I hardly knew her, and I'd barely admitted to myself just how freaked I was about Sebastian's disappearance.

Marge stared at me awkwardly; her eyes darted around as though looking for an exit. I got the distinct impression that I'd overshared somehow.

"I'm sorry," I said quickly—I seemed to apologize a lot to Marge. "Never mind."

I went back to cleaning, feeling stupid. For the first time

since Sebastian failed to show up, I felt as though I might be overreacting. I kept my head down until I heard the bells over the door jingle as Marge left.

Polishing the grain out of the oak counter by the register, I muttered about how ridiculously I'd wound myself up. The door opened, and despite myself, I glanced up, hopeful it was Sebastian sauntering in full of apologies and stories of wild misadventures, but it was just another customer. The warm breeze caused the wind chimes over my head to tinkle.

Lilith twitched. That was odd; she usually only responded to outside stimulus.

I went back to my polishing.

Suddenly, wire and crystal and beads hit my head. One of the strands looped around my neck, and I twisted to try to untangle it. Somehow my movement constricted the beaded wire across my throat. When I tried to shrug out of it, it cut so hard against my skin that I couldn't breathe. I started to panic—it seemed everything I did made the pressure worse. I tried to call William to help, but no sound came out. The customer, a woman with salt-and-pepper hair and sensible shoes, ran up to the counter. I gaped at her to help me.

The woman looked me in the eyes and said, "Try not to move. The wire is cutting your throat."

Of course, the idea of being garroted by a wind chime just made me more frantic. Worse, stars were starting to glitter around the edges of my vision.

The customer came through the gate that separated the customers from the register and put a hand on my shoulder. "I'm going to try to loosen it."

William came around the corner and saw my predicament. "Holy hell," he said, running for the phone.

A black curtain started to drop in front of my eyes. I had the distinct sensation that I was about to faint. Lilith surged in my belly like a bright fire.

4.

Venus

KEYWORDS:

Possessions, Partners, and Moral Character

The next thing I knew, I was on the floor. The woman with the comfortable shoes was telling me to take it easy and not try to do too much. A Hispanic man in a paramedic uniform applied a bandage to my neck. He had a shy smile and a flat top. "It's weird," he was telling William. "It's almost like it's cauterized. She doesn't need any stitches, but I think she should go to the hospital."

"I'm fine," I croaked. I struggled to stand up, but the movement made my neck throb. I tried to hide a wince, but the paramedic noticed and gave me a disapproving shake of his head. His partner, a woman with long blond hair tied back in a militaristic ponytail, stood over me with her arms crossed. I got the sense that if I tried to flee, she'd tackle me and drag me to the hospital.

The paramedic gave William a conspiratorial smile. "They always say that."

"You should go," William insisted. "Your neck is pretty burned. There could be an infection."

I opened my mouth to protest that I couldn't just leave the store.

"I've got it covered." William said. "Marlena is coming in."

I gave up and let them take me into the ambulance past the crowd of gawkers.

Several hours later, I was sitting on a paper-covered metal table listening to my doctor tell me how lucky I was. Apparently, a few more millimeters and the wire would have cut my jugular or some other major artery. He prescribed something for the pain and made a lot of weak jokes about hazard pay for occult bookstore managers.

After thanking him for his time, I wandered out into the lobby, feeling conspicuous with the large, white, slick bandages around my throat. I sighed. I was going to have to walk home, unless I could dig up enough spare change in the bottom of my purse for a bus ride. I'd found a tampon, two pens that had exploded, and forty-three cents when I heard someone call my name. I looked up to see William coming toward me. He gave a little see-ya-later boy wave to the Latino paramedic, who, I noticed, watched William walk away with a wistful expression.

"I thought you might need a lift home," William said, coming up to stand next to me.

"He likes you," I said with a smile at the paramedic, who chose that moment to duck out the door.

"Who?" William said, turning around in time to catch

sight of the door swinging shut. "Jorge?" I nodded, and William blushed. "Oh, yeah, I kind of figured."

Though I was deeply curious what William thought of Jorge's attention, another, more urgent thought came to me. "Who's minding the store?"

"Marlena," William said, obviously relieved I'd changed the subject. "It was dead and she's closed a bunch of times." Apparently, I looked a little distrustful of William's faith in her abilities because he added, "We could always swing by and make sure everything is cool."

I started to nod, but the movement pulled the muscles on my throat. I touched the bandages at my neck. Underneath the cool cloth, my skin felt scorched.

"Are you sure you don't want to just go home?" William asked.

I sighed. As little as I'd been to work this week, my paycheck would be anemic. "I should go in. Double-check those wind-chime hooks. I can't believe one of them broke off like that."

"It didn't," William said. William and I pushed through the doors Jorge had disappeared through. They opened to sunlight so bright it made me squint.

"What do you mean?" I shielded my eyes to glance at William's face. He led me along the sidewalk past a huddle of smokers in brightly patterned scrubs.

"I checked the hooks after you left. The ceiling too. I mean, it was weird how that wind chime just fell on you like that, and I got worried, you know, that there might be water damage or something that made the ceiling weak?"

I nodded. That very thought had occurred to me as well.

"Anyway, the ceiling's solid. I have no idea how that wind chime could have come loose. The wire must have snapped somehow, but there weren't any pieces of it left on the hook."

"You couldn't tell by looking at it?"

William snorted. "Looking at what? The whole thing's melted." I must have seemed a little confused because he started at the beginning. "It was like this, Garnet. One minute that lady and I were trying to get the chime off you and then *ka-blooey*! It bursts into a million pieces. The lady goes to check for the ambulance, and then you look at me with these freaky cherry-red eyes, smile all scary-like, and then pass out. Red eyes, Garnet. Demon eyes. Not cool."

Lilith. I was surprised to hear that she didn't cause more damage or destruction before going back under. She had a tendency to overdo any "rescue" attempts.

"The even wackier part?" William continued. "The wire? It, like, goes all molten, but when it blows—not one drop of hot metal hits me or the lady. Not a drop."

"I guess you finally met Lilith in person," I said. My voice sounded strained and scratched, like the morning after a rock concert. "I think she likes you too."

"Like Jorge?"

"Well, she didn't hurt you. That's kind of amazing."

William, who had opened his mouth to say something else, stopped and gaped. For several moments, William said nothing coherent. Out of his mouth came strings of "uh," and "oh," and "um." I guess it made William a little nervous to have gotten Lilith's attention in that way.

The street was filled with rush-hour traffic and the air smelled of hot exhaust. Heat pressed down onto the concrete and asphalt. The straggly ginkgo trees that lined the boulevard offered little relief.

We'd walked two blocks when William stopped in front of a royal-blue Prius hybrid. A parking ticket was tucked neatly under one windshield wiper. "Nuts," he muttered. Pulling the red-striped envelope out, he slipped it absently into his pocket.

He beeped the car doors open. William lifted a pile of library books from the passenger-side seat and stowed them in the back. I carefully settled in. A lime-green, big-eyed alien toy swung from a chain looped around the rearview mirror.

William deliberately went through the motions of fastening his seat belt, adjusting the mirror, and putting the key in the ignition. I always forgot how careful a driver William was until I got in a car with him. Every motion was separate and conscious, as though he were doing it for the first time or for the licensing test.

After buckling myself in, I closed my eyes and let my head fall against the headrest. William was quiet, clearly still mulling over his encounter with Lilith. He was in what I liked to call his "percolating" stage. There would be lots of thoughtful silence, then pop! He'd ask a question or make a comment. Then, we'd be back to quiet until another something bubbled to the surface.

I let the heat soak into my skin and listened to the quiet hum of the car's engine. We'd pulled out into traffic before he said, "She's kind of scary."

Opening my eyes a crack, I said, "You mean Lilith? Yeah, a little bit."

"No, actually, a lot."

"What were you expecting?" I asked sincerely. I'd talked

to William many times in the past about Lilith. He knew about what She did to the Vatican agents and how horrified I felt about it. It shouldn't really have been a surprise to him that She was anything but the Queen of Darkness.

"I don't know," he said. He paused to signal, check over his shoulder, and execute a textbook-perfect lane change. "I guess I thought she'd be more like a Goddess. Remote. Aloof."

"What makes you think any Goddess is like that? The earliest Goddess sculptures are of pregnant women and are small enough to be carried close, held in your hand—very personal. The Goddess watched over the times when women were most vulnerable, most connected to their humanity—when they started to bleed, when they gave birth—very visceral, messy moments."

William blinked at me. "Wow. I don't think I've ever heard you wax so poetical over the Goddess, Garnet."

I started to shrug, but my neck twinged. "You pressed a hot button, I guess. 'Aloof' just sounded like what people expect the Christian God to be," I said.

"Yeah, I suppose." William mulled this over as pulled into a parking spot a block from Mercury Crossing. "I still think Lilith is creepy."

"She is," I agreed. "Totally."

He walked with me back to the store not saying anything more. When we entered the store, Marlena looked up guiltily from a magazine. Marlena Ito was a slight, short, half-Asian woman with curly brown hair and green eyes. Her eyes widened when she noticed my bandages. "Oh, Garnet," she said. "You look horrible!"

Just what a girl wants to hear.

* * *

The rest of the day passed with the usual sales of books, incense, and jewelry. As we were counting out the till for the nightly deposit, William said, "Oh, hey, don't forget. Coven meeting at my place tonight."

I had forgotten. With Sebastian missing, Mátyás showing up out of the blue, and nearly getting strangled to death today, I was completely unprepared. All I really wanted to do was go home and have a nice hot soak in the tub and find an "I'm fine, sorry to scare you" message from Sebastian on my machine. I didn't really want to go to William's, but this was supposed to be my group. Mine and Sebastian's. Besides, someone there might know where Sebastian might be.

"I'll be there," I said. If I hurried, I could still get in a quick bath.

The bike trip home nearly killed me. I probably should have begged a ride from William because every bit of uneven pavement reminded me not only about the injury on my neck but also all the bruises I got falling off my bicycle earlier. By the time I got home, I felt battered. Sweat stung my neck and the scrapes on my palms. Gritty and exhausted, I hauled my bicycle into the hallway. Climbing my stairs was like ascending Mount Everest.

There was nothing on my machine from Sebastian and Barney mewed at my heels for her kibbles. After I shook out a bowlful from the box, I called Sebastian's cell and told him that I was seriously getting upset and he needed to call me as soon as he got this message.

The apartment was too quiet. I started the bathwater running and then turned on the radio for company, only to discover it still tuned to KCOW, Sebastian's favorite country and western station. I thought about changing the channel, but they played "Bubba Shot the Jukebox." It was a silly song Sebastian had taught me to appreciate and I found myself singing along, imagining he was here harmonizing.

When the bath was filled, I switched the station to Wisconsin Public Radio and let the calm voices soothe my jangled nerves. In the bathroom, I carefully peeled off the bandages. Marlena was right. I looked terrible. There was a puffy, red welt slathered in greasy ointment across my throat that looked even more painful than it felt. Tentatively, I poked at it, and my stupidity was rewarded with a tear-inducing jolt of pain. Going back out to the living room, I dug the prescription out of my purse and popped a pill.

Back at the tub, I lowered myself into the warm water and let out a sigh. I remembered the doctor cautioning me to keep the area dry for a few days, so I soaked without washing my hair. Pushing the door open, Barney hopped up onto the toilet seat and joined me in a bath. She furiously cleaned herself from top to bottom as I scrubbed the day's grime from my body with handmade lavender-mint soap.

After the water had cooled, I got out. As carefully as possible, I added more ointment to my neck. Luckily, the goop made the new bandages stick in place, because my nursing skills needed work. The hospital tape didn't look nearly as neat as when the doctor had done it, especially since I kept underestimating how much I'd need. The pieced-together result made me look a little like Frankenstein's Witch.

I fixed my face and chose the darkest lipstick I had to try to draw the eye away from the bandages. Then I found a deep purple, short-sleeved silk shirt with a high collar that mostly hid my neck and a complimentary, loosely flowing Indian-print skirt that hung nearly to my ankles. I slipped into strappy sandals and then realized that I had an hour to spare before I needed to leave even though I planned to walk instead of ride my bike. I sat on the couch and tried to read a magazine, but despite the voices on the radio and Barney's instant presence in my lap, the apartment still felt too spacious, too empty. Grabbing my purse, I headed out.

The setting sun colored the horizon deep pinks and purples. Gnats danced around lampposts in swirls. Darkness lifted the oppressive heat, though the humidity clung to my skin, making it slick. A mosquito whined in my ear, and I slapped at it, quickening my pace. The air smelled of blooming daylilies and freshly mowed grass.

I'd walked half a block in the direction of William's apartment when I noticed the street name on the sign and remembered it from Sebastian's black book. I dug the book from my purse, losing a lipstick tube and my keys in the process. After scooping up the spilled items, I sat on the short grass of the boulevard and flipped through the pages until I found what I was looking for:

Walter.

In less than a minute, I found myself staring at a two-story Tudor surrounded by a low, stone wall. White, purple, and yellow spikes of foxgloves nodded over the wall, like something out of a storybook. Moonflowers climbed an arched trellis I passed under on the way to the front door. Giant hibiscus stood on either side of the door. I rang the doorbell, already hating Walter. This guy was a much better gardener than I, and I knew that was exactly what drew Sebastian to him. I'd already imagined half a dozen rendezvous between them at the various garden stores around town when the door opened.

"Hello?" The balding man who opened the door dressed in a fuzzy yellow bathrobe eyed me suspiciously.

"Are you Walter?" I asked.

The man shook his head and then called over his shoulder, "Honey, there's some woman here to see you."

"Well, who is it?" came a voice from somewhere inside, "And what does she want?"

Bathrobe looked to me for the answers. "I'm a friend of Sebastian's," I shouted into the interior. Of course, I had no idea if Sebastian gave this guy his real name, or if by naming him all I'd get for my troubles was a door slammed in my face.

"I'll be right there," Walter said.

Bathrobe stared at me distrustfully while we waited for Walter to arrive. Walter turned out to be a short, bespeckled man in his late forties with wiry hair going gray and frizzy at the edges. I blinked at him.

"So what can I do for you, miss?" Walter asked, his voice holding a trace of a Brooklyn accent.

So this was Sebastian's man type? My brain was doing a full-on William-like hiccup as I tried to reimagine the hot, sweaty greenhouse trysts with this guy.

I glanced at Walter's bathrobed companion and asked, "Have you seen Sebastian lately? It's just . . . well, he missed a lecture he was supposed to give at the University Club."

"Yeah, I know," Walter said. "Larry and I were there."

With Larry? Did they both see Sebastian? "You were?" I croaked incredulously.

Larry agreed. "Fifty dollars a head and I never even got to hear about what fun things we could do with the catchfly growing in the back forty."

"The catering was awful," Walter muttered. "Who serves salmon in this heat?"

This was all too surreal. I tried to get back on topic. "Yeah, but, have you seen Sebastian?"

Walter shook his head. "I only see him quarterly."

Quarterly? What did *that* mean?

Larry must have read something in my eye because he laughed. "Oh, darling, she thinks you're his lover, not his tax accountant."

"His lover? In my dreams," Walter said with a roll of his eyes.

I laughed too, if only in relief. "Tax accountant," I repeated. "Of course."

"Look," Walter said, "we're letting all the cold air out, so I'll tell you this for nothing: Sebastian does a disappearing act from time to time." I remembered to nod, and he continued after giving me a once-over. "I'm sure there's someone else who can fulfill your needs in the meantime, eh?"

My *needs*? Did he think I was a ghoul?

My first impulse was to demand to know why he'd jumped to that conclusion, then my hands strayed to the thick, slick bandages on my neck. "Oh, this isn't what it looks like," I said.

"Sure," Walter said skeptically. To his companion, he muttered, "How'd she get our address? Sebastian is usually so discreet, not like some of the others."

Others? What, was Walter the accountant to the paranormal underground? "I'm his fiancée," I said. "I know you're not concerned, but . . ."

Walter gasped, and he and Larry exchanged horrified looks. "Married? Sebastian's getting married? Well, that's a mistake," Walter muttered. "Think of his assets."

"He'll outlive her, remember," Larry said quietly, giving me the you-poor-dear look.

"Still, I think I should insist on a prenup just in case," Walter said. Then, as if he suddenly remembered I was still standing there, he added, "He'll be back, try not to worry. I'll let you know if he calls the office. Go home. Go to bed."

"Uh," I said, not sure if "thank you" was appropriate given how caustic Walter was, but I said it anyway.

I got a surprised "you're welcome" as I turned away and headed down the street as fast as possible.

I didn't know what to make of Walter and company. Despite being a bit of a curmudgeon, Walter seemed in the know, supernaturally speaking. Larry mentioned that Sebastian was immortal, after all.

Still, I supposed vampires had special banking needs. Maybe Walter was some kind of modern-day "Igor," taking care of all of his master's business that he couldn't otherwise attend to during the daylight hours—except Sebastian *could* walk around in the sunshine. Maybe Sebastian used Walter because he did work with other paranormals and he could tell him about those Spanish doubloons or whatever he had sewn into the mattress in 1771.

I shook my head. The more I learned about Sebastian's other life, the stranger it became.

* * *

William's apartment was one block off fraternity row. All the houses this close to the university tended to look completely trashed. William's was no exception. The paint on the trim was cracked and peeling. Beer bottles sprouted among the petunias and wild mustard. The porch sagged nearly to the ground. Creeping Charlie competed with crabgrass for the majority of the lawn. Virginia creeper covered so much of the house that it was almost impossible to tell what style it had been built in.

It was a triplex, and to get to William's place you had to go around the house on a cracked concrete sidewalk to the back. One bare bulb and a string of chili pepper lights illuminated a steep climb up rickety stairs, obviously built by the landlord to comply with some housing code or other.

I always said a little prayer that involved winged feet when I heard the boards creak under my weight. Normally, heights didn't scare me, but I hated that I could see through the slats of the steps. Even though I knew it was impossible, I easily imagined falling through to the fern-covered concrete patio below.

Knocking on the door brought a quick answer. Xylia let me in with a smile. She wore a "Meat Is Murder" T-shirt, denim cutoffs, and combat boots. "No Sebastian?" she asked, looking around my shoulder as though she expected he'd materialize out of the shadows.

"He's . . ." What? Lost? In trouble? On walkabout like Larry and Walter suggested? "Unavoidably detained."

"Sounds important," she said and stepped out of my way so I could enter.

Despite the dilapidated exterior, William had a sultan-chic thing going on. Indian gauze with mirrored coins draped the windows. The couches, of which there were several of various colors and sizes, were velour and festooned with brightly printed pillows. Candles glowed softly in the corners and from on top of bookshelves. Statues of various Indian Gods and Goddesses smiled down beatifically from between books on every imaginable religious/spiritual path, including UFOs and alien abduction.

The room even smelled sweet, though not overpoweringly so, like cardamom and baking bread.

Given all the candles and the amount of people shoved into a limited space, the place should have been stuffy and close, but thanks to a window AC unit, it wasn't.

Once I stepped into the light, Xylia's eyes honed in on the bandages. "What happened to your neck?" Before I could answer, her mouth twisted into a grimace. "Oh. Right. Listen, I understand this is your business, but I just don't think sex that ends up with people getting hurt is a good thing. You shouldn't let him do things like that to you."

"It wasn't Sebastian," I said, consciously resisting the urge to cover the bandages. After my conversation with Larry and Walter, I knew exactly how weak my response sounded. What else could I say? "A wind chime tried to choke me to death" sounded about as convincing as the classic "I walked into a door."

Xylia's expression was both pitying and disapproving. "Vampires, of whatever kind, are parasites. You could do a lot better."

Hey, that was my fiancée she was dissing and, given Sebastian's disappearance, her ire made me instantly suspicious. "Do you have something personal against vampires?"

"Yes," Xylia said, putting a hand on her narrow hip. "Women don't need men like that, men who get off on hurting us."

Us? Was there a story there? "What Sebastian and I do is totally consensual and, as you pointed out, *none* of your business."

Xylia's eyes narrowed. "It's the coven's business if you're expecting to be our High Priest and Priestess."

Xylia was right. It was the role I always imagined Sebastian and myself in. The High Priest and Priestess were the functional leaders of any coven. They directed the rituals and drew the God and Goddess into themselves during the ceremony. Traditionally, the position was held by those in the coven who had the most experience or highest degree. Sebastian seemed an obvious choice given how long he'd been alive, and, well, I was the one with a resident Goddess.

"The group hasn't made that decision yet," I said.

Xylia raised her eyebrows. "Oh, that's up to us?"

"Of course," I said. As much as I'd like to appoint myself and Sebastian, that would hardly be right. For the group to properly function and trust one another, the coven had to be in complete agreement about who its leaders were. Even if Sebastian and I were to be chosen, it's not a lifetime job. Some covens routinely rotated through the members so that everyone had a chance to be High Priest or Priestess.

Xylia nodded, as though satisfied for the moment. I spotted a tray of cold drinks on a nearby table and excused myself to get one. I helped myself to a glass of mint tea, with fresh sprigs of spearmint, no less, and a cracker artfully placed on a silver tray on a foot cushion. I picked up an agenda, and looked around for a place to sit. Then, I noticed a hand waving me over. I did a double take. With wolven features and eyes sharp as obsidian, an American Indian man smiled at me with a sly grin. I knew him. It was the wolf. Or the man.

The wolf-man!

He watched me warily, waiting. He had long, straight, jet-black hair. In deference to the heat, he wore a white tank top that exposed bronze skin, tight muscles, and an amazing tattoo on his left bicep. It depicted a crow in flight. Half of the bird's feathers were an unexpected pearly white, and the others were oily black. The artist had staggered the pattern across the bird's back, as if we were witnessing a transformation.

Tearing my eyes away from him for a moment, I glanced around at the others in the coven. Max and Marge nodded at me around mouthfuls of wheat crackers. Did no one else notice this new guy? Turning back to the wolf-man dude, I smiled politely. "Cool tat."

"Thanks." He patted the seat and said in a growly voice, "I saved you a spot."

I probably should have declined the offer since it was much easier to break into a run when standing, but there was such command in the twinkle of his mischievous smile that I obeyed. Acutely aware of the nearness of his body, I perched myself rigidly at the edge of the cushion and sipped sweet, cool tea. Desperately, I tried to catch William's eye, but he was engaged in a heated discussion with Griffin. Nobody seemed concerned that an interloper lounged against the lime-green velour right beside me—a literal wolf in the fold.

"It's Garnet, right?" I nearly leaped upright when his bass voice purred in my ear.

"Uh, yeah," I said, using my sleeve to mop up the tea I'd spilled onto my lap when I'd jumped.

"You're easily spooked, aren't you?" The smile he flashed me was warmly teasing, impossible to take offense at. "I'm Micah Cloud."

I took the hand he offered and held on to it.

The instant our skin touched, I sensed . . . chemistry? My entire body flushed, like some kind of premenopausal hot flash. Lilith felt it too, rousing from her slumber to sit up, at attention. Her sudden awareness caused the hairs on my arm to prickle, so I got this odd sensation of cold and hot all at once.

He held on to my hand a little too long, his eyes searching mine, as though looking for some kind of answer. The wolf-dog glittered just behind his eyes and I had the uncomfortable feeling of being stalked by a predator. Given that I dated one, I should be used to that hungry look, but this was somehow different. When Sebastian wanted to devour me, I knew it was sexual. Micah's desire seemed more hostile, needier.

Lilith didn't like it one bit. She pushed my hand away from his. Our palms flew apart from each other like a reverse slap with the force of oppositely polarized magnets.

We both studied our hands and then each other with a well-that-was-strange glance. I didn't quite know how to apologize for Lilith's apparent rudeness, or if I really wanted to, given that he *had* freaked me out a bit. Besides, he was giving me another odd looking over. He frowned deeply at me as though he was somehow disappointed, then he wiped his hand on his jeans.

Micah surveyed the room, as if looking for someone specific. I tried to see who he might be searching for when I noticed Blythe staring at me. She stood alone near the door. When she noticed me watching her, she quickly averted her eyes and moved to join a nearby conversation.

"Okay," I said to Micah. "What the hell is going on here?"

"What are you talking about?"

Before I could explain, William cleared his throat. "Now that everyone is here"—he shot me a pointed look—"I'd like to get started. As you see, we have a lot to cover."

I picked up the agenda from where I'd set it on the arm of the couch. Beside me, Micah did the same. I remember telling Sebastian that it would be a good idea if other people hosted meetings right from the start. It would break up the hierarchy, I said. We don't want to establish one way of doing things. We don't want to come off as the boss of everyone. That's not the Wiccan way, I explained.

As I glanced down the items on the sheet, which ranged from setting a meeting schedule to issues of whether or not we'd practice "sky clad" (read: naked), I regretted my insistence.

I let my shoulders slump back against the couch with a sigh. This was going to be a long night.

As I settled back, my arm brushed against Micah's. I felt the heat of his skin. My cheeks burned in response, and Lilith got all agitated and tingling again.

Rephrase: long, *awkward* night.

* * *

If it hadn't been for the constant reminders of how close Micah sat to me, I would have drifted to sleep during the seemingly endless debates about whether or not the coven should engage in civic projects, like helping plant trees on Arbor Day. It wasn't that I wasn't interested, but the tea, good food, and the pleasant sound of everyone's voices reminded me how little decent sleep I'd had in the last couple of days. But every time I started to drift, my body would bump up against Micah's and I'd get an almost electric jolt.

Finally, William called for a break.

I got up and stretched my legs, which had begun to cramp from sitting still for so long. Marge came up to Micah and tugged his arm, and the two of them went off to the corner.

I couldn't help but stare at them a little. They clearly seemed to know each other and they were such an odd pairing. Marge had worn a poet shirt, black straight-leg jeans, and the gaudiest vest I'd ever seen in my life. Fluorescent embroidery floss, geometric designs, mirrors, beads and bangles covered deep purple fabric. It wasn't something I'd wear, but Marge kind of pulled it off. Her gray curls seemed especially puffy today and only served to accent the differences between them. He was tall and lean; she was short and squat. In his barely-on muscle shirt, tattoos, and ripped, faded blue jeans he looked like a Native biker guy. She totally had the hippy matron thing going on.

She also had that dog pendant. Could it be a wolf or whatever Micah was? Maybe Marge was the werewolf's equivalent of a ghoul, except what did werewolves need ghouls for? Had she invited Micah?

Speaking of all that, I still wondered why no one seemed surprised Micah was here. Out of the corner of my eye, I saw William head into the kitchen. I followed him, hoping to get a chance to talk to him alone.

William's kitchen was narrow and hardly larger than a closet. To contain the heat, he'd tacked a sheet over the doorway. When I came in, William was pulling a long, glistening loaf of cardamom bread out of the oven. Despite the temperature, my mouth watered.

The floor was cracked and buckling gray linoleum. Darkly varnished, paneled cabinets stuck to every wall, making the small space even more cramped. Wallpaper flowers looked tired and worn.

I leaned against the stained Formica counter, and asked, "What's the deal with Micah?"

William laughed. He reached around me to grab a bread knife. "Jeez, Garnet, just because the guy's a Native American doesn't mean he can't be into Wicca. For all we know, he was raised a Lutheran."

I stared at William as he cut the bread. Wasn't he as surprised as I that Micah was here *at all*? "No, I mean, who invited him? How did he get in?"

William stopped and gave me a hard look. "What are you talking about? He walked in the door, like everyone else."

It suddenly dawned on me that somehow William thought Micah had been part of the group from the beginning. "He's the wolf!"

"Yeah, he *is* kind of a fox, and I don't even mostly go that way."

I gave up. Clearly, Micah was using Jedi mind tricks on my coven. Enough with trying to convince William otherwise; I was going to the source. Ducking under the sheet, I burst into the living room and made a beeline for Micah. He saw me coming; I heard him make excuses to Marge. Turning away from her startled face, he met me halfway. We faced off over the card table full of crackers with signs of the zodiac done in Easy Cheese.

"I know you've been following me," I said.

A smile quirked at the edge of his lips, like he found my anger amusing. He failed to sound entirely innocent when he said, "Me?"

"You, your wolf, whatever."

Standing this close to him, I discovered that I was mostly looking into Micah's chest, which, thanks to the muscle shirt, I could see most of. I pulled my eyes away from the broad, strong line of his collarbone; it distracted me from my anger.

"Coyote, actually." His maddening smile widened. "I'm used to a lot more denial before we get to this part."

"Yeah, well, I'm special."

His look turned lascivious. "Yeah, I can see that."

I tried really hard not to blush. I didn't want to respond this way and I really didn't want Micah to notice that I was. So I blurted, "Well, I'm used to you supernatural types. My fiancée is a vampire."

Turns out he had slight dimples when he smiled sarcastically. "You're just full of surprises."

"So come clean," I said. "Why are you following me?"

He looked me over from head to foot. "Is everything always about you?"

I thought I was ready for anything he might say, but I wasn't expecting to be accused of being a drama queen. My resolve faltered. I started to wonder if he was right. Maybe I was overreacting; maybe it was all just coincidence, maybe . . .

Maybe he looked awfully smug right now.

My brows drew into a deep frown, and I planted my fists on my hips. "Artful dodge," I said. "But I'm not falling for it. You infiltrated this group. You've fooled everyone into thinking you've always been here. You're after something. If it's not me, why have I run into you on three separate occasions?"

His expression grew serious and the muscle of his jaw twitched. "I want something you have. And you're going to give it to me."

Marge suddenly stood just at my elbow. "Hey," she said. "How's it going?"

Micah and I both gave her the hello-we-were-talking-here glare. Couldn't she see we were in the middle of something? Then, I remembered that this was Marge. If it was social, she had no clue.

"My grandmother says we have Native American somewhere back in the family tree," Marge told Micah.

I pinched the bridge of my nose in sympathetic embarrassment.

"Cool," Micah said without any trace of irritation. Reaching down, he picked up the tray of cheese and crackers. Without a second's hesitation, Micah strode to the kitchen as though he'd been on an errand to refresh the plate all along.

Smooth exit.

I envied him.

Suitably encouraged, Marge began to tell me her entire

family history. I tried to move away, but Marge followed me, talking the whole time. I was pinioned between two sofas when I caught sight of Micah coming out of the kitchen munching on fresh bread. He gave me a little "gotcha" wink.

Luckily before Marge got too much beyond Great-aunt Tillie or whoever, William called everyone back to order. The seats shuffled and I ended up on the floor with my back against the bookshelves. Micah sat in his spot on the couch directly across from me and smirked. Marge and her friend Max had settled in beside him. I noticed Marge taking surreptitious glances at Micah's physique. She shifted, as though to snuggle closer. Our eyes met, and I gave her a you-go-for-it-girl smile. Marge's eyes widened, like she'd been caught doing something illegal. I glanced at Max, who was taking notes on what William was saying. He seemed oblivious or unconcerned or both. When Marge shrank back from Micah guiltily, I figured she and Max must be more than friends.

When William started in on meeting schedules and volunteers for snacks, I decided it was time to give Micah the aura squint.

Light exploded everywhere. Instinctively, I turned and ducked. I probably made some kind of noise. All I know is that for a moment I thought that the sun had gone supernova or the apartment had been engulfed in flames.

When my body didn't atomize, I pulled myself upright. Everyone stared at me. Micah's head cocked to the side curiously.

"Uh, Garnet?" William asked. "So, you think Sebastian will have some problem hosting at his place next time?"

Is that what we'd been talking about? I rubbed my eyes.

I felt like I should have spots dancing in front of my vision, but, of course, there had been no real explosion of light. "I don't think so," I said. "I mean, if he's back. Thing is, I'm not exactly sure where he is."

I don't know why I'd added that last part. Maybe I hoped someone in the room might have a clue as to Sebastian's whereabouts, or maybe I just wanted a little sympathy.

I got it. Everyone was very concerned. They asked all the right questions about when I'd last seen him and whether or not he did this sort of thing a lot. I told the truth, even mostly explaining my surprise visit with Larry and Walter. I wasn't quite up to confessing my fear that Sebastian was off with a ghoul, because I didn't want to seem petty, and anyway, that seemed a bit like airing our dirty laundry. Not to mention that no one believed he was a real vampire.

Marge, the ever socially awkward, pointed to my bandages and said, "Did you two have a fight or something?"

I supposed it was a reasonable question, but I was getting tired of people looking at me like I was some kind of abused wife. "I know you won't believe me, but this was totally unrelated. A wind chime tried to choke me."

People looked away. Marge shifted in her seat, and nervously adjusted her glasses. Xylia seethed.

"It's true," William said in my defense. "I was there. It was the strangest thing."

William took the floor and regaled the coven with the story of the amazing choking chime and how Lilith had come to the rescue. After he finished everyone stared at me again. I nodded confirmation. "Yeah, it was weird."

"Sounds like a magical attack." Griffin said. As usual,

Griffin had ensconced himself in a darkly lit corner. William had a high-back chair that had dark red curtains festooned around it, and Griffin sat in it like a Viking on a throne. He even held his ice tea as though it were a goblet. "Does Lilith have any enemies? Do you?"

Now that Griffin mentioned it, I remembered Lilith's growl just before the wind chime fell. Had Lilith been trying to warn me of a magical assault?

"There's the Vatican," William said. "You said Mátyás was back, Garnet. Do you think he's still working for the order?"

At the mention of the order, the tension in the room spiked. "We haven't been very careful," someone muttered. "We've only been using first names, but we'd be easy to find," Xylia agreed.

I had to raise my voice to be heard over the murmuring. "I don't think it was the order. The attack was too subtle, too magical. They don't like to use their sensitives as offense, only for defense. It's very unlikely they'd engage in supernatural warfare."

"If you've been a target before, you can't rule them out," Griffin said.

"My case is closed," I explained. "They think I'm dead."

I ended up having to explain how Sebastian and I had used a blood-binding spell to fool the order into believing they'd killed us, so it was a while before we got back on track. Micah, I noticed, sat silently through my entire explanation, as had Marge.

William, with his ever-present agenda, steered the conversation back. "What should we do about the next meeting? What if Sebastian is still missing?"

Micah surprised me by saying, "We should plan to meet at his place regardless. You've got a key, right?" he asked, and I nodded. "If he hasn't turned up, we could perform a spell of finding. His house would make a great focus."

"It would," I agreed, somewhat surprised I hadn't thought of it myself.

"Are you sure we should try something so complex first?" Griffin asked. "The group cohesiveness isn't really formed yet."

"Nothing like a baptism of fire, I say," Micah interjected. That wolfish grin held a touch of challenge.

Griffin—none of us, really—could resist. "You're on."

After a few more administrative details had been ironed out, like the fact that we'd need a preritual meeting at my place, the formal meeting broke up. Even though it was well after midnight, everyone was too keyed up to leave.

At some point pizza got ordered and beer materialized. Someone, perhaps Xylia, started mixing Long Island ice teas. People had broken up into groups, and laughter blended with the fusion jazz William had tuned in via satellite radio. I wanted to stay—in fact, I felt sort of like this was one of those bonding moments for the coven—but I was exhausted. The last thing I wanted was a repeat of last night's hangover, plus Griffin's question about enemies had put me on edge.

Could Mátyás be playing me? Was all his niceness an act to lure me into some kind of trap with the order? Had they already nabbed Sebastian?

That last thought made my mind race. What if Sebastian

was in real trouble? I'd been all too willing to believe a ghoul might be involved, but what if it were something even more sinister? The order knew how to transfix Sebastian. They'd done it before. There was still a sawed-off hunk of crossbow bolt stuck in my apartment wall to prove it. The image of Sebastian hanging by a stake completely at the mercy of those creeps from the order freaked me out. I needed to go home and try the astral plane again, anything to see if I could figure out where he was and if he was okay.

So I quickly made my good-byes to William and the others. Stepping out into the darkness, the heat of the summer settled in close after the cool of the air-conditioned apartment. I gripped the two-by-four railing and began picking my way down the steep steps.

"Let me walk you home," Micah said, coming out of the door a moment behind me.

He loped down the steps two at a time, making the whole structure shake. I fearfully scurried down the last few steps to avoid a collision.

"I'm okay on my own," I said, though it was the time of night when it was definitely friendlier with two. Then, I halted midstep as he came up beside me. "Hey, how did you know that I walk home?"

The streetlight that threw harsh light between the houses revealed Micah's wry expression. "I'm stalking you, remember?"

"Yeah, tell me why that is again?"

He turned his head so that he kind of looked at me out of the corner of his narrowed eyes. "You're stuck with a Goddess you don't want, and I can take her off your hands."

5.

Ceres

KEYWORDS:

Creativity, Politics, and Family Bonds

I'd never had an offer quite like that one, and I didn't know what to say to it. "Uh, what do you mean? And, er, how?"

"So you're interested?"

Was I? I'd often said Lilith was a curse. Having Lilith meant always having to watch my temper, lest she escape and kill someone. I put my hand over my stomach, as if I could cover Lilith's ears. "I don't know. Could you really do it?"

Micah jerked his head in the direction of the street, toward which neither of us had made a move. In fact, we'd stood still long enough that a cloud of gnats had found us. "Why don't I explain it as we walk?"

Even this close to the university, most houses were quiet and dark at this hour. Crickets hushed as we passed, resuming their song at our heels.

"I could do it," Micah said after we'd walked a while. "Though it depends. Have you bonded with Lilith yet?"

We walked up a slight hill. The houses on this block were a mishmash of Victorians and more simple turn-of-the-century four squares. The level of upkeep varied, as well. In the darkness, battered gables, torn screens, and listing porches loomed like haunted mansions. I quickened my pace.

What did that mean? Was Micah asking if Lilith and I had traded wacky stories about ex-boyfriends and pets over lattes? "Um, I don't think we have."

"You would know," Micah said cryptically.

It almost sounded like he had experience with having a resident Goddess. Giving him a sidelong glance, I remembered the blast of pure white light of his aura. "What are you exactly? What's the deal with the coyote? Are you a werewolf?"

"Coyote. And, no, among my many talents, I'm a skin walker."

A freight train whistle sounded in the distance. The muffled clack of the rails echoed under the canopy of shadowed leaves.

"So, you shape-shift? How can you"—I waved my arms along the long, lean length of his body—"become something half your size? Where does the rest of you go? Doesn't that violate the law of conservation of matter or something like that?"

He gave a snort of startled amusement. "It probably would, if it weren't magic."

The moon had begun to set. Round and full, it hovered above the leaves of a sugar maple. Lilith shivered across my belly. If there was a true believer, it was me. Still, I had a hard time with the idea. "Seriously?" I asked him. "You shrink down and sprout fur?"

He shook his head. "No. I don't shrink. I am Coyote."

This was deeply Zen Native. He "became" coyote in some metaphorical, yet not, way. We'd come to my place. I stopped in front of the concrete steps that led up the hill to the short walk in front of my front door. Mulberries from the neighbor's bush left pungent purple splotches on the pavement. A light had been left on in the kitchen, and I could see Barney's plump, furry silhouette in the tower window.

"This is me," I said.

He gave me that wicked grin and asked, "Are you going to invite me up?"

It wasn't that the offer wouldn't have been tempting under other circumstances, but with Sebastian missing and possibly in danger, not to mention the fact that I didn't know the first thing about this guy or where he came from . . . "Sorry," I said. "Not this time."

"Does that mean I get another chance?"

I shook my head. "I have to find Sebastian."

He nodded like he understood, but he didn't make a move to leave. Barney's soft mews drifted down from the window above. Finally, Micah said, "How long did you say you've had Lilith?"

I hadn't. "About a year and a half," I said. "Why?"

"The longer together, the more you become one."

There was a frightening thought. Lilith's personality could be summed up by the words "death" and "destruction." Her gloom and doom didn't really jive with my whole perky Goth lifestyle. The idea of becoming more like the Queen of Hell with every passing year seemed a bit daunting. "Are you sure?" I asked. "I mean, how do you know all this?"

In the darkness, Micah's face became inscrutable and he said, "I can read it in your eyes. It's already beginning."

Normally if a guy gave me a line as cheesy as that, I pointed fingers and laughed at them. But my eyes were the scars left from the night Lilith entered me. They'd changed from light blue to deep purple, a physical reminder of the deal I'd struck. "When . . ." I dropped my voice, even though I knew it was kind of foolish to whisper, as if the Goddess couldn't hear me. "How soon would I have to excise her? That is, if I wanted to."

"The sooner the better. You have to ask yourself, Garnet. Why does she stay? What does Lilith get out of your little arrangement? Is she satisfied with what she has?"

Now I was really nervous. More than once Lilith had shown an interest in taking over more of our body "time share," as it were. I'd already had to magically contain her once, lest she start moving my body around like a puppet. Was that what Micah was talking about with "bonding"? Had I bound her to me with my spell? "What are you saying exactly? Are you saying Lilith is planning some kind of takeover?"

He cocked his head to the side quizzically. "She's already tried, hasn't she?"

My mouth was dry. I nodded.

"You need to do this."

"Maybe," I said. I still wasn't sure. There was so much about Micah that seemed, well, untrustworthy. For one, I didn't know why he was so concerned about me. What were his motivations? What had he meant by saying he'd "take her off my hands"? Was he planning on trying to keep Lilith for himself?

He shook his head at me as if he could read my thoughts. "It's the power, isn't it?"

"What?"

"The power," he repeated. "Raw. Elemental. Heady stuff. I can't really blame you. A lot of guys wouldn't want to let something like that go."

I pursed my lips. "Are you saying I'm keeping Lilith because I like having access to her magical strength?"

"Aren't you?"

Before I could formulate a response, Micah turned and walked away. I watched him bound down the stairs. The trees cast deeper shadows along the sidewalk where the streetlights couldn't penetrate the dense leaves. I watched him move through the strobe of dark and less dark. In one lighter patch, I saw a man turn to look at me. In the next, there was a coyote, nose to ground, padding silently away.

I was so preoccupied with the questions Micah had left me with that I almost walked past the blinking red light on my answering machine.

I hit play. My breath caught as I heard what sounded like Sebastian, but I couldn't be sure since the message was a weird, slow-mo amalgam of voices that I couldn't understand at all. Very *Exorcist*. It took me a second to realize that somehow my answering machine had chosen this moment to stop erasing previous recordings. Instead, it had recorded new messages on top of previous callers. So, it sounded like the dental office was reminding of an appointment from a month ago, while Sebastian was trying to communicate to me.

I screamed in frustration. Sure, I was a cheapskate for reusing the microcassette tapes, but have you tried to find those little buggers since everything has gone digital? Why now!? Of all the bloody times?

I picked up the answering machine and banged it on the bookcase.

"Stupid, stupid, stupid." I punctuated each word with another slam, not entirely sure who I was yelling at—myself or the machine. I took some pleasure in watching pieces of plastic fly off it, since I knew I'd be at Target tomorrow buying the goddamn top-of-the-line (in my price range) replacement. Which—bang!—would not—bang!—take—bang!—tape—crunch!

In the kitchen I heard Barney sneeze and make a hacking sound like she was tossing a hairball. I gave the answering machine one last withering glance as I dropped the pieces on the table and went to check on the cat. When I entered the kitchen, Barney sat primly in front of empty food bowls and looked at me with sorrowful eyes. "All that noise just to get fed?"

She blinked innocently. I filled up her bowl. I sat down at the table, still covered in my astrology books and papers. Remembering the sight of Sebastian coming into the kitchen, I felt tears stinging my eyes.

He'd tried to call. At least I knew Sebastian was still alive. Or was when he left the message, anyway.

My neck ached, and my hands rubbed absently at the

slick bandages around my throat. The surgical tape itched, so I picked at it. Goddess, what a day!

I considered the idea of luck as I traced the letters of Dane Rudyard's *Astrology Now*. Didn't I look for patterns in the tides of fortune? Wasn't that part of what I believed— that everything happened for a reason? Maybe something was happening in the stars, something that if I knew about, I could counteract.

Even though my eyes were gritty from a lack of sleep, I pored over my chart, ephemerides, and my entire astrological library for the next two hours. I found nothing. In fact, progressing my chart only showed that this was supposed to be a pleasant, benign time for me. I checked transits. I unearthed Sebastian's chart from my notebook, our combined relationship chart, and anything else I thought might be useful. Still, I found no illumination, no clue. Finally, my eyelids drooped and the words I scanned blurred into senselessness.

I gave up. Dragging myself into my bedroom, I didn't bother to change into pajamas. I was out before my head hit the pillow.

The alarm didn't go off and I overslept for the second time in two days. I probably would have slept the day away, but Barney decided she'd waited long enough for her food and knocked a pile of paperback novels off the bed stand. The crash brought me to my feet. When I noticed the time, I frantically undressed from the clothes I had fallen asleep in last night and redressed in the first things I grabbed out of my closet, cursing the entire time because

somehow every movement twisted my neck muscles in just
the wrong way. I called William to tell him I'd be there as
soon as possible, threw food in Barney's bowl, grabbed a
breakfast bar and a protein shake for me, and ran downstairs and out the door.

Halfway to the store, it started to drizzle. Even as my
bike kicked a stripe of wet up my back, I wished the sky
would just open up into a full-fledged thunderstorm. At
least then there would be a chance that the humidity
would drop afterward.

I parked my bike in the alley behind the store and used
my key in the back door. Stopping at the employee bathroom, I attempted to style my soggy hair and retouch my
makeup. The bandages on my neck had mostly peeled off
in the rain, so I removed them the rest of the way. The burn
marks on my neck looked puckered and sore, but not horrific. I had a tendency to heal a bit faster than your average
girl thanks to a blood transfusion from my vampire ex, Parrish. I adjusted my collar to hide the marks as best I could.
Taking a deep breath, I felt ready for the day. Confident, I
walked out into the front only to see Eugene, the owner,
waiting for me with a frown on his face.

Oh, crap. I'd forgotten I'd asked him to come in so I
could talk about buying this place. Well, two and a half
hours late made me look really responsible. Way to impress
the boss.

We meandered through the store negotiating as Eugene
compulsively rearranged materials to his liking. I resisted
the impulse to fix them back to their original order as we
discussed cost (Oh, my god, really? That much?), financing
options, and contracts.

Eugene looked more like a customer than the owner in his striped short-sleeved shirt and what could only be referred to as a man skirt or, perhaps more generously, culottes. He had quite the look going with his knee-high, dark-colored socks that showed through open-toed hemp sandals. By the end of it all, we were standing in the pagan greeting card alcove having come to a tentative agreement.

After seeing Eugene to the door with many hearty hand-shakes, I felt like my day had turned around for the better. That's when I saw Mátyás leaning against the political slo-gan display—his head framed by a poster that read, "My other car is a broomstick."

"We have to talk," he said, putting a vice grip on my el-bow and steering the two of us toward the coffee shop next door. "Now."

I looked around for William, who had conveniently found busywork to do when Eugene was nosing around the store. I wanted to let him know I'd be stepping out for a few minutes, but I didn't spot him anywhere. "No need to shove," I said, wrestling my arm out from his grasp. "Hon-estly? I could totally use a triple espresso right now, espe-cially if you're buying."

Máytás looked startled for a moment, then said, "Yeah, right. Sorry."

Sorry? Did Mátyás just apologize for being rude? "Are you okay?"

Mátyás shook his head. "I'm far from okay. That's why we need to talk."

The scent of French roast made my head throb with desire as we stepped across the threshold into the adjoining coffeehouse, Holy Grounds. Until I walked into the place,

I'd forgotten that I'd skipped my usual morning caffeine. I was really starting to regret it. I'd done most of the negotiating with Eugene on pure adrenaline—had he really agreed to consider it? Gulp!—and now the days of little or no sleep were catching up to me. I needed a lot of caffeine and I needed it now.

Despite large windows and tall ceilings, the place seemed cavernous and dark after the extreme glare of summer.

I sent Mátyás in search of a spot to sit while I ordered our drinks. My friend Izzy was behind the bar. Izzy, who had been experimenting with her hair for a few months, had given up and decided to go au naturel. Her hair puffed around her head in an Afro, making her look a bit like Beyoncé in that Austin Powers movie—except Izzy seemed more regal, more solid.

I pointed to her hair. "Cute."

She pointed to my neck. "Ugly. Dang, girl, what happened to you?"

Reflexively, my hand reached up to cover the burn marks. "A crystal wind chime tried to kill me," I said trying to sound casual.

"A flaming wind chime? Because you look scorched."

"I am," I admitted. "Lilith kind of, well, melted the chain."

"Hm. She should be more careful with the body she inhabits." Izzy handed me my "velvet hammer with a depth charge" and Mátyás's iced chai.

I nodded, thinking of Micah's comments last night. I totally expected Izzy to grill me about what had happened with the wind chimes, but maybe she'd just gotten so used to the crazy in my life that she decided it was something better not known.

"So, who's the new hottie?" Izzy asked as she made change for my twenty.

"Hottie?" I looked around to see who she might be talking about. Had Micah walked in?

She pointed her chin in the direction of Mátyás. "The guy you came in with."

I looked at Mátyás in horror. Izzy thought he was sexy? "That's Mátyás Von Traum. Sebastian's son," I said, trying not to sound as disgusted as I was that someone might find him attractive.

Izzy actually purred. "So, you're not into him?"

"No way."

"Is he single?"

I couldn't help but gape. "I have no idea."

"Find out and your next latte is free."

"Okay." I mean, I had to keep myself in lattes, didn't I? Still, did I really want to encourage my friend to date my fiancé's son? Why did I suddenly envision extremely awkward double-dating?

Mátyás had chosen a spot in the back on the comfy couches. Prime real estate, and usually the first spots to be filled, which was a testimony to how slow things were at this hour during the summer. I only hoped things were equally as dead over at Mercury Crossing; I was going to owe William some time off.

I must have unconsciously checked my watch because Mátyás said, "Am I keeping you from something?"

"Well, my job, actually," I said dryly.

"This is about Papa."

The store could wait. "Did you hear from him? What's happened?"

"I think Papa's in hell," he said seriously.

"No way," I said, not waiting for an explanation of that strange little gem of a conversation gambit. "I heard from him last night. He left a message. At least, I'm pretty sure he did." Dang, I thought, looking at my watch again. The day was slipping away from me, and I'd really hoped to go to the department store over lunchtime to buy a new answering machine.

"Maybe he went to hell after he called you," Mátyás said casually, as if we were discussing the latest Badgers game. "I'm pretty sure he's there."

I took a long sip of my coffee. It was true to its name: smooth and vaguely painful. I could feel my brain start to kick into a higher gear, which was helpful since Mátyás seemed to insist on talking in riddles. "What are you talking about? Literally in hell? And, how do you know?"

Mátyás's gaze slid from mine and focused, instead, on the painting on the far wall. The featured artist of the month apparently attempted to explore the darker side of the subconscious. Eyes, beady and yellow stared hungrily at me out of inky, oily canvases. They were spookily realistic—glistening and intense, especially given the sketchy blackness that surrounded them. There was one that portrayed some kind of hairy, demonic, twisted-up man-beast crawling across the lonely stretch of highway, its eyes mournful, like a lost puppy. I was horrified, yet captivated. It was well-done but disturbing stuff.

"Beast of Bray Road," Mátyás said when he saw my eyes had followed his. "Who knew Wisconsin had its very own werewolf, eh?"

I'd heard of the supposed werewolf that lived just northwest of here. It was in the news several years ago, but I'd never put much stock in it. Now that I'd met Micah, I wondered. I was curious what Mátyás knew about skinwalkers, but I'd ask him later. I knew a diversionary tactic when I saw one. "How can you be so sure Sebastian's in . . . trouble?"—I couldn't quite bring myself to say "hell," especially since I got the impression Mátyás *did* mean it literally—"Did you have some kind of magical contact?"

"I have a . . ." He pursed his lips as his finger traced the grain on the tabletop. He opened his mouth as if he were about to say something more, but then his eyes met mine and he stopped. "No. You're not family."

"What?" I was livid. By Mátyás's own reckoning Sebastian was in danger, and now he wasn't going to tell me the whole story. "I've been worried sick. How can you come here and say something like that and not back it up?"

"You're just going to have to trust me."

"The heck I am. Tell me how you know."

We locked gazes. The muscle in his jaw flexed as he clenched his teeth. "No."

Izzy chose that moment to come over and ask flirtatiously if we needed anything else. She batted her eyelashes at Mátyás, but he mostly continued to glare at me.

"Well, there is one thing you need, hon," Izzy said bluntly. "And that's my phone number. Here." She slapped a business card down in front of a startled Mátyás. "Call me."

Even though her timing was less than impeccable, I had to appreciate her style. Mátyás's baffled expression was priceless. As was his sudden attention to Izzy's curvaceous form as she sauntered back behind the bar. "She just gave me her phone number," he told me as he stuck it in the pocket of his jeans.

"I know. She thinks you're cute. Goddess knows why."

"You know her?" He seemed both skeptical and impressed.

I nodded. "I wish you'd talk to me about Sebastian."

He stood up to leave. "It was a mistake to come here."

"Please," I said, taking his hand as he started to move past me to the door. "We both care about him. Tell me why you think he's in trouble."

"I can't."

His hand slipped from mine and he walked to the door. I stood up and shouted angrily at him, "It has something to do with the Vatican, doesn't it? You're still working with them, aren't you? Come back here, damn it!"

The bells over the door jangled ominously as he walked away.

When I got back to the store I was greeted by a sudden influx of customers. I was grateful for the work. Taking care of business kept my mind from drifting back to Sebastian. Occasionally, I even allowed myself a quick daydream about the things I would change about the store once it was mine. I was actually happily musing the ways I could bring more customers into Mercury Crossing when a young, freckle-faced woman cleared her throat. Bright red hair fell in loose ringlets to delicate, birdlike shoulders. My first impression was: brittle.

"Sorry," I said, with an apologetic smile. "I was miles away."

She returned my smile nervously. "I'm Alison," she said without any preamble. She reached up and ran a finger across the bottom of one of the wind chimes. The soft cascade of bells made my throat ache.

"Alison?" It took me a second to place the name—one of Sebastian's ghouls, the one I'd called yesterday with the Britney Spears voice mail. Goddess, how did she find me? I had a flash of telling her the name of the store during my flustered babble. "Oh! Alison."

I looked at Alison again, this time searching for clues as to why Sebastian chose her. I supposed she was pretty in a breakable, fragile way. She had that kind of porcelain, pale skin that a lot of Irish women naturally had, the kind, I might add, I used a great quantity of makeup to replicate. The sky blue of her eyes reminded me of glass too. She wore a patterned, vintage sundress and white, heeled sandals. She looked cool and effortlessly stylish.

"I'm Garnet," I said and I offered a hand because I felt I should.

She inspected my hand momentarily, and then, with a sigh that seemed very put out, reached over. It was a clammy, halfhearted shake, but she must have shuffled her feet on a rug or something, because a static electric shock arced between us when we touched. Strangely, it reminded me of when I'd shook hands with Micah.

Sebastian had said that ghouls, in general, were discouraged from practicing magic. Practice and talent were sometimes two different things. What if someone were naturally inclined toward the occult?

I gave Alison the squint. Her aura was hazy and blurred. I'd never seen anything like it; it was almost as if there was a brighter one that a dark film had settled over. I couldn't quite get a bead on it. Was this what Sebastian had meant when he said they had ways of keeping ghouls from doing magic? Was her natural talent being hobbled in some way?

"Is something wrong?" she asked.

"It doesn't seem right," I said. What if she was meant to be the Einstein of Witches? Although I supposed if she stopped being a ghoul, she could start being a Witch.

"What doesn't?"

Did she even know? Should I tell her? "Uh, nothing. Never mind."

"O-kay," Alison said with that look I'd seen a million times whenever I got all woo-woo. "Anyway, you tried to sound casual on your message, but I could tell you were worried." She looked over her shoulder as if to check to see if anyone was listening in.

No one was. William was in the storeroom sorting out a recent order. The last rush of customers faded after the lunch hour.

Satisfied, Alison turned back to me. "None of the others has ever contacted me before in person. I figured it had to be some kind of an emergency."

Others? She thinks I'm another ghoul, like her. I started to bristle with the desire to correct her assumption, but stopped. I'd let her think I was one of them for now. "When did you last see Sebastian?"

"Day before yesterday."

Oh Goddess. She was the one he'd gone to after being with me.

I was still reeling from this revelation when she continued. "He told me he was getting married. Can you believe that shit? Married? What does he think? His need is just going to go away because he's giving a ring to some norm?" She made an exasperated sound. "Did he tell you that too?"

Well, he had. "Yeah, he did."

"It's fucked up is what it is. I mean, what's he going to do? Start knocking over the Plasma Alliance?"

What she was implying finally hit me through the onslaught of her constant babble. "Wait a minute. Did he break up with you?"

She frowned. "He thinks he did." Then she actually snapped her fingers. With her too-thin fingers, pasty complexion, and two-hundred-dollar casual wear, the gesture looked like a parody of urban hip. But, her eyes narrowed fiercely as she continued, "Just wait until he discovers that he can't get enough from one woman, even if she is a willing donor, which I doubt she is. They never fall for one of us, have you noticed that?"

Alison didn't wait for my answer. "Anyway, I bet he made the rounds, you know, cutting everyone off. So, what's the deal? Did, like, one of us pop a cork or something? Do we need to go rescue him?"

Talking to Alison made my head spin. "You think one of the others is holding Sebastian hostage or something?"

She stopped short, and gave me a quizzical look. "Isn't that why you called me?"

I suddenly had *no* idea why I'd called her. "Uh, he's really only been missing a couple of days."

Alison gave me a very curious looking over, then said, "So I was the last one to see him? Are you accusing me of something?"

I didn't know what to say to that, but luckily, I didn't have to.

"Well, that's just silly," she answered her own question again. "I'd never hurt Sebastian. You know who I think did it?"—I didn't, but I was sure Alison was about to tell me—"I think it was Traci. That girl's a freak. She seems like a White Rose to me. Don't you think?" Think? I had no idea what a White Rose was. But before I could ask, Alison answered herself. "Yeah, totally." Then she glanced at my black, spiked hair and bloodred T-shirt with a vampire bat centered over my breasts. "No offense."

"None taken," I said easily since I had no idea just how I'd been insulted. I was still surprised Alison knew the others' names. What, did they have a newsletter? A LiveJournal community?

William came back from the storeroom with a box of books for shelving. He gave Alison and I a cursory glance and then did a textbook double take. "Ali?"

William knew one of Sebastian's ghouls? Did I even want to know how?

"Oh, William, hey," she sniffed, like something about William smelled badly to her.

Undaunted by the obvious brush-off, William continued toward us. "Do you keep in touch with Feather? How is she?"

Of course! I'd forgotten that William's ex-girlfriend Feather was a bite junkie. Was Feather one of Sebastian's ghouls too?

"She moved to Chicago a couple of months ago." And then, as if we were all thinking about the larger percentage of vampires living there, Alison added, "For school."

"Right." William's tone conveyed that he didn't buy that last bit either.

"I'm not supposed to talk about the business to you anymore, remember?"

Anymore? I looked to William askance. He looked away guiltily and scratched at the hairs at the back of his neck. I had a vague memory of William being nearly seduced by Sebastian's glamour. "You weren't . . . ? With Sebastian, were you?"

William raised his hands quickly. "No. I'd never do that to you. Honest. It was Parrish."

I remembered William had gone all black-haired and Goth after discovering that vampires were real, but I had no idea he'd become anyone's ghoul, much less my ex, Parrish's. That just seemed so wrong. It would almost be better if William had said he'd ghouled for Sebastian. At least I knew Sebastian was a gentleman and would have treated William well; Parrish was a bad boy to the core.

Alison turned to me conspiratorially. "Do you have somewhere private we can talk? Now that he's left the fold, we need to uphold the vow of secrecy."

"Uh, right." To William, I mouthed "later."

"Yeah, okay. Anyway, Ali, it was nice running into you," he said, as he continued to the back of the store where we kept a small alcove of pagan-friendly kids' books.

Alison and I watched him go. "It's too bad he's out of it. I hear he was always in demand. He'd be cute if he did something with that hair."

I nodded absently, still trying to wrap my head around William as a ghoul. Anyway, William's hairstyle changed as often as his religion. Currently, he seemed to be trying to emulate the side curls that some Orthodox Jews wore, except his sort of looked like messy sideburns heading toward muttonchops.

As Alison still seemed to be considering William's finer assets, I tried to steer her back on track. "Do you really think this Traci character could hold Sebastian against his will?"

Her theory went with Mátyás's strange statement this morning that Sebastian was "in hell." Maybe that was some kind of dhampyr code word for "stuck in a ghoul's basement," but why he couldn't just come out and say that I'll never understand.

"Totally. She's always talking about leather and chains and things."

Leather? The more Alison spoke, the more certain I was that there were things I did *not* want to know about Sebastian's life. Being face-to-face with this fragile, non-sequitur spewing woman was hard enough, but now I had to think about Sebastian in S and M dom mode too? Or as a bottom? I shook my head to clear it of half-formed images involving shiny buckles and leather. I shouldn't jump to any conclusions. After all, I'd been wrong about Walter. Maybe Alison was wrong about Traci.

Alison was giving me a curious look. "You want to go kick some butt right now?"

If Alison was right, and somehow Traci had captured Sebastian for some bondage fantasy, I did.

Definitely.

As it happened, Slow Bob came sauntering in at that very moment to relieve me. With all the chaos of being late, making the deal with Eugene and such, I'd half forgotten that I'd asked him to cover for me this afternoon. I told Alison to wait for me at the coffee shop next door for a few minutes, and I got myself ready. William whined a little at being left with Slow Bob, but I reminded him that he could have Bob take care of the orders while he staffed the register. While Slow Bob was painfully deliberate with every transaction he undertook in inverse proportion to the number of customers waiting in line, he stayed on the store's roster because he was an absolute whiz when it came to alphabetizing and sorting. Besides, I swore he'd read every book and tested every product in the entire place. Despite the fact that Slow Bob worked irregularly, sometimes it seemed he knew more about my inventory than I did.

With William thus mollified, I gathered my things and skived off. A twinge of guilt hit me as I punched out. It felt a lot like playing hooky given how late I'd come in. Still, if Alison was somehow right and Sebastian might be trapped at some ghoul's house, I didn't want to wait around until after close to check things out.

Izzy was chatting up Alison when I came in. When Alison turned at my wave, Izzy flashed me the international cuckoo symbol by twirling her finger near her temple. I widened my eyes in the I-know-but-she's-all-I've-got-to-work-with glare.

Alison, now armed with some frothy-looking caffeinated drink, met me halfway across the room. "Where do you want to look for Traci?"

"How about her place?" I asked, fishing Sebastian's book out of my purse.

Seeing the black book made Alison's pert lips form a perfect O. "Is that *his*?"

You would have thought I was holding the Shroud of Turin the way her hands reached for it reverently.

Since I didn't know how to deal with her creepy admiration, I ignored her and flipped to Traci's entry. "Crap," I said. "We're going to have to call a taxi or something. She's way out past Lake Monona."

"Taxi? Why not just take my SUV?"

I quickly schooled my expression before the sneer surfaced. I chose to ride my bicycle year-round because I generally tried to live an ecologically low-impact life. I'd mellowed considerably from my hemp/natural-fibers-only days, and I consciously tried not to judge people on their choice of transport. After all, Sebastian drove a car built before emissions testing. But SUVs made my eye twitch.

"Sounds great." I managed to smile. "Lead on, Macduff."

The drizzle had stopped, and the sky was now robin's-egg blue. Stepping out into sunlight, the brightness made me squint after spending so much time indoors. The heat of the afternoon felt good against my artificially chilled skin. The air smelled of city and dust, but the clear sky begged me to inhale deeply. Alison pulled a pair of oversized sunglasses from her clamshell purse.

She led me around the corner to a Cadillac Escalade. This vehicle was a behemoth of newly washed and waxed midnight-black steel. She beeped the engine on before we were even within five steps of the thing. Exhaust bellowed out in an oily cloud that slithered up into the clear blue sky.

Goddess, you could just *watch* it killing rain forests.

The interior smelled faintly of McDonald's take-out and leather, which the air-conditioning instantly recycled at a subzero setting. As I buckled in, I shivered slightly from the sudden temperature shift.

Alison went through the motions of getting herself situated. Then she asked, "Okay, where are we headed?"

I read off Traci's street address.

She pulled out like an expert into the traffic that circled around the capital square. I gripped the door handle with white knuckles.

"So," she said conspiratorially, eyeing the book that rested in my lap. "How did you get it? Did you lift it from him?"

Well, I kind of did. It wasn't exactly laying out in plain view and I certainly had it without his permission. "Yeah."

"Cool," she said, nodding to herself as if deciding something about me. Then, in yet another conversation jump: "It's nice to finally meet someone else. I only know the others from online."

Oh my great Goddess, they *did* have a Yahoo! group. What was it? Some kind of vampires' MySpace? "So, how did you find Sebastian anyway?" I asked.

Her narrow shoulders rose in a shrug. "The usual way." For a second, I didn't think she was going to elaborate, and then she added, "You know, a friend recommended me to him."

I wondered what *that* application process was like; what did you have to have on your résumé to have someone say they thought you'd make the ideal candidate to have your blood sucked on a regular basis?

"How about you?" she asked.

I thought about lying, but I wouldn't even know how to construct something plausible. "He came into my store."

She nearly snorted the latte she was sipping, and I thought she might swerve into the median. She recovered and gave me a quick look over, before returning her attention to the road. "He picked you up? No way. Oh my god, you are *so* lucky. I've heard about that happening, but I thought it was some kind of fairy tale. You're a Sleeping Beauty."

What did that make Sebastian, my Prince Charming with fangs?

"You need to join our group," Alison insisted. "The other girls would love to hear your story. It'd inspire them, especially now that he's talking about marriage . . ." The dots connected, and her face hardened. "You bitch. You've been letting me think you're one of us. But you're not. You're the norm. You're the one he's going to marry. Jesus," she spat. "I can't believe I didn't notice the rock."

Too late, I covered my left hand. With abrupt apprehension, I realized that I was barreling down the streets of Madison with a hostile stranger, and the gigantic SUV suddenly seemed too confining, too small, and too . . . locked.

Alison was still carrying on a conversation with herself, though she seemed to be winding herself down a little, at least. "Of course, that's how you got the book. You're sleeping with him."

The bitterness with which she said that made me wonder if that meant that she was *not*. I wanted to ask for clarification, you know, just to be sure, but Alison was accelerating so fast I thought we'd miss the turn onto Traci's street. "I think this is it," I said.

The SUV cornered better than I'd have expected for something of its size. I guessed that was down to the "sporty" part of sport-utility vehicle. "I'm only still helping you because of him," Alison informed me as we sped down the residential street. "If I didn't think that Sebastian might be in real danger, I would have pulled this car over and kicked you out by now."

I nodded, mentally calculating the route of the bus ride home. It would take three transfers, but I had enough cash. "It's cool," I said.

"Cool? Are you fucking kidding me? This whole thing is so not cool. I can't believe you're his . . . his . . . *lover*." She said it like it was the ugliest word in the English language, which was strange since I got the impression with the whole Sleeping Beauty comment that what all these ghouls wanted was Sebastian's adoration.

I knew this was volatile territory, but I had to know. "So, you're not? Lovers, I mean."

"I love Sebastian," Alison said with frightening resolve. Then her lip twisted. "But there are rules. I agreed to the terms before I became his supplier."

Terms? Like a contract? "And what are those terms exactly? No sex?"

"Bloodletting only," Alison sniffed, keeping her eyes averted from mine, ostensibly checking the house numbers we cruised past. "Not that it's any business of yours."

"Is that the same for all the ghouls?" I asked, more to myself than to Alison.

"I'm not privy to the arrangements Sebastian has with the others. And, 'ghouls,' by the way—not nice."

Alison pulled up alongside a vintage black Trans Am, complete with phoenix decal. Then, with a series of rapid motions that made my muscles tense, she parallel parked the boat like a pro.

"I'm sorry. I didn't mean to offend you," I said once we'd stopped.

Alison's lips were so tightly pressed together that there was a white line between them. "I'm not supposed to talk about this with outsiders. I only corrected you because Sebastian has been remiss in your education. Clearly, you didn't know any better."

I hadn't. As long as I'd know about vampires, I'd heard them refer to their blood donors as ghouls and/or ghoul-friends; I hadn't known they preferred another designation. I could see why Sebastian didn't call them suppliers, however. Despite Alison's insistence that she liked it better, I found the term somewhat forced, like they were desperately trying to find something more dignified to be called.

We stepped out onto a neatly mowed boulevard. Traci's address matched a ranch-style house with an attached three-car garage. Given the vintage vehicle parked out front, I suspected Traci and Sebastian had more than one passion in common. Despite everything I'd just learned from Alison about Sebastian's platonic relationship with his ghouls, or, excuse me, suppliers, I still felt a twinge of jealousy.

When I started for the house, Alison put out a hand. "You should stay in the car," she said. "This is a supplier matter. Private. Personal. Besides, you're out of your league here."

"I can take care of myself."

"Against a vampire who may be starved?" She gave me a very dismissive look. "Please. You don't have a clue."

I'd been with Sebastian when he'd been nearly bled out by the Vatican witch hunters, and he'd almost killed Feather with his need. Feather would have died without my magical intervention. "I've had some experience with that. You might need me, actually."

Alison snorted. "What, are you a nurse?"

"No," I said. "A Witch."

Alison's face pinched even tighter. If she got any angrier, I though her face might implode. "Oh," she said in a voice clipped and cold as ice. "I see."

"If we're going to do this, we should probably go in," I said. Besides, the heat was starting to be stifling. I could feel the sun sinking into my black shirt and burning my bare arms.

Her lips stayed jammed shut, but her eyes strayed to the house. I could tell she was weighing the discomfort of having to work with me and the necessity of rescuing Sebastain.

Wiping my palms on my black, sequined jeans, I was reminded of something Alison had said about Traci. "What's a White Rose?" Her eyes strayed to the vampire bat on my T-shirt. My eyes followed. Before Alison even opened her mouth, I got it. "A Goth," I said.

"A vampire wannabe," she said, with a nod. "Someone who's secretly craving to be turned."

"You'd think there'd be a lot of those," I said. We'd paused in the shade of a cottonwood. It was the only tall, well-established tree in the cul-de-sac. The rest were no more than a few feet high and still mounded at their bases with mulch.

"There would be, if we weren't all carefully screened." At my blank look she sighed. "It's a closed community," she explained. "We're all recommended by someone who takes responsibility for our indoctrination. We have to be discreet, after all, and keep a fairly tremendous secret. There are, of course, exceptions. The Midwest area group just happens to be very well organized."

"Plus, Sebastian can't 'turn' anyone, anyway."

The muscles of Alison's tightened jaw jumped a little bit more. "What do you mean he can't?"

Oh, was that a secret? "Uh, because of how he was made, you know."

Where they rested on her hips, hands clenched into fists. I thought she might actually take a pop at me, so I stepped back a pace.

"I suppose you know his whole life story." There was a challenge in her tone and her stance. One thing was certain, I was definitely taking the bus home.

I shook my head slowly, trying to keep a calm demeanor to defuse the situation. "I don't," I said. Her face turned bright red and I sensed she was going to explode with any number of rude epithets regarding my moral character. "I didn't know about you, did I?" I reminded her.

Alison squared her shoulders, causing her glossy red curls to flounce. "None of this matters. We should focus on rescuing Sebastian."

Her sundress was a brilliant white flash as she marched resolutely toward the door. A dragonfly skimmed above the lawn, its iridescent wings shimmering in the heat. We stood together on the narrow concrete pad only large enough for two. A little roof extending from the line of the house provided a bit of shade. I punched the glowing orange doorbell button. I could hear a faint chime though the vinyl door.

Minutes later, a woman in her late fifties answered. She had short-cropped hair and deep smile lines on a tanned face. Dressed in jeans and a Grateful Dead T-shirt, I could see the hint of faded ink of tattoos on both arms. "Can I help you?"

"Is Traci home?" Alison asked.

"I'm Traci," the woman replied.

Not exactly the "White Rose" Alison was expecting, but then I reminded myself that they'd never met in person. Given the hot rod out front, maybe Alison had misconstrued this whole "leather" business. It was possible Traci had been referring to things like motorcycle chaps—in the dark it wasn't always easy to differentiate the hard-core bikers from the leather queens.

"I'm Garnet, Sebastian's fiancée," I said. "This is Alison."

"Garnet." She smiled, offering a hand for me to shake. I could feel calluses on fingertips that made me suspect she played guitar or some other stringed instrument. "It's nice to finally meet you."

Unless this woman was a supremely good actress, I didn't think that we'd find Sebastian in chains in her basement. "I'm sorry to barge in on you like this, Traci, but Sebastian's missing."

I watched her face for any flicker of guilt. Instead, I saw growing concern. "Missing? For how long?"

"Since Wednesday," I supplied.

"You'd better come in." Traci stepped out of the way so that we could enter. The interior of the house was cool and extremely . . . white. Spotless carpeting in a brilliant ecru blanketed the floors and stairway. Beige-painted walls framed tall, broad, echoing spaces that felt profoundly empty despite the immaculate furniture and crystal light fixtures.

Alison followed on my heels, not saying a word.

"Your home is lovely," I murmured trying desperately to mean it. The place smelled new, like carpet glue or drywall mud.

Traci laughed. "You want it? It's for sale. I'm putting it up on the market tomorrow. It was my mother's. I was living in the garage apartment until she died."

"Oh," I said. "I'm sorry to hear about your mother."

"She was ninety, and she lived on her own the whole time. Pretty good life, I'd say."

"Yeah," I murmured, though I couldn't help but think about how hard it would be to deal with Sebastian's immortality when you'd just lost someone.

"Muh," said Alison, who seemed to have been stunned speechless by Traci. Admittedly, I hadn't expected someone who seemed old enough to be my mother either, but Sebastian had been alive a long time.

Traci led us into a kitchen, which, unlike the rest of the house, looked lived in. There were dishes in the sink and car parts on the table. The smell of strong, black coffee permeated the room. I tried to imagine Sebastian sitting in one of the straight-back wooden chairs; unfortunately, it was all too easy, especially given all the copies of *Custom Rodder* scattered about.

"Where is he?" Alison demanded. "What have you done with Sebastian?"

Traci and I both looked at her askance.

Alison had no problem elaborating. "Look at you, Traci. You look nothing like your online persona. You're clearly living some kind of lie, and you're probably desperate for Sebastian to turn you since you're so old and your mom just died. So, where's the basement in this place? Or do you have him chained up in the bedroom?"

Traci's eyebrow arched. "Old?"

The two of them stared at each other as though in a minute a ghoul slapfest might break out.

"Look, obviously, Alison is mistaken about all this. Do you have any idea if there's someone in the . . . uh, supplier community who might want to kidnap Sebastian?" I said, hoping that I could bring them back to the important issue at hand.

"Mistaken?" Alison said, her voice raising an octave and a decibel level. "We need to search floor to floor. He could be here. He could need us. Sebastian?" She started shouting, as she began to move around the room. "Sebastian? I'm coming, Sebastian!"

Too shocked to do much else, I stared as Alison began roaming through the house, opening every door, even the one with the frosted glass clearly marked "pantry." I glanced at Traci, expecting her to try to stop Alison's frantic scavenger hunt. Instead, I found that she was filling up a coffeepot with water.

"Do you want some coffee?" she asked around Alison's constant screams for Sebastian. Traci noticed my hesitation and added, "She won't be satisfied until she's searched every corner. It's a big house. It'll be a while."

Traci and I sipped a very fine Colombian blend as Alison continued to rip through the house. Traci asked a lot of questions about Sebastian's disappearance, and in the course of retelling the events of the past few days I unthinkingly outed myself as a Witch.

"A real Witch?" she asked, awe beginning to creep into her voice. "A real Witch that really works magic?"

"Yeah," I said. "For real."

"Omigod!" Traci didn't notice my slight mock, she was too busy going all fan grrl over me. The expression I'd mistaken as the disapproval of a religious conservative was actually the adoration of a devotee discovering her idol. Turns out Alison had been right about one thing: Traci was a "White Rose" of a kind, except instead of being a vampire wannabe, she wanted to be a Witch. "Oh my God," Traci was still saying, only slower this time. "That's just so awesome."

"Uh, yeah," I said.

"Would you do some?"

"Some what?" I asked, concerned about the sparkle in her eye as she asked. Her words almost seemed like a come on, the way she said them.

"Magic."

"Uh." Again, I wasn't exactly sure what Traci was requesting, especially the way she leaned closer across the table with each sentence. "I'm not sure I'm supposed to," I said. I mean, ghouls weren't supposed to do magic.

"Oh, we wouldn't do it together. But, you could scry," she said. "You know, to find Sebastian."

I couldn't believe this woman was asking me to stare into a crystal ball for a clue as to Sebastian's whereabouts. Then, just as suddenly, I couldn't believe I'd never thought of it myself. "Good idea," I said.

After Alison had satisfied herself that Traci didn't have a secret S and M dungeon squirreled away in her house, we explained our plan—or rather, Traci did in breathy excitement.

Alison pulled herself up to her full height. "It's forbidden."

"We'll just watch," Traci said, hopping on the balls of her feet with unrestrained glee. To me, she asked, "What do we need to do this?"

"This is unacceptable," Alison said. "I won't be party to it." With that, she turned on her heels and slammed the door.

Traci and I looked at each other. "Are you going to get in trouble?" I asked her.

"Don't worry about it. Sebastian has called it quits. I'm not a supplier anymore. Rules no longer apply. Anyway, there's no harm in watching, is there?"

Other than the fact that it seemed a bit voyeuristic? I shook my head. "I'll need something reflective. Traditionally, scrying was done with a crystal ball, but I could use a mirror or even water in a bowl."

"I have a crystal ball," Traci said. "Let me go get it." Traci returned with a concrete statue of a dragon wrapped around one of those garden "gazing globes" of metallic purple. "Will this do?"

"It's, uh, fine," I said. I grabbed the statue. "Let's do this," I said, thinking that I wanted to get it over with as quickly as possible.

Not ten minutes later, Traci and I sat on a stiff uphol-stered couch in a chilly living room staring at the dragon's ball. Traci had insisted in getting dressed in a belly dancer skirt and shawl that dripped with bangles and beads. She also put some kind of humpback whale song on the stereo to get us "in the mood," and I guess because she thought I needed it to be magical.

I felt vaguely silly. Still, if it would help find Sebastian, I was all for it. Traci asked me what else I might need, and I just raised my hand dramatically to hush her. I closed my eyes briefly. I could feel Lilith loosen within me, like a spring uncoiling. I focused my thoughts: Where are you, Sebastian?

I opened my eyes. There was only a reflection of darkness, and then I caught the flash of a wolfish grin. It was there for only a second before it was gone. But I instantly knew it wasn't Sebastian's.

It was Micah's.

6.

Mars

Violence, Power, and Animal Nature

I stood up. "I've got to go," I said.

Traci was thrilled. "You saw something! Ohmigod! What did you see?"

Explaining Micah was far too complicated. "I'm not sure, but I saw someone I know. I think he might have some answers."

Traci nodded solemnly. "You have to go," she agreed. "Do you need a ride anywhere?"

Even though I wanted to find Micah as quickly as possible, the thought of spending another awkward ride in a stranger's car—particularly a stranger who was quite so into me—made me shake my head vehemently. That kicked-puppy look threatened to surface on Traci's face, so I said, "This is something I have to do alone. I saw it in the crystal."

Of course that was a lie, but Traci bought it. She thanked me several times and offered, very solicitously, that if I needed anything—*anything*—I should call her. I took the business card she offered politely. Glancing at it, I noticed a LiveJournal blog address. "Is this the supplier group's blog?"

She shook her head. "That site is locked. Do you want me to get you in?"

"I do."

When it was revealed that I didn't have a LiveJournal account, Traci said she'd be more than happy to set one up for me. I gave her my work e-mail—it was the only one I had—and she said she'd be in touch. She hugged me a little too tightly for just a little too long, and we parted ways.

Outside, the afternoon had turned into a storybook gorgeous summer day. The temperature had leveled out somewhere in the mideighties, no clouds in the sky, and the rhythmic sound of automatic lawn sprinklers filled the suburbs.

I needed to get back to the city. Micah knew something about Sebastian's disappearance, I was certain of it. Not only had I seen his smile in the scrying bowl, but he'd been standing at the junction where Sebastian's astral cord frayed.

Bright yellow school buses made their rounds, and the clusters of mothers waiting at street corners gave me suspicious looks as I walked down the wide-paved sidewalks. I took advantage of their stares to ask for directions to the nearest bus stop. I was informed that the best spot to pick up public transport into town was the strip mall about a mile and a half thataway. *Good luck, good-bye, and don't come back* was the subtext. Even so, I thanked them cheerily and went on my way.

The big square houses that I passed, which all looked

much the same, made me want to sing Pete Seeger's "Little Boxes." Even the gardens had a cookie-cutter feel, tending toward hydrangea, sedum, and hosta. Occasionally, some brave soul would break out and have a tall stand of sunflowers or a riot of deep purple wave petunias spilling from hanging baskets, but they were rare. All the trees were approximately the same size and shape, being all the same variety and having been planted at the same time.

In my spangles and black jeans I felt conspicuously different. My shoulder blades itched like I could feel eyes watching my progression through this Stepford community.

There was a reason I lived in the city.

When I reached the busy intersection near the mall, something akin to relief washed over me. Shoulders I didn't remember hunching, relaxed. It was as if a tiny bit of "city" chaos had encroached into the sterile orderliness of the suburbs, and I felt much more anonymous among the billboards and neon. Even the smell of fast food and exhaust comforted me with its familiarity.

The bus stop proved difficult to find. Foolishly, I assumed it would be somewhere convenient for shoppers, like right at the main mall entrance. I walked up and down the mile-long mall twice until I finally broke down and asked someone. Of course, they didn't know, having driven there like everyone else. Just about ready to give up and do a no doubt equally fruitless search for a pay phone to call a cab, I spotted an information desk inside. The bored security guard directed me to the back alley. She also told me the wait would be nearly an hour, since I had just missed the bus a minute and a half ago.

Great.

Frustrated and tired, I made my way to the food court. With any luck there'd be a Subway, which at least had a veggie sandwich option. If not, I could get something to drink and sit down for a while.

My pace quickened when I noticed the yellow and green logo, pleased that at least this one thing had worked out for me today. I ordered and paid, gleefully splurging on chips and a drink.

That's when I noticed Micah Cloud sitting two paces away. A Wile E. Coyote T-shirt hugged his sleek frame, and his hair was loose and unruly. Apparently in an attempt to ward off the muted, neon glare of the mall, he wore sunglasses. He looked like some kind of fugitive from the law; or he would have, if he weren't reading a book and eating a meatball sub.

The coincidence was too much. I stormed over to him so fast the soda nearly slid off the slick plastic tray. "You're stalking me again, aren't you? What did you do to Sebastian? I know you're involved somehow."

He looked up from the pages of *Coven Craft* by Amber K. and smiled lazily. "Garnet, it's nice to see you again too."

I held my tray in shaking hands. "I'm serious, Micah. I saw you in the scrying ball. I know you have something to do with Sebastian's disappearance. Quit screwing around with me."

He removed his sunglasses to give me an appraising look. His eyes twinkled, and I realized I'd handed him the perfect opportunity to be flirtatious. So, I was already blushing by the time he said, "Unfortunately, I haven't had that particular pleasure."

I hid my embarrassment by settling down in the plastic chair opposite him. He moved his book aside to make room for my food. "You're avoiding the issue."

"Which is?"

"Sebastian," I said.

"Sorry, wrong tree." He looked me directly in the eye, though the fluorescent light made him squint at me.

Too smooth; I didn't buy it. "You were there when I was searching for him on the astral plane, and I had a vision of you when I was asking for clues for Sebastian's whereabouts. Explain that."

He stared at me for a beat. It was just long enough for me to sense the coyote behind his eyes, that unblinking, inhuman gaze. "Maybe the Higher Power is telling you that you need my help to find him."

Oh, he was good. So good, in fact, that I found myself entertaining the possibility. The image in the ball had been a flash of his smile, nothing more threatening than that. "But, on the astral plane, when I met you . . . it was a place where Sebastian's cord split."

"Fate," he said simply, taking a bite of his sandwich. When it became obvious that I had no idea what he meant, he finished chewing and said, "Clearly, I represent some kind of apex of choice. You join forces with me; Sebastian's fate goes one way. You don't . . . ?" He spread his hands indicating a wide open future.

"That sounds like a threat."

"It's not. It's just a possible explanation."

I frowned. Either he was playing me or he was being sincere. I couldn't decide. His easy, unruffled demeanor wasn't helping either. Somehow Micah managed to crook his smile in a way that looked untrustworthy and charming at the same time. I unwrapped my sandwich. Oil had made the paper slick and transparent. My mouth watered at the tart scent of banana peppers and onions. Micah watched me surreptitiously from behind long lashes. We munched as I tried to decide whether or not to trust him.

"Have you decided what you want to do about"—he jerked his head in the direction of my stomach—"you know."

My weight problem? I glanced at my tummy for a second before it occurred to me that he must mean Lilith and his offer to release her. "I haven't had much time to really consider it. The last few days have been a little crazy."

He raised his eyebrows, but went back to his book. I, meanwhile, tried not to dribble lettuce down my shirt and considered Micah's motives. What was he up to? Did I really believe that fate wanted the two of us to try to find Sebastian together?

"Every day you become more like her," he said without lifting his eyes from the text.

"You said that before, but I don't see it. I haven't sprouted chicken legs."

He looked up from his book. "But you could be sterile."

"What? Seriously?"

Micah shrugged. Flipping a page, his eyes went back to the text. "Or you could be growing more judgmental and cruel and not even realize it. Your morals could be eroding so slowly you won't even notice the change until it's too late."

I frowned. Had I become colder? Living with a vampire had made me a little jaded, it was true—I mean, blood no longer made me squeamish. But could that also be Lilith's influence?

"Think about it," he said, glancing at me briefly. "How often do you tap her these days? Is it more than before? Are you using her for simpler and simpler magic? The kinds of stuff you used to do on your own?"

Bristling, I put my sub down. "I'm a strong Witch on my own."

"I'm sure you are," he said without inflection.

He finished eating and returned his attention to the book, content to let me stare unabashedly at him. "Why are you reading a coven primer?" I asked.

The eyes that peeked over the edge of the covers were quizzical. "Seriously? You can't guess?"

"You've never been in a coven before?" I ventured.

He put a finger on his nose. "Got it in one."

I found that hard to believe. With all that raw power roiling under his skin, Micah could hardly be a newbie to magic. I wanted to check his aura again, but remembering how devastating it had been last time, I didn't dare. Maybe he'd been a loner up to now. That made a kind of sense.

"You said you thought that the 'Higher Power' wanted us to try to find Sebastian together," I said. Rolling up sub detritus in the paper that I'd used as a makeshift plate, I stuck it in the plastic baggie. "I'd be up for that."

Micah nodded. Putting down his book, he seemed to be waiting for me to say more.

"So are you busy?"

He laughed. "You mean now? Boy, you don't waste any time, do you?"

"I guess not," I said. "So are you? We could go to my place . . ."

"I thought you'd never ask."

"A Jeep Cherokee?" I asked when he led me to the spot where he'd parked. "Not seriously. Aren't you offended or something?"

He shrugged. "Do you think there's a bunch of naval officers pissed off that there's a Jeep named the Commander?"

"Ha-ha, but they're not . . ."

"And I'm not Cherokee," he said over the red hood. It sounded like one of Micah's quips, but I thought I detected a slight edge. He'd parked underground and I couldn't read his expression in the stark, fluorescent light. "Get in."

For the second time in so many hours, I slid into the seat of a stranger's car. Broken in but well kept, the seats and floors were clear of major clutter. There were a few library books—fiction, mystery or thrillers from the looks of them—stowed in the back and a paper bag half full of Coke bottles and other typical car garbage.

Wisconsin Public Radio came on when the car's engine sprang to life. He glanced at me almost apologetically as he switched it off. He probably expected me to say something snarky about his choice in stations, but my horizons had expanded a lot since dating a vampire who loved country and western. I could hardly point fingers. Besides, NPR was comfort radio to me. My hippie folks tuned in every Saturday for *A Prairie Home Companion* for as long as I could remember.

Micah powered down the window on my side a little bit,

as a way of indicating that natural air flow was the driver's preference. There was something inviolable about the prerogative of the owner of the vehicle and the use of AC. One didn't question it, at least not the first time you rode—maybe after you had dated several months. For instance, Sebastian and I could argue about it—well, we *could* if any of his cars were new enough to come standard with a cooling system.

Not that I minded the fresh air. I'd gotten used to it with Sebastian to the point of preferring breeze, no matter how warm, over the ultra chill. Besides, this way there was less shock going from car to building.

Even though he'd been parked underground, the Jeep still smelled of overheated leather. I found the control and dropped the window another inch or so—just enough to catch a breeze. Because I knew we'd be taking the highway, I resisted opening the window all the way and hanging an arm out. Like a dog, I loved the feel of the wind on my skin, and, if it were socially acceptable, I'd ride with my face blasted with sun and speed.

"You're not Cherokee," I said, even though I knew it might be a sore subject. "What are you?"

He glanced at me out of the corner of his eye, as he backed us out of the parking space. "I'll tell you what, Garnet. You tell me your flavor, and I'll tell you mine."

I was probably supposed to buy a clue that he didn't want race on the table, but I forged on cheerfully. "Scots-Irish, English, German, and Latvian."

"Latvian?"

I nodded. "My grandmother Apsitis."

"Me too," he said. "That is, I'm lots of things. But the answer you're looking for is Ojibwe."

Being a transplant to this area, I had no idea if there were Ojibwe in Wisconsin. However, I did know there were a lot where I was from. "Are you from Minnesota?"

"Yeah, you?"

For the next ten minutes, Micah and I bonded over Norwegian bachelors, "Minnesota Nice," butt-freezing winters, lakes "up north," and how much we both loathed the movie *Fargo*.

"Yeah." He laughed. "Except, one time when I was trying to make the point that most people in Minnesota don't talk like that, this guy comes into the café and we have this conversation. 'Hot enough for you?' he asks. 'Yah,' I go, 'At least it keeps the mosquitoes down.' "

I laughed so hard I nearly peed. I'd had conversations just like that. "It's embarrassing isn't it? I once overheard my grandfather, who was standing around watching my dad put up a fence, say, 'Other guys might have measured that twice.' "

" 'Other guys might have.' " Micah snorted. "Oh, yeah, I've heard that one a lot too."

We pulled up to my apartment. My front gardens—really a wide tangle of purple-blossomed oregano, foxgloves, and yellow snapdragons—looked a little droopy in the afternoon heat.

"Your place is certainly, uh, bright in the day," Micah said, miming shielding his eyes from the horrendous Day-Glo hot pink my landlord had painted the exterior in a misguided attempt to be historically accurate.

I grimaced. I'd actually tried to plant flowers I thought would help soften the color scheme, thus all the soft indigos of violets and Johnny jump-ups and bluebells of the creeping bellflower. It didn't help. "It's better inside, I promise."

Micah followed me up the stairs, making admiring noises at the woodwork and leaded glass. His hand traced reverently along the plaster, as though acknowledging the hardships of a noble, worn sanctuary.

As I dug my key from my purse, I heard Barney yowling. She sounded like the time she'd been cornered by a neighborhood cat that had slunk up the back stairs into the apartment. "Barney? You okay?"

I cautiously opened the door a crack, not wanting to startle her. I was greeted by more deep-throated warning growls and a hissing spit.

"You've got an attack cat?" Micah asked, amused, from above my shoulder.

"Not usually," I said, still trying to catch sight of what was going on inside. "It sounds like there's something inside she doesn't like."

"Maybe it's me," Micah guessed.

As if in answer, Barney let out another territorial yell—not unlike the "I don't want to go to the vet, you can't make me" screaming I hear annually.

It occurred to me that Micah could be right. Barney didn't like magic and, given that the last time I peeked at Micah's aura I nearly fell over, Barney might be pitching a fit over that much raw power waltzing over the threshold. I closed the door. "Let's do this in the backyard."

Micah stiffened. "You take orders from a *cat*?"

Ah. That could be the other part of Barney's literal hissy

fit. Micah spent part of his time as a dog—or at least a dog-like being. Barney did not like canines of any sort. Magical dogs—well, she'd just see that as insult on injury.

More to the point, besides the fact that Barney rightly considered the house half hers, she *was* my familiar. As such, she acted as guardian. If she put up this much fuss to keep Micah out, maybe she had a reason. Given my trust/not trust in him, I was apt to agree. "In this case," I said, "I do."

He shook his head at me as if he couldn't quite believe the absurdity of it all. "It's your call."

After tucking my purse inside of my apartment, I shut the door without locking it and guided Micah back down the stairs, through the communal hall to the back door. A cedar privacy fence surrounded my backyard. I had a clay chiminea on cinder blocks in one corner, a little too close to the house and the wood to satisfy the fire marshal. But my landlord liked it, so we both pretended we used it "for cooking," which was the exception that would make its placement fall into legal parameters.

He also gave me free rein when it came to gardening, being especially thrilled that Sebastian was a "Master Gardener" and a part-time horticultural instructor at UW.

The pride of our efforts this season was the herb garden along the far wall. Tufts of sweetgrass and mounds of curly parsley formed the edges of the garden. Tall, stiff stalks of white betony poked up among pink, puffball onion chive flowers. Dark-leaved chocolate mint aggressively crowded the delicate red, tubular blossoms of the peach pineapple sage. The air smelled of French thyme and basil.

"Oh," Micah said, after taking it all in with a deep breath. "This is lovely."

"Thanks," I said.

Though we had no trees in the yard proper, much of the lawn was shaded by the neighbor's oak, whose thick branches stretched high over the fence, nearly touching the spire of the tower. Even on hot days, the backyard stayed relatively cool. When it was really scorching, I commandeered the kiddy pool that the downstairs tenants had bought and mostly forgotten about. Currently, it was stashed under their kitchen window, filled with brackish water, leaves, and dead and/or drowning bugs.

"Where shall we . . ." Micah started, and then looking down at his feet, he added, "Never mind, I see. Here is good."

We stood in the center of a natural circle. Early in spring, Sebastian and I had dug a nine-foot diameter ring and filled it with creeping thyme, which had stayed mostly invisible until the white, star-shaped flowers began to bloom. Now the image stood out starkly from the blue-green of the grass.

"Cool, isn't it?" I couldn't resist a little brag, but not wanting to force flattery from Micah, I quickly continued. "I haven't gotten a chance to really use it yet."

Something about that made Micah's perpetual smirk deepen. I could see the hint of dimples. "Virgin, eh?"

I rolled my eyes at him, but I felt a twinge of guilt at the thought of using this circle first with someone other than Sebastian. I reminded myself that we were planning on casting a spell to help find him, and if any place was invested with Sebastian's energy it was the garden he'd planted with me.

"Let's get started, shall we?" I said.

"Au naturel too, I like that," Micah said as though we

were talking about sex instead of a magical ritual. "No fancy tools or special outfits. I like that kind of rough-and-ready witchcraft."

"You would," I said with a smile, despite the sense I had that encouraging him was a bad idea.

"So let's get down to it, girl," he said, holding out both hands for me to grasp.

I took them and felt a hard shock, like static. Between our feet, a small eddy of wind like a dust devil swirled. Startled, I glanced up into Micah's eyes, and saw the obsidian glint of Coyote looking back at me.

"Bring up the Goddess," he demanded in a sinister, yet soft, almost loving, command. "Let me see Her."

I hesitated. There was too much power here. The grass stood on end under my shoes, shivering in the preternatural breeze.

"For Sebastian," he reminded me. "You want to find him, don't you?"

I did. Even if Micah had only offered to assist me because he wanted to see Lilith in action, it didn't negate the fact that adding his strength to Hers was an expedient solution. If Sebastian was in trouble somewhere, this would help.

Closing my eyes, I woke the dragon.

It began as it always did, like a sudden jolt of heat between my legs. Myth would have it that Lilith was a seductress, a succubus, that entranced men in their sleep, and I could believe it. Her rising within me bordered on arousal.

Micah seemed aware of the changes inside me. He purred appreciatively, and his grin grew impossibly more magnetic and tempting. I could feel my body reacting under his gaze.

Lilith surged along my nerve endings. My muscles trembled with fiery awakening.

Micah stepped closer, so that our bodies touched. He was hard and hot, and my knees began to tremble with a desire to merge with him sexually and magically. I tipped my head back, and my lips parted without my volition.

He leaned down. I could feel his breath tickle my skin. I started to push away, but an unseen force held me firm, willing me to submit. The more Lilith rose, the less control I could exert. I felt my arms weakly push against him, even as the rest of my body began to yield. When his lips touched mine such intense fire reared up I thought I might orgasm on the spot. His tongue darted inside me, first tentative, then hard, almost violent, violating.

Wind roared in my ears for a split second before I surrendered my consciousness.

I dreamed of running. Wolves surrounded me. Jaws snapped and teeth glistened yellow in moonlight. Spruce trees, erect and dense, blocked the starlight. The pack closed in. Terrified, I sprinted. Feet pounded on uneven ground. Leaping over a fallen log, I fell onto four feet, running faster now. The night brightened, and the air tasted crisp and clean. Those who had pursued became companions, running closely alongside, encouraging me to greater speeds, to test limits, dance on the edge—play. Something that had been held back released with a crash of thunder.

Rushing faster than ever before, the world blurred. The forest turned into a green smear, objects barely discernible, except one that caught in the corner of my eye—a saint, tied to a tree, pierced with arrows.

"Sebastian!"

Rain poured down in sheets from an eerily green-yellow sky. I blinked the water from my eyes. Soaked to the bone, I shivered and looked around for Micah. I stood alone in the circle. My flowers were battered to the ground by drops of rain so heavy and fast that mud splattered. The tops of the trees bent in the wind. A pop of lightning flashed, followed by a boom of thunder so near it rattled the fence.

Then, I heard a wailing sound so low that it took my brain a few moments to distinguish the noise from the spray of rain and rush of wind. Then, it came through clearly: sirens.

Tornado sirens.

I bolted for the back door, slipping in the slick, oversaturated grass. Water flooded in as I swung the screen open. The wind ripped the handle from my grasp and banged the aluminum frame against the house. I scrabbled for it, wrestling it closed. As I secured the lock and shut the heavier wooden door in front of it, the sky outside blackened ominously.

I flicked the light switch several times before I realized the power was out. I took two hesitant steps into the darkness. Thunder rattled the house again, and this time I thought I could hear a thin, plaintive meow.

Oh, great Goddess—Barney!

I galloped up the steps, my clothes pressing heavily

against my skin. My shoes soaked the hardwood. The wind screeched around the gables. My ears popped.

That did not seem good.

I wrenched the knob on the back door and nearly pulled my arm out of its socket before I realized the door was locked, and I'd left my keys in my purse. I could go around to the front, but the tornado was imminent; there was no time. I rattled it several times uselessly. "Barney," I yelled. "Oh Jesus, Barney!"

I knew I was freaked when I reverted to my pre-Wiccan oaths. My verbal slip jolted me out of my panic momentarily. I felt I couldn't run back down and around to the front door in time. I had to break down this door. Lilith had helped me crack locks before. She could do it again.

Trying not to hear the sound of tree limbs splitting from the force of the gale, I closed my eyes and reached deep down for the familiar strength.

Nothing.

My hand stroked my abdomen. "Come on," I whispered. "I know you're in there." But suddenly, I wasn't so sure. A cold fear settled in my guts in Her place.

A sound came like someone emptying a gigantic bag of ball bearings onto the roof. Hail exploded against the landing window so hard I thought the glass would shatter any moment. Barney cried pitifully somewhere beyond the door.

Fuck Lilith. I braced my back against the half wall of the stairwell and gave the spot just above the doorknob a swift kick. Dumb luck and a cheap lock conspired in my favor for once, and the door burst open with a bang.

"Barney!" I shouted once I recovered my footing. I wasn't quite sure what I was expecting—my cat had never before come when I called. Despite the danger, she didn't this time either. I raced through the apartment checking all her favorite hiding places. Under the bed? No. Behind the couch? Damn it all, no.

"Where are you?" I shouted, as menacing white clumps of hail burst against the windows. I checked behind the fridge, grateful she hadn't squeezed herself back there. I'd moved one mountain for her already today; I didn't think I had enough muscle to move another. Just when I was beginning to think I'd have to abandon her, I remembered my bedroom closet. I found her wedged on top of the boxes of my winter clothes. I grabbed her, despite her protests, and scrambled for the basement.

Downstairs, three skanky-looking guys sat huddled around a flickering tea candle. One with greasy curls drooping from underneath a dirty stocking hat cradled a bag of Doritos like a teddy bear. Another, whose shaved head showed off blue-ink, abstract tattoos, drank deeply from amber liquid in a Mason jar. The last had a blond Afro and a soul patch on his chin. Soul Patch waved at me. "Fugitive girl," he said.

I let Barney slip out of my arms, and she disappeared into the shadowy corners to hunt up spiders. To Soul Patch, I said, "Sorry?"

"That's you: fugitive girl," he said, emphasizing the last as though it were my superhero moniker. "Running from the FBI and stuff?" His tone shifted as though he suddenly didn't trust his memory.

I probably should have denied my past dubious involvement with government agents, but I felt sort of sorry for the guy. Besides, he was my neighbor, and it was the one bit of shared history we had in common. "Yeah, that's me."

He broke into a loopy grin. "Dude!"

My eyes strayed to the plant stalks whipping frantically in the wind outside the basement window. The stems bent this way and that, and suddenly stood straight up. When a tree branch crashed somewhere outside everyone ducked in sympathy.

"Man, I hope that didn't bust up the house," Tattoos said, taking another swig and passing the jar to Doritos.

"Dude, you don't even live here," Soul Patch said.

"Right," Tattoos said, as though the fact had only just now occurred to him.

Leaving the brain trust, I started searching the room for a radio. Last time I did laundry I thought I remembered seeing an AM/FM radio stashed along one of the shelves above the washing machine. Instead, I found a flashlight missing its batteries, two dead sow bugs, a jar full of coins, and a lot of empty bottles of detergent.

My hand rested on the wet fabric of my shirt near my tummy while I scanned the shelves. Could Lilith really be gone? I hugged myself tighter as water sluiced from my soaking clothes.

"Are we supposed to leave the windows open or something?" Doritos asked around a mouth full of chips.

"Southeast corner," said Soul Patch. "I think we're supposed to go to the southeast corner."

I smiled to myself listening to their chatter. Honestly, I was surprised they had made it to the basement, what with the state they were in. I continued shuffling though the shelves, automatically cleaning and organizing as I moved along. I unearthed a single ice skate, a terrarium with a dusty rodent wheel, and a roll of paper towels.

Pushing a clump of dripping hair from my eyes, I shivered. I found myself still clutching my abdomen, as though protecting an open wound. I hadn't been without Lilith's presence for over a year and a half. She was part of me. How could She disappear?

"Under the doorway, I think. Or is it a staircase?" said Tattoos.

"I think we're supposed to get in a bathtub."

"Man, that's only if you don't have a basement."

"Ditches are bad."

"No, ditches are good. Bridges are bad. And mobile homes, nobody wants to be in a trailer. You're doomed."

They all bobbed their heads in agreement to that. As the wind made a sound like a jackhammer, I rubbed my arms. My clothes clung to me, cold and soggy. Where had Micah run off to? Did he take Lilith with him? A crack of thunder made me jump. Was this weather a result of our magic somehow?

My dream/vision had left me more certain than ever that Sebastian was in trouble, possibly even being held captive somewhere. I wanted to go out to find him, but I was stuck in a basement with a bunch of stoners desperately trying to remember their weather safety courses from sixth grade.

"This is kind of weird, right?" Soul Patch was saying. "I mean, ten minutes ago it was sunny and shit, and I didn't think this part of Wisconsin had that many tornados. You know, because of being on the edge of the Driftless Zone and that."

Everyone, including me, stared curiously at Soul Patch.

"The Driftless Zone?" He seemed to ask us for confirmation, but no one said anything, so he continued hesitantly. "You know, where the glaciers split during the second Ice Age. It's why we have standing rocks and the Dells and stuff."

"Man, you're like a geologist or something," Doritos said in awe.

"Dude, it's my major."

Okay, so I was impressed too. Thunder crashed, but the wind seemed to push the grass around less frantically now. Hail turned back to rain.

"What we need is a meteorologist," Soul Patch said.

"Or a radio," suggested Tattoos.

"Don't you have one of those weather-alert radio things up in the bathroom, Tom?" asked Doritos of Soul Patch.

"Yeah," he said, and so they all decided to head back upstairs to fetch it. I pressed my chin up against the crumbling, wet basement wall to try to peer up at the sky through the window well. All I could see was crabgrass and gravel and lots of rain. Still, I thought the stoners' instincts were correct; the danger of the storm had passed.

A quick search found Barney asleep on top of the dryer in an empty plastic basket of mine. I scratched her head, and she gave an annoyed chirp at having been awakened and laid her head back down as if to say, "Five more minutes."

"Now," I said.

"M-now?" she repeated, sounding unhappy about the prospect.

"Yes, now." I was anxious to figure out what had happened to Lilith and Micah. "We have a dog to track down."

Barney squiggled as I held her against my wet shirt and

headed up the stairs. I snuggled her tightly as I stepped gingerly around the shattered remains of the backdoor. The apartment was dark, though from the blinking, red twelve o'clock on my kitchen radio and microwave, I guessed that the power had come back on at some point. Letting Barney leap from my arms once I got to the dining room, I felt for the wall switch.

The light revealed a figure sleeping on my couch in the living room. I screamed, thinking it was an intruder, which it was, but as he sat up in alarm, one I recognized, "Mátyás?! What are you doing here?"

He reached over to flip on the floor lamp near the couch. It was an overly-familiar-with-my-stuff kind of gesture, especially given that I'd never, ever invited him into my home before. Rubbing his eyes, he stretched. "I let myself in. Your door was wide open. You really should be more careful. Anyone could wander in."

He'd said the last bit sarcastically, and I rolled my eyes. "Clearly. Seriously, why did you come all the way here?" Then, fear seized my stomach. "Has something happened? Have you heard from Sebastian?"

"In a way," he said, though he looked strangely embarrassed about it.

"Tell me," I demanded. "Or are you going to spout a bunch of malarkey about hell again and go all cryptic and silent on me?"

With a sneeze, Barney shook the water from her fur onto Mátyás's crisply pressed pants.

He crossed his hands in front of his chest. "I have information about Sebastian. Do you want it or not?"

"I do."

"Then you should put on a kettle for some tea and while you're at it may I suggest that you change clothes?" he added dryly. "I can see right through your shirt. Not that I've never seen you in the buff before, but, well, it's distracting."

Ew! Nothing like having your lover's son point out that he's seen you naked before. I crossed my hands over my chest; I wasn't wearing a bra. I rarely did, since I was small enough that major support wasn't an issue. Trust Mátyás to take this opportunity to remind me that when we first met, I was sitting naked in Sebastian's kitchen. I stomped off to my bedroom, wondering once again why I bothered being nice to him.

Once safely behind closed doors, I slid out of my wet clothes and dumped them in a pile near the foot of the bed. While raiding my drawers for a sports bra, I came across the clothes Sebastian had left at my place. I unfolded one of his T-shirts—a black one, a souvenir from an Iron Maiden concert—and buried my face in it, trying to catch his scent. Pulling the shirt over my head, I snuggled into it, hugging the fabric close. I stomped into a pair of bright red, cotton underwear and loose-fitting black jeans with wide cuffs. I found red, fuzzy socks accented with glittery, silver metallic thread and put them on. I was chilled enough from the wet that I almost considered unearthing my winter sweater box and finding something woolly to throw over my shoulders, but I knew the temperatures would warm up again soon enough. After a quick stop in the bathroom to fix my makeup and run the blow-dryer over my hair, I felt ready to face Mátyás again.

Almost. My fingers brushed my belly again. I felt strangely unarmed, like I should have a gun at my hip and suddenly didn't. The absence of Her presence, Her missing weight was its own kind of sensation.

Taking in a deep breath, I squared my shoulders. I was still a Witch. I'd called a Goddess to my side once, I could do it again need be. Right?

Right. Too bad I couldn't quite convince myself.

I found Mátyás in my kitchen. He'd located my teakettle, filled it, and put it on the left front burner—the one that sputters. Mátyás fiddled with the knob, trying to make the flames come out evenly.

"That one needs to be cleaned or something," I said, frowning to myself at the general state of the kitchen, as I took the kettle off that burner and put it on the right. My astrology stuff cluttered the table, and morning coffee cups littered the sink. "The whole stove should probably be looked at."

"Or thrown away. It's got to be twenty years old, if a day."

I bristled. "It's okay for what I need."

"It's dangerous. You'd be well rid of it."

"I can't just throw it away. Besides the fact that I can't really afford to put in a new gas stove, I think my landlord would have something to say about it."

"I meant when you move in with my dear papa." Mátyás leaned casually against the counter, giving me a curious, yet judging look.

Despite the change of clothes, I felt much more naked without the security of Lilith's presence. It made me prickly. "What?" I snapped.

"You have cold feet," he stated. "I hope you're not

planning on doing a runaway bride, jilting my poor father at the altar."

"He's the one who's disappeared, remember."

"I haven't forgotten," Mátyás said solemnly, and giving me a look that suggested perhaps I had. "So, about the dream," Mátyás said so quietly I almost didn't hear him over the drumming beat of the rain on the gutters.

"Yeah," I said suddenly remembering the strange images that flooded my mind before the storm. "It was weird. More of a vision, I guess, while Micah ran off with my Goddess."

The teakettle whistled. I brought down two mugs from the cupboards. Handcrafted and uncommonly wide, each had a pale pear painted in the center which, in the wrong light, looked a little like a vulva. I liked the cups anyway, because you could pour nearly three normal-sized servings in each, making them the perfect companion for long conversations or lazy Sunday mornings. I had a feeling this might be the former. I handed Mátyás one. He peered at it skeptically and smirked at the pear. Only when I went to get myself some honey from the cabinet did I realize Mátyás hadn't responded. He was filling up his cup and giving me the are-you-completely-insane? eyebrow lift.

I rested my hand against my stomach, but I still felt only emptiness. "He did, you know," I said to make the whole thing a joke, despite the shiver racing up my spine. "That skinwalking so-and-so absconded with Lilith."

"Garnet, what the hell are you talking about?"

I shook my head. "A were-coyote from my coven talked me into doing a spell to try to find Sebastian. But I think it was a ruse to waken Lilith. I think he convinced Her to run away with him." And I was a little freaked out about the prospect. Scratch that, make that a lot. I felt so empty without Lilith's warmth coiled around my belly, like a sleeping snake. Her power frightened me, but it was always there, ready to protect and defend me.

Mátyás poured himself tea and added a dash of milk, just like Sebastian liked it. "Coyote steals fire," Mátyás said as he settled into my chair. "How very mythical."

Coyote? With a capital C? No way, Micah was a real person, flesh and blood, not some Trickster God straight out of myth.

Like Lilith.

Oh.

How stupid did I feel? I'd been tricked by the Trickster.

7.

Jupiter

Micah was Coyote.

Well, that certainly would explain the intense brightness of his aura and, strangely enough, his perverse sense of humor. Wile E. Coyote T-shirt. Oh yeah, I got it now. Very funny. Ha-ha.

Still, I wasn't used to capital-letter Gods that walked around corporally—not full time, anyway. I'd thought that to come to this earthly plane, Gods and Goddesses needed human vessels. That was the role that the High Priest and Priestess played during most rituals—they opened themselves to the presence of a God or Goddess. It was a meditative channeling and part of how I'd called Lilith into me. Lilith didn't exist on the physical plane, except within me, which is always why I assumed She stayed. For her own reasons, she liked having a body and being part of this place.

Maybe Coyote had commandeered Micah full time, like Lilith occasionally tried to do with me. If that were true, I had to find him. Because if he released Lilith, where was she now? Was she riding inside Micah now too? Holding on to that much deity for that long would burn him up, exhaust his human body.

Mátyás tapped the table with his finger. "Excuse me," he said to my stunned, open mouth as I tried to process the concept that the man I'd ridden home with from the mall might be a Native God, and not just in the damn-you're-hot-small-"g" kind of way. "But can we talk about *me* for a minute? I did just drive through a tornado to tell you why I think my father is in mortal danger."

"Uh," I said, trying to remind myself that really, what was a God, when I dated a vampire and had dealt with zombies and ghouls? "Yeah, sure."

Mátyás took a sip of his tea and I noticed his hands trembled a little as he set the cup back down. "Thing is, I don't . . . that is, I've never spoken of this with anyone outside of my family."

I momentarily forgot about Gods that walked around in blue jeans and muscle shirts that showed off tattoos. "Spoken of what?"

He pursed his lips, and his eyes slid away from mine and back to the rain. "I walk into other people's dreams."

He'd said it as though he just told me had some kind of dread disease, so I waited for more. It sounded like clairvoyance to me, and having "real" or prophetic dreams was pretty common among Witches, so I thought maybe for Mátyás it was the kind of thing he got only if he drank goat's blood or made some kind of virgin sacrifice under a dark moon.

When the moments stretched and he didn't offer anything, I prompted, "And?"

"And it's my curse, you wouldn't understand."

Clearly, I didn't. I took a sip of my tea while Mátyás brooded at my windowpane. "Well, so?" I asked. "Did you talk to Sebastian? What did you see?"

Mátyás snapped his attention back to me and blinked, like I'd given him angst whiplash. I guess he'd expected me to join his pity party and hardly knew what to do when I didn't. "Uh," he said. "Well, I saw Saint Sebastian with the arrows piercing him, except it was my father, of course. He was bleeding, but he didn't seem to know it. When I called to him, he didn't answer, which is unusual. Honestly, that's why I came to you at the store the other day. I wasn't as sure before, but I think he's under some kind of spell."

Mátyás's eyes watched mine to see if I'd understood him. He seemed to be implying that he and Sebastian spoke to each other in dreams sometimes. Again, it seemed like pretty standard Witchy stuff to me. Honestly, I was more surprised to hear that Sebastian tolerated even that much communication from his son. "Do you talk to him a lot?"

The table became suddenly very interesting. "No. Perhaps you've noticed we're a bit dysfunctional? But . . ." His gaze met mine. "He's always noted my . . . intrusion into his dreams, and we often exchange a glance if nothing else. This time, it was as if I wasn't there." He shrugged. "He totally blanked me."

"Wait a minute, are you saying the dream of the saint is Sebastian's dream?"

Mátyás nodded. "And that's the thing, it's the dream he

has when he's in the long sleep or, more rarely, in physical pain."

"You see *other* people's dreams?"

Mátyás squared his shoulders. His jaw flexed as though preparing for a blow. "Ah, so *now* you get it. With my mother's people, I'm called *budjo shon*—literally 'moon swindler,' dream thief."

"Can you see anyone's dreams?" I asked suddenly wondering what Mátyás would think of that one where I'm in a hotel that's really my old high school and I'm late for a test or a job interview, only I can't find the room because all the stairs are Escher-esque and backward.

Mátyás sighed, setting his cup down gingerly in the only spot on the table not covered in paper or books. "I don't know. I can't really control it."

"How do you know the dreams aren't yours? I mean, how did you figure out you weren't just dreaming your own dreams with other people in them?"

He studied his hands. "I'm always the stranger. The dreamers are always aware that I'm not supposed to be there."

"Holy crap, Mátyás, you're the boogeyman," I said. "You're the monster that I can't run away from. That guy whose always trying to break into my apartment."

"In the flesh," he said with a grim smile and a salute of his cup.

"Does it happen every night?"

"Nearly."

I tried to imagine what it must be like to never have a dream all your own and instead restlessly wander through other people's unconsciousnesses. It would be disconcerting, at best, I'd think, never understanding the symbolism, always wondering what was up with the old lady in the corner or whatever. How would you get any real rest? Especially if your presence changed the dream into a nightmare. "Wow," I said. "That totally sucks."

He laughed. "Yeah. It does."

I drank my tea down to the honeyed sediment. Barney strolled in past us on her way to the adjacent tower room. She hopped up onto the window ledge and jammed herself into the narrow open crack. Her flabby fur hung over the edge of the sill, but somehow she clung there. The rain had mostly quit, leaving behind the fresh smell of ozone.

"Did Sebastian's dream give you any clue as to where he was or who might have captured him?"

Mátyás started, seemingly lost in his own thoughts. "What makes you think that he's being held?"

"You said you figured he was under a spell. We both had visions of him stuck to a tree. What do *you* think that means?"

The overhead light in the kitchen bathed the room in an artificial yellow. Mátyás's finger traced the edges of the papers piled on the table. His eyes don't meet mine.

"Pretty strong magic to hold a vampire."

He sounded scared, but it was clear he was trying not to. I didn't have a good answer, though he looked up at me, wanting one. I shrugged. "I don't know. Your buddies in Rome figured out how to pin him against the wall."

Mátyás's gaze dropped.

"You told them," I surmised. "They had no clue how to deal with a real vampire until you told them."

Glancing at the darkened windows, Mátyás's jaw muscles worked. "At the time I wanted him dead." He laughed a little at his choice of words, then added, "I mean, all the way."

"And now?"

Gold-brown eyes finally connected to mine again. "He's my *father*." I thought for a moment that was all he was going to say on the subject, but then he let out a breath and said, "Blood is blood, isn't it?"

I nodded, staring into the bottom of my mug at the dregs.

Apparently gathering his thoughts, Mátyás watched the rain. With his shoulders slumped and hair falling into his eyes, he looked lanky and young sitting at my kitchen table. He wore a silvery-gray silk shirt that clung loosely to his narrow shoulders. Black tapered pants led in a straight line to polished, Italian leather shoes that marked him as a foreigner—no bright white, American brand-name tennis shoes for Mátyás.

At this moment, he looked surprisingly like Sebastian. Sebastian was more solid and much less pretentiously Eurotrash, but there was something of him in Mátyás's expression, his carriage and mannerisms. They were clearly related.

I thought about my own mother and father. I hadn't called them yet to tell them the big news. They didn't even really know about Sebastian, even though we'd been dating for more than a year now. My folks and I were benignly estranged, but that was no excuse. Sebastian and Mátyás actively hated each other and Sebastian had made the call. I sucked. "It is," I said, resolving to call them first thing in the morning.

I must have telegraphed what I was thinking because

Mátyás squinted at me like he suspected I'd dropped the ball. "What does your family think of you marrying a vampire?"

"They don't know," I admitted, since trying to deny it would only get Mátyás curious.

He was anyway. "Don't know? As in they don't know your lover is a bloodsucker or they don't know about Sebastian, period?"

I waved my hand embarrassingly indicating the latter. "That last one."

Mátyás laughed, and I felt stupid.

"In my defense, he only proposed a few days ago. I haven't really had time to call home." And Sebastian knew he was going to ask me, so he contacted Mátyás and started dumping his ghouls . . .

Sebastian had been totally setting his affairs in order. Maybe there was a clue to his disappearance there. It was still possible one of his ghouls held him captive out of jealousy. I'd only met two and there were several more that seemed on the active list in his little black book. But if those options didn't pan out, I had to start asking myself who else might be upset by my marriage to Sebastian.

Looking at Mátyás, I could think of one.

"So what ever happened with Teréza, your mommy dearest?" I asked.

Mátyás, who had been smirking, faltered.

His jaw flexed. I'd clearly hit a nerve. Last I'd heard, Teréza was stuck in some kind of postdeath suspended animation. She'd been dying of consumption when Sebastian tried to save her by turning her into a vampire. Unfortunately, Sebastian discovered that, being made by science and magic, his blood didn't work that way. He can't make other vampires. But Teréza didn't die all the way either. She was something in between—dead, not-dead. Sebastian and Mátyás fought about what should be done with her body. Sebastian wanted her buried somewhere peaceful; Mátyás kept unearthing her and searching for a "cure." In fact, Mátyás had been willing to sell out his father to have the Catholic pope exorcise the "demon" blood from Teréza.

If it had worked and she was up and wandering about, Teréza wouldn't be too pleased about our upcoming marriage. She was Romany, a gypsy. It wasn't out of the realm of possibility that she might lure Sebastian away in order to keep him to herself.

"Yeah," I said. "How'd that whole thing with the pope work out?"

Mátyás's eyes narrowed and his lips flattened into a thin, menacing line. "Leave my *daia* out of this," he said.

This was twice tonight that I'd heard him say something in his native language.

"I just think it's interesting that you showed up at the same time Sebastian disappeared. Did you bring Mummy with you?"

Mátyás stood up slowly with his hands at his sides, like we were facing off at the OK Corral. "I already told you why I came here. I came to talk him out of marrying you."

"You didn't answer the whole question. What about Teréza? Where is she?"

"Mother is . . . convalescing. Elsewhere."

Well now, didn't that sound just spooky? "Convalescing?"

"Yes." He watched me from where he stood in front of the kitchen table. He continued to hold himself wary, as if ready to fight. I could tell he wasn't going to give me any more details about Teréza. I wasn't sure I wanted to know anyway, as long as she wasn't anywhere near Sebastian. "Just tell me she's not in this country."

"She's in Italy."

Though the sky was still dark outside the windows, it had lightened to a less threatening overcast. Rain pattered softly against the glass. Though it was possible that Teréza was in on Sebastian's disappearance without Mátyás's knowledge, I doubted it. Could she even be capable, having been not-dead/dead for so long? Even if she made some kind of recovery from that state, certainly Mátyás watched over her like a mother hen. It surprised me that he left her so far behind. "You left your mom in Italy?"

His jaw twitched again, and he sighed. "She's with friends. People I trust."

Mátyás had friends?

"Look," he said. "I know what you're getting at, but my mother simply isn't capable right now. I don't know if she ever will be. She spent a long time . . . in the darkness. She's not well."

Trapped between life and death for over a hundred years could easily make a person insane. "But she's awake?"

His lips pressed even tighter. "Some days."

Did that mean that sometimes she was alive and others she was dead again? Things sounded very complicated, to say the least. I began to understand why Mátyás didn't want to talk about this.

I suddenly had a pang of sympathy for the guy. As if his life wasn't bizarre enough—he had a vampire for a father, whose blood had made him a perpetual teenager, cursed to

wander through other people's dreams—now his dead
mother was back from beyond, kind of.

I started to say something supportive when we heard the
impact. All the lights went out with a pop. The house shook
with noise. The door between the kitchen and the living
room banged open, bringing with it a cloud of plaster dust
and oak leaves.

"What was that?" Mátyás asked, pulling a keychain
flashlight out of his pocket and shined it into my face.

I blinked helplessly. It sounded like my living room had
just exploded.

A gigantic tree killed my couch. Its massive trunk
smooshed the frame into two separate halves, and stuffing
erupted from the tears in yellow gobs. The tree's branches
also took out three windows, half of a 150-year-old lath-
and-plaster wall, my end table, a lamp, and knocked over
my bookcase.

Cold, rainy breeze ruffled the pages of my *Mountain
Astrologer* and *In Touch* magazines, which now littered the
room like confetti. The room had a strangely pleasant
smell of tangy sap, like a forest. Oak leaves blanketed
the floor.

I couldn't believe it: a tree had crashed into my living
room.

Barney, having appeared from somewhere to survey the
damage with us, twined around my ankles. She paused, taking a sniff, and let out a delicate, wet sneeze.

Magic?

Mátyás apparently had a similar thought. "Shouldn't this

have happened a half hour ago, when there was actually some wind?"

Barney crouched low and took a step toward the branches, as though she was stalking the tree. She sneezed again, more forcefully. I scooped her up, afraid I'd lose her in all the debris. She sneezed on my shoulder and rubbed her nose in my armpit. The rain continued its gentle tippity-tap through the hole in the wall onto my hardwood floor.

Stepping over scattered books and a shattered statue of Kali, I touched a gnarled branch. I half expected the wood to evaporate like a dream, but it was solid, real.

There was a knock at the tree-blocked door. "Are you okay, fugitive girl?"

"Fugitive girl?" Mátyás asked, an amused smile twitching across his lips. "Another persona?"

"I'm okay," I shouted to Soul Patch, ignoring Mátyás. "A tree fell into the house."

"No shit, man. Where the hell'd it come from?"

Then I heard another voice from behind the door. "Tell her about the light."

"What light?" I asked.

"Before the tree hit," Soul Patch said. "We saw a buzzing purple light."

"Lavender," came the other voice.

"Mauve."

"Whatever, it was spooky," Soul Patch said. "How'd this tree come down, anyway? I thought the storm was over."

"It *was* over," Mátyás said as he gave me a hard this-isn't-what-it-seems glare. "This was deliberate. You're under attack."

"What? I didn't catch that," asked Soul Patch. "Anyway, I just wanted to make sure you were okay and stuff. Oh, hey, and I called the landlord."

"Thanks," I shouted back.

I heard a muttered "No problem" and the clomp of heavy shoes on the stairs.

Mátyás had his cell phone to his ear. "I'm calling the utility people about the electricity. You've got a breaker box in the basement." I nodded. "I'll head down there and make sure everything is off. I'll shut off the gas too just to be safe."

I nodded, happy to let Mátyás deal with that sort of stuff. I shut Barney up in the bedroom and came back to try to salvage what I could from the living room. By the time he came back, I'd cleared up most of the books and was sitting on the floor trying to decide if the statue could be rescued with some glue or if it was beyond repair.

Mátyás knelt beside me and handed me a silk handkerchief. I hadn't realized I'd been crying, but his kind gesture crumbled the remains of my resolve. I sobbed and leaned heavily into an awkwardly offered hug.

When I finally pulled away, we didn't talk about it. Mátyás silently helped me shift the important things into my bedroom and out of the way, and he waited patiently while I packed Barney into a kitty carrier and put together a bag for myself. How ironic that I'd been so reluctant to move in with Sebastian. Now his was the only place I really had.

"We can come back for the rest tomorrow," I said.

"Of course," Mátyás said softly, taking my duffle bag from my hands. "Let's get you home."

If he didn't stop being so understanding, I was going to start bawling again.

At Sebastian's, Barney refused to come out of the carrier. She crouched flat with her ears pressed against her head and kept up a constant growl that occasionally morphed into a pitiful-sounding moan.

Mátyás watched my attempts to cajole and comfort her from where he lounged on the leather couch with his stocking feet propped up on the glass coffee table. He tipped a martini glass in the direction of the carrier and said, "Sometimes I quite agree, my dear."

I placed a bowl of tuna several steps out into the open of Sebastian's living room. "You know you want it," I told her teasingly.

She hissed at me.

The house ghost, Benjamin, who apparently felt similarly about the feline intrusion, rattled the windows.

"You guys are just going to have to learn to get along," I said to them both. Giving up with a sigh, I took Sebastian's favorite chair near the fireplace.

I eyed Mátyás's martini with a touch of envy. He'd offered me one, several actually, but the thought of going to work with a hangover again didn't appeal to me. Still, the sharp, evergreen smell of juniper reminded me of Christmas trees, which in turn made me think about the oak that tore through my apartment . . . and suddenly, I wanted to drink until I couldn't see straight. Which was something, apparently, Mátyás already had on the agenda from the peaceful, vacuous look in his half-lidded eyes.

"Someone magical wants you dead," he said distinctly, twirling the stem of the glass between his fingers. "Given that you said he stole Lilith, I'd guess it was that coyote friend of yours."

"He hardly qualifies as a friend," I snapped. "Anyway, Micah got what he came for."

It was hard to believe that Micah had set me up to steal Lilith. He'd offered to take her from me, but I didn't realize he wanted her so badly that he would just take her. I hugged myself around the waist, feeling small and hollow. Mentally, I kept reaching down within to feel her presence. Every time it was a surprise to find nothing but emptiness.

"He's the only deity after you right now, though, right?" Mátyás asked, lifting an eyebrow and his martini glass in my direction. "Because it takes damn strong juju to uproot a tree and hurl it with that kind of force," Mátyás continued. "If he's not a God, then your enemy is one serious sorcerer."

We hadn't spoken about the whole killer-tree incident in the car. Mátyás had let me chatter away to Barney about how everything would be okay, and how the landlord was sure to fix things up soon, we'd move back in, it would all be normal, and did I mention we'd be okay? Even though it was clear to me that it could take months to finish the repairs on the apartment, I kept inanely repeating myself because I still couldn't deal with the fact that the place I lived in was ruined, gone.

"Well, they're not *that* good," I pointed out. "They missed."

Mátyás grunted an amused assent. "Although you're assuming what they want is for you to be dead. You have to admit they've scored a lot of points." Setting his drink down, he held up fingers as he counted, "One, they kidnapped Papa. Two, stole your Goddess. Three, destroyed your house. And in your column, you're 'still alive.'" He held up his other fist to indicate zero. "I'm not sure you're winning this one, Garnet. Especially given the state of your neck."

"Bleah," was all I could think of for a reply. Leaning my head against the back of the chair, I accidentally pressed into the welts on my neck. I winced.

Absently, I magically reached for Lilith again. When I noticed myself doing it, I stopped. She wasn't there. No matter how often I looked for her, I wasn't going to find her. She was gone. Possibly for good.

"You're shrinking," Mátyás noted.

"What?"

He tipped his martini glass at me. "Can you actually crawl inside yourself, I wonder?"

I'd pulled my feet up onto the couch in a fetal position. My arms held my knees so tightly they ached. Even with Mátyás smirking at my uptight body language, it was difficult to unwind. Without Lilith, I felt so exposed and vulnerable. "Sorry," I murmured as I shifted a bit, trying to act as though I was a lot more comfortable than I felt.

Mátyás pulled at his lip. "I should say something useful here, like 'there, there,' shouldn't I? I mean, your apartment, it'll get fixed. I know it's upsetting. But it really will be all right." He swallowed a mouthful of martini, draining the glass to the dregs. Mátyás looked at the empty glass for a moment before setting it on the glass-topped coffee table between us. "Are you sure you don't want one? Being numb is really the only coping skill I have a lot of practice with."

My lips quirked into a feeble smile. It was sweet of Mátyás to try to comfort me, but it only served to make me miss Sebastian even more. He'd have some plan of action right now, some idea to try to figure out who wrecked my place or how to get Lilith back. Best, he'd offer to do it all himself while tucking me into bed.

"No, I'm okay," I lied.

"Suit yourself," he said, getting up to refresh his glass.

Once again I noticed myself poking around mystically for Lilith. I started to feel a bit pathetic, like a junkie who unconsciously rubs at the crook of their elbows when they're jonesing. I had to pull myself together. Sebastian needed *me* this time.

My fingers absently stroked the cool leather of the chair. Glass clinked in the kitchen as Mátyás refilled his drink. The central air conditioner hummed.

If Sebastian and I were under attack, I needed some kind of protection. I couldn't walk around so exposed. What I needed was another Goddess, someone whose expertise was protection.

Benjamin, or maybe the wind, screeched around the gables. Cool breeze ruffled my hair, despite the closed windows. Lightning lit the sky.

I closed my eyes. When I'd called Lilith before it had been completely unconscious, a gut reaction born out of desperation and fear. There had been no complicated spell weaving or bells or whistles, just me crying out for help with every fiber of my being.

I needed help now too. There might not be anyone with

a pistol pointed to my head, but I'd lost my house, my lover, and someone very powerfully magical was gunning for me.

Instead of trying to suppress my fears, I let them grow. I allowed myself an unadulterated moment of sheer panic. My muscles began to tremble, but I pushed myself even deeper. I imagined the worst. Sebastian dead. The Witch with the vendetta ready to kill me . . . or Barney. Then, I opened my astral body and my mouth and screamed, "Help!"

Thunder clapped. Dishes fell to the floor as Mátyás swore and shouted my name. Then, without warning, my skin felt afire. Pain seared along my nerves, concentrated in a knot in my abdomen. With a cry, I doubled over.

8.

Saturn

❧

KEYWORDS:

Limitations, Sorrows, and Delays

In my peripheral vision, I saw Mátyás leap to his feet. He was shouting something, but I couldn't hear him over the sound of my own agony. Air swirled through the room, picking up newspapers until they danced around me like my own personal tornado.

Barney yowled and streaked back into her kitty carrier.

Newspapers crinkled in the air. They bent and shifted, circling me, until the form of a woman's face pressed through them in relief. My stomach clenched again, and I doubled over, but not before recognizing wide screech-owl eyes.

Lilith had come back.

The house shook on its foundations. Lights flickered, and then went out.

No doubt thinking that I was under attack, Mátyás tried to step into the circle of spinning air—only to be tossed out like a rag doll. The force of the gale sent him crashing into the stair railing. I heard something break, and I hoped it was a rail spindle and not one of his ribs. He lay where he fell, moaning.

Out of the magical corner of my eye, I sensed Benjamin entering the room, called by my cry. He looked ready to try to come to my defense as well, but I didn't need help. Though the expression in the newspaper face mask hadn't changed, somehow I understood that Lilith was still being held to Micah in some way. She needed a magical boost.

I faltered. It had been a long time since I'd done magic like this solo. Did I have the strength? I'd called Lilith here, but a capital-letter God held the other end of the leash.

Static electricity crackled along my limbs as I lifted my arms into the Goddess position. Blue and silver sparks flashed out from my body like a mini electrical storm. I took a deep, welcoming breath, turned my palms upward and said, "Come to me, so mote it be."

The wind whirled faster, but the image of Lilith's face began to break up. Holes appeared in her image as sheets tore off. Her mouth opened up into a wordless scream, as she continued to collapse in upon herself.

I was losing her.

I didn't know what to do. Lilith had been the source of my magic for so long. My hands grasped uselessly at the air. I swore the hollow of her eyes looked disappointed as the swirling air ceased. A bang rattled the air, like the rush of thunder, and then quiet. Newspapers drifted slowly to the ground, landing in a perfect circle around my feet.

The lights snapped back on.

Inside her carrier, Barney hacked up what sounded like a

gigantic hairball. Then she let out a dainty sneeze and a quiet, mournful meow.

Mátyás groaned, pulling himself upright. He held on to the railing, as though it were a crutch. "What the hell was that?"

"Me," I said, trying to sound plucky, "being a loser."

"Ah. Right." Mátyás's jaw twitched, as he ran a hand through his hair. The same nervous gesture Sebastian had.

My plucky façade cracked. I crumpled onto the couch and buried my face in my hands. Hot tears constricted my throat. "Oh God, I don't have the strength to get Lilith back. I'm never going to see Sebastian again."

"I've been thinking about that," Mátyás said. He came and sat beside me. Despite my loud sniffles, he plopped down as though we were settling in to watch the game. His feet went up on the coffee table and his arm flopped loosely on the back of the couch. "I think I might have a solution, though I've never tried it before and . . ." He coughed into his fist and looked away. Mumbling, he added, "I might need your help."

I shook my head and wiped broadly at the tears that streaked down my face. "Didn't you just witness this disaster? I'm not going to be much help to anyone."

When I'm upset, I clean. Pulling myself upright, I started picking up the papers and tucking them under my arm. Consciously, I started in the east and worked my way around counterclockwise, as though opening a circle. I reveled in the simple physical actions—bend, pick up the smooth, slick newsprint, straighten, tuck, repeat.

"Don't you even want to hear my brilliant plan?" Mátyás said, lifting his legs as I grabbed for a sheet that had fallen between the couch and the table.

"Sure," I said. "Whatever."

The truth was I was despondent. I couldn't stop the tears leaking out of my eyes and I felt exhausted. Beaten.

"I take the fight to them. Use my powers for good," Mátyás said.

I'd gotten a huge wad of newspaper tucked under my arm. I looked around for somewhere to deposit it. Seeing none, I clutched the crumbled ball to my abdomen. "What are you talking about?"

"If you can figure out who might have Papa, I'll invade their dreams. The unconscious is a funny thing. The guilty often dream of their crimes. Maybe with a little magical nudge from you, I can get them to show me where—or how—they're holding Papa."

It wasn't a bad idea, actually. I sat down again, this time on the couch kitty-corner from Mátyás. I tucked the newspaper between me and the arm of the couch. "The problem is I don't have a clue who it might be."

"You must have a list of suspects. Let's do a little detective work." Tapping his feet, he twiddled his thumbs. He looked at the bookcase crammed with books. "What we need is a whiteboard."

"What?"

"You know, like they always have in those crime shows."

I smiled. "We can probably just think this through."

He tapped his index fingers together thoughtfully. I got the feeling Mátyás enjoyed the idea of being a detective. His socks made a soft padding sound on the rug.

"What we need is some kind of motive that ties all the events together. Who do you know that has a reason to be rid of Sebastian and hates you enough to want to kill you or at least damage everything you hold dear?"

Chewing my lip, I considered. "Well, Xylia and I got into kind of a fight about Lilith. She implied that it was kind of unfair that I had a Goddess because it automatically meant I'd probably be chosen to be the High Priestess of the coven. She seemed kind of down on vampires too, for that matter."

Mátyás brightened. "A lead. Okay, anyone else?"

I heard the sound of wet munching coming from behind the couch. Barney, apparently, decided to come back out to sample the tuna. My fingers touched the welts on my throat gingerly. "Well, Marge was in the store just before the wind chime jumped me and was looking for books on Lilith."

"So, what does that make? Xylia, Marge, and Micah— three suspects?"

"Uh, at least," I said. Frowning, considered other options. Who else had seemed into Sebastian? Well, there had been Blythe. Suddenly, I tried to remember if I'd seen Blythe at the most recent gathering. Micah's appearance had so completely distracted me I couldn't remember if she was there or not. She'd said she was just a comparative religion major; but she had to have some magical talent in order to see the invitation. "There is another covener. Her name's Blythe. She seemed pretty fascinated by Sebastian."

Okay, so that was an understatement, but I could hear Mátyás making another one of his chew-toy references again, speaking of which: "Oh," I added. "And probably every one of Sebastian's ghouls hate me. I guess he was breaking up with them."

"Jesus, Garnet. Is there anyone who *doesn't* want you dead?"

I let out a little, sad laugh. But thinking of the ghouls again reminded me that I had the LiveJournal address from Traci. I should check in and see if she got me an account. "Would you take me back to the store?"

He glanced at my neck. "Do you want to do some kind of magical detective work? To see who tried to do you in?"

I hadn't really considered that, though I could look for residue trails. "Yeah, plus I need to check my e-mail."

He laughed. "Interesting priorities you've got."

"It has to do with Sebastian's ghouls, er, suppliers. They have an online community."

Mátyás shook his head. "Of course they do."

I was surprised when we got into Mátyás's Jag that the dashboard clock read 6:30 p.m. I made him give me the keys, since he'd been drinking. The sun hadn't even begun to set yet. The thick cloud cover made it feel much later in the evening. When my stomach growled, I realized I'd skipped dinner.

The car was cool inside, almost chilly, and the air that came in from the open window brushed warm and wet against my skin. The moisture brought out the scent of alfalfa and clover.

I put the car in drive. It purred smoothly. Oh, I could get used to this kind of ride.

He sat grumpily in the passenger seat. "I'm fine, you know."

"Better safe than sorry," I said, noting how smoothly I made the turn out of the drive.

"Fine. After you check in on the ghouls, we should make some house calls to your coveners. Did you bring the black book?"

I did, but I wasn't planning on using it. I put my hand up. "No, I've been doing far too much of that spur-of-the-moment stuff." The direct approach hadn't been working very well for me lately. After all, it had led to a very awkward misunderstanding with Walter, the accountant, and a strange, convoluted confrontation with Alison and Traci. "We need to think this out in advance. Maybe, you know, try a little subterfuge."

I think Mátyás would have protested, except that my stomach chose that moment to rumble even louder than it had before. Mátyás arched a thin eyebrow at the sound and tried to hold back a smile. "Maybe we should think things out over dinner."

I grinned in return. "I like that plan."

On the way, I drove past my apartment. The damage was even more impressive from the outside. The tree's roots buckled a portion of the sidewalk and upturned most of the boulevard. Broken branches and leaves littered the undamaged section of the roof, the yard, nearby cars—everything. The place where the tree and the house met was a huge, gaping, dark pit.

"The downstairs is completely untouched," Mátyás noted once I'd accelerated back to normal speed. "Not even a window cracked."

I craned my neck to confirm his observation. He was right. It was completely whole. Though they'd be without utilities, the downstairs neighbors could sleep under their own roof tonight, if they wanted. "Thank Goddess," I said. "I'd hate to think that anyone else got hurt because someone was after me."

"So," Mátyás said, as I smoothly steered the Jag around a corner, "we should look for a considerate enemy, someone not willing to cause collateral damage."

In the darkness of the car, I couldn't read Mátyás's expression. "Are you serious?"

"I'm trying to work out a profile of your attacker," he said. "Maybe he or she is someone who's been in the army and is sensitive to the idea of civilian casualties."

I glanced at him out of the corner of my eye. "You watch entirely too much TV," I decided.

He grimaced at the road. "It's not TV. I dated a detective from Scotland Yard. She got me interested in crime solving. I nearly got a degree in criminal justice."

"Nearly?"

He shrugged his shoulders. "Didn't work out. I'm not really the bookish sort, am I?"

Mátyás was certainly no mental slouch, and he seemed to have a lot of, well, determination when he wanted to use it. I'd been on the receiving end of that, hadn't I?

The bluish dash lights reflected the sharp edges of Mátyás's imperial features, and I recalled it wasn't that long ago that he'd actively tried to betray Sebastian and me. Now here we were going out to dinner. Hell, we'd spoken civilly to each other for over an hour. Desperation made strange bedfellows, as it were.

The sun shone fuzzily behind heavy clouds. Sebastian and I had driven this route so many times. "Goddess," I said, rubbing my arm despite the warmth. "I hope he's okay."

"Me too," breathed Mátyás.

William looked surprised to see me walk into the store. His eyes widened even further when he noticed Mátyás trailing behind me. William's eyes darted between us, and finally he said, "Uh, hey, Garnet. Mátyás."

"I just need to check my e-mail quickly," I said.

"Uh, yeah, okay," William muttered, his eyes still glued on Mátyás, then he shook his head. "Wait, Garnet, did you just say, 'check my e-mail'? Do you even know how to do that?"

Have I mentioned that I'm a complete techno-dork? "Hey," I said with faux protest. "I'm not that bad."

"Oh, yes, you are," William chided.

Both men trailed me back into the office. Slow Bob, who had his nose pressed into a book in the primal myths aisle, nodded as we paraded past. The office was barely big enough for three. I sat at the swivel chair, and William and Mátyás crowded shoulder to shoulder behind me.

As I went through the motions of logging on, William said, "So, Mátyás, it's been a while."

"Yes," came the curt, barely civil response.

"How's things?" William tried again.

"Fine."

Leaning in, William whispered in my ear, "Is he on our side now?"

I glanced at Mátyás, who raised an eyebrow as though he was interested in my answer as well. "Yeah," I said. "He is."

Mátyás gave William a gloating told-ya-so smirk.

Traci had sent me the invitation as promised. I activated it and then got sent to the world's longest questionnaire about my hobbies and best friends. I filled out the bare minimum, anxious to get to the ghoul's community.

"You're joining LiveJournal?" William asked when he glanced at the screen. "Are we going to have a store blog? Sweet!"

I heard Mátyás explain everything about the ghouls as I scanned the most recent entries on the bulletin board. I tried not to be disturbed by the various icons people used—necks, fetish wear, *South Park* characters, and unicorns—and read the posts. There were birthday congratulations and other stories of everyday life. Then, I noticed, several screens down a screed left by someone called "luvslave," with an icon depicting a close-up on an impossibly high leather heel with chains looped around the ankle, who complained bitterly about how Sebastian had told her (or him?) the news of the upcoming wedding. It had garnered a lot of responses. I clicked on the "leave a comment" link. A few counseled understanding, but most responses seemed equally shocked and upset. The words used to describe me would make a sailor blush.

"Wow, are they referring to you?" William asked.

I nodded. Well, if I'd hoped this would turn up a single villainess, I couldn't have been more wrong. It seemed that violent hatred of me was pretty universal in the local ghoul community.

My fingers hovered over the keys. The empty box for comments begged me to tell these women what for. I was just formulating a zinger of a first sentence, when Mátyás cleared his throat. "If we're going to get dinner in, we should go."

"Right," I said, starting to close up the window. Then, seeing William still trying to read some of the posts, I said, "Can I ask a favor, William?"

"Anything," he said.

"Would you mind taking a moment and reading more on this blog? It's possible one of the people who post here might be party to Sebastian's disappearance."

William glanced at the clock. "Yeah, sure, I can look through it for a while. I'm leaving early tonight, remember?"

"Oh, right," I said, though I had absolutely no recollection of giving William part of the night off. "Whatever you could do would be a big help."

"Of course," he said, sliding into the seat as I got out. He started clicking through messages like a pro. "What am I looking for, exactly?"

"Someone who's overly attached to Sebastian."

"You mean, like 'luvslave'?"

"Well, yeah, see if you can find out more about her."

"Will do, boss," he said with a smile.

"Thanks, William," I said sincerely, even though his grin was pure I-can't-believe-I'm-getting-paid-to-surf-the-Internet. "I'm really worried about Sebastian."

Mátyás tapped my shoulder and whispered in my ear, "Which is why we should go make plans for his rescue."

They were getting ready to close when we walked into Noodles & Company on State Street. The guy mopping the floor gave us an annoyed glance when the chimes above the door jingled. I knew that expression, having cast it upon plenty of customers myself. It was the oh-man-I-was-hoping-to-get-home-early-for-once look. Still, like a trouper, he plastered on a more pleasant demeanor and dutifully took our orders.

"Since you have such a long list of suspects, what we need is something that would smoke out our villain," Mátyás said as we took a seat near the window. I set the placard with the number six in the center of the table.

"But what?" I asked, trying to consider who might want something from Sebastian or me. Neon and fluorescent lights gave the pedestrian mall its own kind of eerie brightness in the fog. The rain had energized a swarm of gnats that darted frantically around an overhanging light. An enterprising spider had built a gigantic web under the awning.

Otherwise, the street was quiet. With many of the college students away for the summer, the foot traffic consisted of tourists and natives, and there weren't many tonight. Only one couple strolling slowly, hand in hand, window-shopping. I looked away. "We've got to find him," I said. Fear tightened my stomach. "What if we're too late? What if Sebastian is dead?"

Mátyás must have heard the tremor in my voice because his eyes met mine and held them steadily. Reaching across the table, Mátyás put a hand on my shoulder. It was surprisingly confident and comforting. "You and Sebastian are close. You'd know if he was gone."

I closed my eyes and felt for the silver cord that connected Sebastian and me. It was weak, but it was still there. I hadn't been able to follow it to its source the last time I traveled on the astral plane, having been intercepted by Micah, but I took comfort in the fact that the thread seemed taut. The other end was anchored in Sebastian, I was certain. He was alive. If he wasn't, the cord would be limp or gone completely.

"See," Mátyás said, removing his hand. "You can feel it."

Opening my eyes, I said, "But the strand between us is so thin."

"That's why we're going to come up with some kind of Witchy sting."

"A sting?" I repeated, as the noodles arrived. I'd gone for simple buttered noodles with freshly grated Parmesan cheese sprinkled on top. Mátyás had ordered something exotic and curried, which he deftly ate with chopsticks.

"Yeah," he said around a mouthful of green pepper. "But we'd have to be sure of what they want in order for the trap to work."

I looked up at the spider's web I'd noticed earlier. It bobbed and swayed with the multiple impacts of the gnats getting snared. "Something bright and shiny," I said.

Mátyás's eyes followed mine to where the bugs encircled the light. "Yes, we need bait."

I frowned at my own bland dish and wished I'd ordered what Mátyás had. I poked at the macaroni with my fork, watching the sheen of buttery sludge ooze between the noodles.

"I couldn't get Lilith back, Mátyás. I don't have anything anyone wants anymore," I said. It seemed true. If the ghouls wanted Sebastian, well, someone else had him. Micah stole the Goddess. Hell, even my apartment was wrecked. I couldn't even offer real estate as bait.

"Don't be so sure," Mátyás said. "I've been thinking about the order of events and something doesn't add up.

First, Papa disappears. He's clearly not the main target because if that's all the attacker wanted, he'd be done—no need to go after you. So, whoever put a spell on Sebastian wanted him out of the way to get to you. Which makes sense if Micah is your bad guy and he's after Lilith. You said there was someone at the store just before the wind chime fell on you, someone interested in Lilith?"

"Yeah, Marge," I supplied, taking a tentative swallow of my pasta. The cheese was actually very tart and the congealed butter nicely spiced.

"So one possibility is that she's connected somehow to Micah."

I had seen them talking at the meeting at William's place. "Yeah, I could see that."

"All good so far: Sebastian is taken out of the picture somehow by Marge and Micah, which is also plausible because Micah being Coyote might have the strength of a God at his disposal."

"Oh Goddess," I interrupted, the noodles sticking in my throat. "Just before the wind chimes fell, I'd asked Marge if she'd seen Sebastian. I thought she looked panicked at the time, but I chalked it up to her poor social skills. What if she dropped the chimes on me because she thought I was on to her?"

"Maybe she was trying to scare you off the scent," Mátyás said. "See, this all makes a kind of logical sense. Then Micah lures you into letting the Goddess out, and whammo, they've absconded with their treasure."

"Yeah, this is good," I agreed, remembering how Micah promised to help me find Sebastian and how the silver cord had frayed in the astral plane when I'd seen him there.

"This makes sense. A lot of sense. You should have stuck with the whole detective thing, Mátyás. Seriously."

His lips quirked slightly and I could tell he was pleased by my compliment. His only acknowledgment, however, was a slight tip of his head. "Here's the wrinkle: the tree. A magical attack so powerful it smells like the handiwork of your coyote, but he has no reason for it at that point. Lilith was in his hands. Why would he toss a tree at you?"

"To finish me off?"

"Because you're such a threat now that you're back to being a plain, old Witch?"

Ouch. That hurt, especially since it was true. "Yeah, well, I don't know then. Why else do it?"

"See, that's the thing. I'm not convinced it was Micah or Marge. I mean, okay, maybe they're tidy little Goddess-stealing serial killers and they want to leave no trace of their mystical crime behind. But if that was the case, why aren't you dead? You pointed out that they missed. Don't you think a God would have better aim?"

There were plenty of trees in the backyard. If the attacker was a God and omniscient, then he'd have known I wasn't sitting on the couch. Maybe Coyote's power didn't work that way; I had to focus Lilith's energy and she was only as effective a force as I made her. It was possible that Micah missed because he didn't channel Coyote's energy properly. "Not necessarily," I said. "What are you trying to say, there's someone else after me?"

"Your list was a mile long, darling."

I winced. Hearing Sebastian's pet name for me on Mátyás's lips surprised me. "Don't call me that." Then realizing how harsh I must have sounded, I added a soft "please."

"Right. Sorry," he said. "The point is, you might make perfect bait. Maybe someone in the coven wants you dead, someone jealous or power hungry like that Xylia woman you mentioned. Maybe at your next coven meeting . . ."

My fork clattered into the porcelain bowl. "Oh crap! That would be tonight! At my place! That's why William was taking an early night!" I smacked my forehead. Suddenly, I imagined the scene: people showing up with crab dip and corn chips and finding a tree slammed into my apartment. They'd all be milling around, wondering if I was okay. William would try my cell phone, only it wasn't working. He'd try Sebastian's house and get no answer. I found myself standing up. "Great Goddess, everyone probably thinks I'm dead."

"Everyone except the person who tried to kill you," Mátyás pointed out from where he sat. He took a long drink from his water. I could hear the ice knock against his teeth.

"We should go," I said. Not only was I anxious to put any rumors of my untimely demise to rest, but I was also getting tired of the mop guy giving us more and more openly hostile looks. I glanced around for a clock on the wall. We had about six minutes until people would be arriving. "It's not too late to catch them if we hurry," I said.

Mátyás stood up and gathered his things together on a tray. He pulled his phone from his pocket. "Call William," he said. "You should at least warn him."

While Mátyás bused our dishes, I dialed William's cell phone.

"Hello?" William sounded very skeptical when he answered, probably baffled by seeing an unfamiliar number on his caller ID.

"It's Garnet," I said. "Have you gotten to my place yet?"

"Uh, yeah. I don't know if you know this, but there's a great big tree in the middle of your house."

"I know. Listen, we need to have everyone meet at Sebastian's tonight. Do you think you can direct everyone?"

I heard some fumbling. "Yeah, what's his address?" I told him and he said, "I'll just pull it up on my Black-Berry. Doesn't look too bad. Let me read you what MapQuest says."

I listened. As someone who is usually a passenger, I had no real idea if the route was the most direct, but it certainly sounded familiar enough.

Mátyás came up and mouthed, "Wards."

"I'll be waiting outside the place," I added. Or maybe I could do a little counter-magic just for one night.

"Are you okay?" William asked after we'd confirmed everything. "The house looks totaled. Maybe we should postpone this."

"No," I said. "I think the storm damage had something to do with Sebastian's disappearance—"

"You're telling him?" Mátyás cut in.

"It's William," I protested. "Anyway, I really want to do the spell of finding tonight."

"Okay," William said. "Oh, hey, people are arriving. I've got to go."

Mátyás and I walked out into a cocoon of a yellowish haze of streetlights. The inky blackness of the sky above pressed close. Our heels echoed on the empty sidewalks. The air carried the fragrance of cooling asphalt.

"You know," Mátyás said, as we reached his car. Leaning

on crossed arms, he stared at me over the roof. The paint reflected a deeper metallic under the streetlamps. "A sting only really works if you have the element of surprise."

"William isn't trying to kill me," I said, my hand on the door handle he hadn't unlocked yet. "Besides, he was going to cancel the meeting. I needed to give him a sense of urgency."

"Which he could be sharing with the whole coven right now. You didn't ask him not to tell anyone."

Oh. "I'm not used to being a spy."

"Clearly," he said dryly, opening his car door. I heard my lock click open.

I slipped into the passenger seat, feeling a little stupid. "Maybe William won't say anything."

Sarcasm oozed from Mátyás's tone. "Because William is the soul of discretion."

I looked up at the crescent moon barely visible through the cloud cover and prayed, for once, he was.

"We'd better have a plan," Mátyás said as we pulled into Sebastian's driveway. He put the car in park and turned to face me, an arm resting casually on the steering wheel. "Can you act arrogant?"

This was one of those questions I dreaded answering. "Uh, I don't know, why?"

"You need to irritate the attacker into making a move," he said. "That's the whole bait thing."

"Don't they already hate me just the way I am?"

"Who doesn't?" He smiled softly, and for the first time I actually thought he might be teasing and not trying to insult me. "I was thinking that maybe you should try to take control of the coven or something. If the issue is really jealousy, maybe one of them will out themselves."

Oh boy. Well, it was a better plan than no plan at all.

I stood out at the end of the long, gravel road that served as Sebastian's driveway and swatted mosquitoes. They seemed particularly attracted to my ankles and the wounds on my neck. Slapping another one, I scanned the county road for headlights. Crickets chirped softly in the tall grass that grew wild in the drainage ditch.

A lone highway light illuminated the county cemetery next door. Most of the few, scattered markers were at least a hundred years old, knee-high obelisks that listed to the side or were overgrown with plants once left as offerings. Names had worn off the soft stone now riddled with lichen and moss.

Except one. At the edge closest to Sebastian's farm was a brand-new marble headstone bearing the name Daniel Parrish, no dates. Parrish had "died" in order to help clear my name with the FBI. Even though I woke up to discover his body gone, I had insisted on buying a gravestone. For me, it was a place to grieve, and more important, I wanted some kind of acknowledgment of Daniel's bravery, his sacrifice.

Honestly? I was pretty sure he'd managed to escape the grave. It would be weird to think of him buried alive there, even if he was in torpor.

The sound of a car's tires woke me from my reverie. I waved at what looked like William's Prius. Once the car was close enough, William powered down the window. Xylia's friend Robert sat in the passenger seat, and Marge and Max huddled together in the back. Max waved at me.

I smiled and waved back.

"Are you sure this is right?" William asked.

Sebastian's wards made his house looked like an abandoned farm, a common enough sight in the back roads of Wisconsin that most people drove past it, even in broad daylight. At night the illusion was especially strong.

"Trust me," I said. "Mátyás will let you in."

William looked doubtful but he pulled into the drive. I continued my vigil.

Wind rustled the stiff stalks of corn that surrounded Sebastian's farmhouse. Though it was June, the phrase "knee-high by the Fourth of July" came into my head. In straight rows, the broad leaves reflected moonlight like sword points.

Across the road, I could see the stalks shiver and shake as something passed through them. The rows parted for silver fur and a black-tipped tail. Four legs took the coyote quickly into the steep dip of the drainage ditch filled with tall fronds of white sweet clover.

Up onto the road came a man: Micah.

"What are you doing here?" I sounded angry, but my stomach tightened with fear. Had he come to finish me off, after all? Instinctively I reached for Lilith for protection. I felt her, though not where I expected to find her. Her presence stretched between Micah and I, like a rubber band.

She wasn't mine, but neither, I could tell, was she entirely his.

His eyes glittered obsidian-hard under the streetlight. In black-and-white relief, he looked otherworldly.

And angry.

Maybe Mátyás was wrong about the second party that wanted me dead. Maybe, somehow, I still had a connection with Lilith, one Micah couldn't break. Perhaps in order to get complete control over her, Micah needed me dead.

"Uh, William?" I called behind me, taking a step back. "Mátyás?"

Micah started slowly across the street.

Just when I was considering making a run for it, a rusty Honda slowed its approach, coming between Micah and me. Xylia stopped at the top of the driveway. Over the roar of a shoddy muffler, Xylia said, "This must be the right place." She smiled. Then seeing Micah on the other side of the road, she turned and said, "Hiya, Micah. Want a ride?"

He flashed a dark grin as he got in.

Well, that seemed ominous. Talk about a wolf in the fold. But Micah wouldn't be crazy enough to try to kill me in front of the entire coven, would he?

As I waited for the stragglers, I considered my options. I could stay with the plan as Mátyás outlined it, although given how pissed off Micah already seemed I didn't think I needed to add the whole "act annoying" shtick. Or I could run away and hide. Frankly, I was kind of liking door number two. But really, where would I go that a God wouldn't be able to find me? And, if Mátyás was right about Marge and Micah, then one or the other was responsible for Sebastian's disappearance.

After directing the last of the group, I walked up the long drive now lined with cars. I felt a little like I was headed to the gallows, and it was hard to believe that I'd talked Sebastian into starting a coven because I thought it would ground me, help me settle in. I should have known things would end badly; we'd started off on such a wrong foot with Sebastian's flirtation with Blythe.

Hey, Blythe never showed!

Had I been wrong about Sebastian? Was it possible that the day after he proposed to me, he ran off with another woman? I shook my head. Not Sebastian. There had to be another explanation. Quickening my pace, I was determined to find out.

I walked into chaos. Books were flying everywhere. Windows were slamming open and closed. Lights switched on and off, like a strobe.

I pushed past a clump of people who stood near the doorway covering their heads with their hands and screaming.

William and Xylia sat in the middle of the floor in the lotus position, chanting something. Griffin stood off to one side shouting, "What the fuck?" over and over. Mátyás, who sat on the steps with his head in his hands, looked up with a long-suffering sigh.

Micah, meanwhile, lounged on the couch, calmly eating from a bag of potato chips, watching the whole thing like it was the best show he'd ever seen.

Benjamin. He was in full attack mode. I'd totally forgotten to warn him that there'd be company.

"Garnet," Max said, tugging my sleeve. "What is it? What's going on?"

I raised my hand. "I'll take care of it. Everyone just needs to calm down." Not that anyone heard me, though Max did start letting people know that I had some kind of solution. I only hoped I did.

Closing my eyes, I exhaled a slow, steadying breath. I rose into the astral plane. Having forgotten to sit down first, I felt my body fall face-first onto the Persian rug. The pain of smacking into the floor nearly jolted me back into my body, but I held on.

"Smooth move," said a voice that was more growl than words. I opened my magical eyes and saw Coyote. Superimposed over Micah was the image of a coyote-headed man wearing a traditional beaded buckskin robe. Black eyes glinted with mirth and mischief. His long snout lifted in a slight sneer, showing sharp yellowed canines. The tufts of fur at his ears were gray and coarse. He looked old, but very much like a God. I shrank back a bit in awe. I might even have fallen down on my knees in supplication had not Benjamin chosen that moment to toss another book.

Benjamin picked up another pile of books, shouting, "Get out. Get out of my house."

Several coveners rushed over to where I'd seemingly passed out on the floor. Marge shook my shoulders gently and called my name. I ignored them. I had a poltergeist to deal with.

"Benjamin," I said quietly, but firmly.

Book raised over his head, he stopped. Bringing it down slowly, he stared at William's skull like he still desperately wanted to do him bodily harm. "Garnet?"

"These people are here to help me find Sebastian."

"Interlopers." He shook his head, as though he didn't believe me. "I only like dead things in this house. The dead . . . and you." He glanced at me with a glint in his eye I wasn't especially comfortable with.

O-kay. Sebastian had told me that Benjamin got crazier the closer it was to full moon.

"Um, well, that's sort of sweet." And sort of odd. Best not to dwell on the implications of that. I cleared my throat. "They'll only be here for a few hours. You want Sebastian back, don't you?"

Benjamin's shoulders drooped and he let the book drop to the floor with a bang. Everyone in the room jumped, except Micah, who sat in Sebastian's chair with his feet up on the table, watching the exchange between Benjamin and me.

"Out," I commanded Benjamin as I'd heard Sebastian do many times before. Then, on impulse, I added, "Please."

"All right," he said. "Since you asked so nicely." Benjamin walked past Micah and said, "You're not welcome here."

Micah smiled sweetly, though I saw his astral tail twitch. "I was here long before you."

Benjamin stiffened and I thought he might give in to another tantrum, but he simply narrowed his eyes at Micah and stalked out. He pushed the kitchen door open forcefully, and then went outside and slammed the back door shut like a petulant child.

I lowered myself back into my body slowly. The hardwood was cool against my cheek. Inhaling, I came back into the sensation of the heaviness my body. I felt the weight of skin and bones and all the pressure of all the little aches I'd been subconsciously carrying with me over the past few days—the dull throb of my swollen, burned neck, bruised knees, and skinned palms.

My head was partially propped on someone's knee. Craning my neck, I noticed it was Max. Marge knelt over me, though her attention, like everyone else's, had shifted to the noisy retreat of the ghost.

Max, however, looked ready to administer CPR.

"I'm okay," I told him, pushing myself up on my elbows. "Really."

"Lifeguard training in high school. I guess it all comes back to you in a crisis situation, eh, Garnet?" A beat. Then he added, "Jeez, was that a real ghost?"

We had the attention of the whole room, many of whom, no doubt, had the same question on their minds.

"Poltergeist," I said. I pulled my knees up to start the process of sitting up. Marge scooted out of the way and a few others stepped back to give me room. With more effort than I would have preferred, especially given the audience, I got my feet under me and myself upright. "I'm sorry about him," I said, rolling my shoulders to ease the sting from falling. "Benjamin kind of came with the house."

"You live with a ghost?" Griffin asked unbelievingly. "On purpose?"

"Sebastian does," Mátyás said from his spot on the staircase. "Garnet just sleeps over."

I shot Mátyás a glare. What was with the sudden hostility again?

"Aren't you going to introduce us to your new friend, Garnet?" Micah asked from where he lounged in the chair.

"Uh, everyone," I said. "This is Mátyás Von Traum, Sebastian's son."

There was a chorus of ohs and heys and nice-to-meet-yous. Mátyás stood up and edged a little closer to the group.

Since Mátyás stood there looking somewhat at a loss as to what to say next, I introduced each covener by name. Plus, this way Mátyás could connect names and faces to all the people we'd put on our suspect list. I saved Micah for last.

"*Enchanté*, I'm sure," Micah said with a tip of an invisible hat.

"*Et vous, júckal,*" Mátyás replied.

"Now, now, no need for name-calling. You hardly know me," Micah said with a lazy smile.

"It's kind of mystic, isn't it?" William said to no one in particular. "There are always twelve of us. Sebastian goes missing and Micah joins us. Blythe dropped out and now Mátyás is here."

"Yeah, what happened to her anyway?" Xylia asked. "She was kind of cute."

"Cute?" Mátyás mouthed to me. "And she's been missing how long?"

"She's been AWOL since Sebastian disappeared," Marge said, stepping closer into the two of us uninvited. She gave me a sheepish glance and added, "I kind of figured they ran off together, honestly."

"No," Mátyás and I said simultaneously and with nearly the same vehemence.

Marge took a step back. "Oh, well, I thought he was a vampire and that maybe she, well, you know, thought that was cool."

That seemed like just the sort of thing someone might suggest to try to cover up her part in Sebastian's disappearance. I was just about to call Marge on it when I got cut off.

"Wait a minute," said Xylia, joining in the conversation that I'd originally intended to be private. "Are you saying we're doing a ritual to find a guy who's off having kinky vampire sex with Blythe?"

"Sebastian ran off with Blythe?" someone at the far end of the room repeated. "Seriously? When did this happen?"

Mátyás continued to act as though he were only talking to me. "She could have," he said. "Maybe she's the one who put the spell on him."

The door opened. Every head in the room turned to watch Blythe walk in. She had a motorcycle helmet under her arm, and she shook out her long blond hair. "Hullo, everyone! Sorry I'm late."

9.

Uranus

❦

KEYWORDS:

Electricity, Magic, and Rebellion

The room was silent for a heartbeat as we waited to see if Sebastian would stroll in behind Blythe. Necks craned to see around her, and Blythe started to have that concerned look you got when you thought you might have a piece of broccoli stuck in your teeth or your fly might be open. "Um," she said, "am I missing something here?"

"We were all just talking about you," Micah said from his spot on the couch. "By the way, did you kidnap a vampire?"

"Actually, I think that was *you*," Mátyás said.

"Oh God," I heard Marge say. Her face drained of color and her eyes darted toward the door. She couldn't have looked guiltier if she'd tried.

"Right," Mátyás added. "And you."

"What is this, Miss Marple?" Griffin asked. "Who is this guy who comes in here and starts accusing people of vampire-napping, anyway?"

I had to admit this wasn't exactly what I'd hoped for from our plan to draw the bad guy out, but if anyone could irritate someone into expressing their guilt, it would be Mátyás. Still, I wasn't sure what he was thinking, poking at a guy who harbored not one God, but two. I could only hope he had some kind of ace up his sleeve.

"Mátyás is my friend and"—I started to say that he was Sebastian's son, but Sebastian was my fiancé, not just some guy I knew. That made Mátyás—"family. Besides, I think he's right."

Micah stretched his arms over his head languidly, as though he were getting ready for a nap. Scratching the back of his neck, he smacked his lips together. "Well, isn't this exciting," he murmured sleepily.

Marge, meanwhile, had inched her way closer to the couch and now stood beside it, watching Mátyás and me with wide, wary eyes. She pulled nervously on her fingers and clutched herself for support.

Micah stood up slowly. Despite everything, the room veritably crackled with the threat of his movement.

In response, the rest of the coven seemed to huddle closer to me and Mátyás, as though closing ranks. Griffin came up behind me and put his hand on my shoulder. He gave me a reassuring squeeze and I could feel his magical strength adding itself to mine. "So, is it true?" Griffin asked. "You got the lady's boyfriend stashed somewhere?"

"Fiancé," I corrected quietly.

"Fiancé," Griffin repeated louder.

Micah's gaze swept the group as though he were measuring his ability to take us on collectively. When his gaze lit on mine, I had no doubt he could. I squared my shoulders anyway, bolstered by the hand on my shoulder and the nearness of the others.

Micah seemed ready to respond when lightning struck the house. A sizzling crackle made my hair stand on end, followed by an explosion of light. Someone screamed. A loud boom, like standing in the middle of thunder, shook the walls. Plaster dust fell from the ceiling. Several people ducked, including Micah.

The lights went out.

Lighters flicked on around the room. William and Mátyás switched on keychain flashlights. Neither Marge nor Micah had taken the opportunity to disappear dramatically. In fact, both of them looked surprised and startled. Marge whispered to Micah, "Did you do that?"

A cold breeze tickled my eardrum. "The house is under attack," it seemed to say. Benjamin.

Mátyás either heard Benjamin or intuited the same conclusion. "The second party has made their move," he said.

Xylia and a couple of other people with lighters lit the decorative candles around the room. Soon we were bathed in a soft, flickering glow. "It's weird," William said, after lighting a kerosene lamp Sebastian had on his mantel. "There's not even any rain, but the sky is kind of green. Only right above us."

I peered out the window into the inky darkness. Mostly I saw my worried reflection on the glass, but William was right. I could make out a strange swirling greenish light over the house.

The airs on my arm prickled. I looked down to see the

fine hairs sticking straight up. It was happening again. Dropping the curtain, I shouted to everyone, "We're under magical attack. We need to counter this, now."

I held out my arms indicating that people should join hands. Griffin, Xylia, William, Mátyás, and the others quickly linked up. Marge and Micah stood outside the circle. I could hear a buzz, like the buildup of static, and I knew the next strike was imminent. We could do the spell without them, but . . . Micah was a God. "Get in here," I said, letting go of Mátyás's hand to reach for Micah.

Though surprised, Micah stepped up to take it. "Who is it?"

The lightning stuck again. The floors trembled. William, who held my other hand, nearly crushed it in shock. Everyone made a nervous noise of some kind, even Micah. "I don't know," I said. "But let's stop this before it gets too serious."

I felt something cold settle in directly behind me, like when you wander into a chilly spot in a lake. I knew it must be Benjamin. Apparently, he decided there was safety in numbers too.

Normally a coven will take months to get to the point where they can work together seamlessly. We didn't have time. Luckily, magic on the fly was kind of my specialty.

The wind rattled the windows.

The room hummed with anticipation. The candles flicked with each exhalation, so that the light pulsed in rhythm with our breath. When we were perfectly harmonized, I began to cast the circle. Starting in the east, I slowly moved in a clockwise direction behind the group, making sure to include Benjamin. I visualized a sphere of dark amber light, like the color of the center of Sebastian's eyes, forming behind me. At each cardinal direction, I called a guardian. Normally, I brought forth aspects of Lilith, but I could feel Micah's eyes on me, so instead I chose Hecate, Queen of Witches. In the east, she appeared as a warrior maiden, leaning casually against a two-handed sword. When I reached the south, I met a Hecate with hair the color of fire and bright embers flashing in her eyes. She was full-bodied with the swell of pregnancy, stirring a cauldron in the west. At the north, I saw her as the crone, bent with age, leaning on a staff.

I went around again. As I passed each covener, I could feel their energy join in the circle. Individual colors swirled in the amber sphere that surrounded us, like the oily sheen of a soap bubble.

Micah's energy joined subtly at first, like a tingle at the edge of my fingertips. I wondered at first why he didn't lend his full strength, but then I felt a familiar presence.

Lilith.

She was still with Micah. My heart quickened at the thought of her so near. Mentally, I reached out and was rewarded with the sensation of invisible, icy fingers stroking my hair lovingly. My body ached with longing. I wanted her inside me again.

Lightning crashed the roof again. The sound of shingles sliding from the roof ricocheted across the ceiling.

"Seems she wants to bring the house down on you," Micah said in his usual droll tone. "You certainly have powerful enemies."

"She?" I asked. I quickly rejoined the circle. Taking Micah's and Mátyás's hands, the circle was complete. Normally, I'd say some kind of pat phrase to mark the moment, but the energy was tight. I felt the hum of the others the instant my fingers linked.

Benjamin's presence was like a cool breeze at my back. I could sense Lilith's nearness, but her energy was somehow muted. I wanted to search for her, call her in, but I could feel the other building up another electrical attack.

"Oh yeah, definitely a 'she,'" William nodded sagely, and I wondered if he was just playing along or if he really had sensed something. "Another Goddess, I'd say."

Everyone's attention was drawn to the ceiling. I looked too. A swirling cloud had condensed above us. Miniature lightning strikes flashed, lighting the air deep purples and reds.

Thunder rolled and suddenly, something rained down on us. Hard, small, white pellets clattered in a rush. At first I thought it was hail, but when I shook some from my hair they were obviously—"Maggots!"

10.

Neptune

❧

KEYWORDS:

Delusion, Trances, and Mystery

Panic moved through the circle, and I could feel peo-ple starting to pull away. "No," I shouted. "We have to stay focused. Keep your hands together," I implored, but it was too late. People frantically brushed at the larvae, trying to get it off themselves. I could feel the circle breaking. The attacker, whoever she was, would have her opening in a minute.

Electricity sizzled through the air. I cringed.

"Enough of this," Micah said, stepping forward. He held his arms out open wide, spread-eagle. The silhouette of a black bird hovered over his heart. Larger and larger it grew until I could swear that I could make out the image of slickly glittering feathers. The bird-ghost-shadow burst into the air.

A powerful stroke of its wings made the evil maggot-hailing cloud dissipate.

With Micah distracted, Lilith took the opportunity to show herself. Lilith's warmth enveloped my stomach. An image began to materialize in front of my face, smoky at first. Strands of her long, gray-streaked raven hair swirled in the gale. Eyes, like burning coals, flashed darkly in the candle-light. If I was going to get her back, I needed to act quickly.

"Benjamin. Get the intruder. Get Micah!"

Benjamin acted quickly. I saw a blur as he sped toward Micah. Then, there was a bang, as he passed through Micah's body. The air pressure dropped. My ears popped. For a split second, I caught the image of a very surprised coyote-headed man knocked out of Micah's body. Benjamin, however, came out the other side in flames. He shrieked with the sound of wild wind across the prairie and fled through the floor into the basement.

Micah gave me an imploring look. He looked sick. His eyes seemed sunken, his skin hung loosely to bones, and his hair turned completely white. No, strike that, Micah was dying.

Just as I started to ask him what I could do to help, the black cloud that was Lilith rushed into my open mouth.

I breathed her in, nearly gagging on the scent of fecund compost and the taste of death. She filled my lungs until I thought they would burst. Then, she spread outward, sinking back into the recesses of my being. A sensation of homecoming filled me. Lilith glided into my body, softly, comfortably. I felt a sigh of familiarity, and the warmth of kindred-spiritedness slid through me.

In that same moment, I saw the ghost Coyote step back into Micah's body. Micah's features hardened. His youth returned, and suddenly I understood. Coyote possessed

Micah the way Lilith did me, except where She came and went in short bursts, Micah was always Coyote.

Focusing on me, Micah's lips lifted in a sneer. Closing the distance between us, he grabbed me by my shirt and slammed me up against the wall hard. Air rushed from my lungs. "Didn't your mother ever tell you it's wrong to steal," he growled in my ear.

He might be a God, but he was also a guy. So I kicked him hard in the most sensitive part of a man's body: the knees. He went down with a yelp, just as three of the more burly guys from the coven and William descended on him. They pulled him the rest of the way off me.

He shook them off easily. "I helped you, and you repay me by taking what is mine?"

"Yours? Lilith was mine first." Oh my Goddess, that sounded childish. I stuck with the theme. "Finders keepers."

"I need her," Micah said, and I saw that desperate look flash, momentarily, across his eyes.

"You need to get lost, pal," Griffin said.

Mátyás stepped between Micah and me. "Yes, I think you should be going."

Micah eyed the men suddenly surrounding me with a look of derision that clearly implied they were all boys compared to him. He let out a patronizing chuckle and said, "We can talk about this later, Garnet. Privately."

He stomped out.

It was difficult to release the circle we'd created in any kind of controlled way. Though everyone resumed their spots and did their best to focus on the task at hand, the energy was chaotic at best. I could hardly concentrate myself.

The circle collapsed in on itself with a wobbly thump.

The guardians stepped backward into a mist with disapproving looks on their faces.

Everyone in the coven started talking among themselves. Someone produced a Tupperware container filled with chocolate chip cookies, obviously meant for the "cakes and ale" section of the ritual.

Mátyás handed me a cookie. "Well, that didn't go as we planned, did it?"

"No," I said. I leaned against the wall and watched the coven as they broke up into small groups and started debriefing among themselves. William and Griffin appeared to be engaged in a debate about something, and Blythe seemed to be catching up on everything she missed from Xylia and some of the others. I bit into the cookie, barely tasting it. "But I guess the second party revealed themselves."

"They did?" Mátyás asked. "Was it someone here?"

"No. I don't think so. I would have felt a power surge from someone as I cast the circle, even without Lilith." I touched my stomach reflexively, gratified by the feeling of her heaviness just under the surface. "I'm pretty sure everyone here was fighting *against* the attack, even Micah."

"But not Marge," Mátyás pointed out. "She slipped out early."

She had? I'd been so focused on Micah's participation, I didn't even track to see if Marge had joined or not. "You think she's the second party?"

Mátyás shook his head. "No, it's someone outside this coven, like you said. Who else did you say wanted you dead? One of Father's ghoulfriends?"

"They're not supposed to practice magic."

Mátyás licked chocolate from his fingers. "Someone's a rule breaker."

I had to agree. "I wonder who," I said.

Mátyás shrugged. "Did you ever call the ghouls?"

"I met one," I said. "Two actually. And his accountant."

"Walter? I love Walter," Mátyás said with a nod and a fond smile. When I gave him a curious look he added, "What? He administers my trust fund."

I nodded absently. Lilith shifted inside me, settling. Having been without her for so long, I now noticed how her presence heightened all my senses. The subdued colors of Sebastian's living room glowed in the flickering candlelight. I could smell the faint scent of red rot from the ancient books that filled the shelves and a trace of someone's sandalwood perfume. The soft murmurs of everyone talking washed over me gently, like waves lapping the lakeshore. I was more aware of my body: the tautness of skin under my shirt, the ache of the scrapes on my knees.

Magically, the sensations were even more intense. Without even intending to I could see the auras of everyone in the room. William's deep purple, the brassy flash of copper that was Griffin, and Xylia's dappled mossy green, all swirled together in the air.

How had I ever lived without her?

"I took the liberty of 'borrowing' something from Marge's purse," Mátyás said conspiratorially.

I looked at him. "What are you talking about? Why?"

He held up a comb. It was one of those black, utilitarian types you find next to the tiny tubes of toothpaste in the travel section of department stores. "For you," he said, handing it to me. "To help me focus tonight."

I looked at the unremarkable thing. It had a few strands of curly gray hair stuck in the teeth. "Are you saying you stole this from Marge? And what am I supposed to do with this thing, exactly?"

"I can't really control whose dreams I enter," Mátyás explained. "I can reach out to my parents, but we're connected by blood. I'll need you to help me direct my abilities tonight so we can see if Marge dreams about where she might have stashed Father."

I looked at the comb and at Mátyás. "Do I know how to do that?"

"Improvise. You're good at that."

11.

Pluto

❧

KEYWORDS:

Disappearance, Kidnapping, and Crime

After all the excitement of the magical attack, it was difficult to get people to leave. Everyone wanted to quiz me about who might be so desperate to kill (or at least fry Sebastian's shingles) and to get details of what was going on with Micah.

"So he stole Lilith," William repeated, after I'd explained it to a new group of curious coveners. I was beginning to think I should have just issued a statement as if for a press conference. I was getting weary of repeating myself to each new group that came up to me. This must have been my sixth time through the whole thing.

I nodded, taking a sip of iced tea. We'd raided Sebastian's pantry for snacks. A lot of people had gotten the munchies after all the magical energy we'd expended. I'd owe Sebastian a week's worth of groceries once we found him. Goddess, I hoped he was okay. I prayed Mátyás and I would be successful tonight.

"Why?" William asked. "To what end?"

"What?" I blinked, having lost track of the conversation.

"Why did Micah steal Lilith? What purpose did that serve?"

It was an excellent question and one no one had asked me before. I frowned, considering. "I don't know," I admitted, though I remembered how old and exhausted he'd looked when Benjamin had knocked Coyote out of Micah for a moment. "But I think maybe he needed Lilith's energy."

"Like a battery recharge?"

I shrugged; that seemed as good a metaphor as any. "You wouldn't think a God's energy would run down though, would you?" I thought of my own resident Goddess. Was I in danger of tapping her out some day? Micah and Coyote seemed to be closer linked than I was to Lilith. In fact, they seemed almost merged. Was it possible that they needed more energy to sustain that bond? Or, if Coyote was more on the surface, perhaps existing that way siphoned off this godhead somehow.

"Lilith seems more powerful the more you use her. Or, maybe more in focus."

It was true that I'd learned to tap Lilith's power for little bursts of strength or magic.

"Maybe the Gods need magic," Griffin said. He'd wandered up to join our conversation. He was chewing on a peanut butter sandwich. "Like we need food."

"So you're saying Micah's God has run down because he's not a sorcerer? He's not feeding it magic like Garnet does with Lilith," William said, sounding ready to debate Griffin again.

"No," Griffin said, "I wasn't. But that's a good theory."

It was.

"I'm ready if you are," Mátyás said with a yawn. "Actually, I could have slept several hours ago."

We'd decided that since we didn't know when Marge went to sleep we might as well let everyone trickle off in their own good time. I had no idea it would be near dawn, however. I said good-bye to the last straggler as the sky was brilliant indigo, glowing with the hint of the sunrise to come. With nothing else stirring, the chirpings of tree frogs and sparrows echoed loudly over the cornfields.

I gripped Marge's comb in my hand. As I walked back to the house, the breeze brought the scent of cow manure and clover. My shoes made dark patches in the dew-covered lawn.

Mátyás lay down on the couch. He had a pillow and some blankets; he'd been sleeping there since arriving in the States. I perched on the glass-topped table. "I'm not feeling very sleepy with you staring at me," Mátyás said.

"Should I go in another room?"

"No, you need to be in here to help direct me to Marge." He scratched his eyebrow. "Maybe you could sing?"

"Are you kidding me?"

He looked embarrassed. "It used to work when I was a kid."

I tried to imagine Sebastian singing to Mátyás as a child. It was strangely easy. Sebastian had a beautiful voice.

He sang in the shower. Usually in German. "I don't think I know any traditional Austrian songs," I said, "though I could chant. It might help start the spell."

"Sounds nice," Mátyás said.

Feeling a little sheepish, I started to sing. I picked something simple. "We are a circle, within a circle." It was a song I learned when I first started practicing witchcraft. "With no beginning and never ending," the line repeated endlessly. It was meant to help bring a person to a trance state. The way Mátyás's eyes were drifting closed it seemed to be working. It was time for me to try to nudge him in the right direction.

I held Marge's comb and concentrated on it. I pictured Marge in my mind—her long, wavy gray hair and tendency toward Hawaiian shirts. I could see her pretty well in my mind. The only problem was that I had no idea how to convey this information to the now-snoring Mátyás. I tried thinking at him really hard, but I had no idea if he got the image or not.

Going to the astral plane might help. I let myself slip the rest of the way into a trance state I'd started with the song. I was exhausted. It'd been a long time since I'd gotten a decent night of sleep. My head slumped to my chest. When I opened my astral eyes, Mátyás was waiting for me with his arms folded across his chest. "Took you long enough."

We were somewhere I'd been before, though I couldn't have named it. It was an empty plain with grasses bending in the wind. The sky was large, purple, and black. Mátyás too looked darker, more sinister. Dark hair fell over hooded eyes and his skin hung to a rail-thin body. His astral image wore a trench coat, ragged at the edges, and it blew in a mystic breeze. I thought his reputation as a boogeyman might be well deserved.

"Which way?" he asked.

Good question. I looked around. The field was unremarkable until I noticed giant, plastic comb teeth, like the bones of some ancient behemoth leading to the horizon.

I led Mátyás along the row of spikes. We moved quickly, faster than walking somehow. His image appeared to flicker as he moved on the opposite side of the black obelisks. "You're different here," he said. "Did you know you picture yourself as blond?"

I hadn't until he mentioned it, but once he did, I had vivid images of my dream-self as the Garnet I was before Lilith. Glancing down, I saw that I had on my favorite sundress—batik images of the Venus of Willendorf patterned the material.

"Lilith looks different than I would have expected too. Younger. More beautiful," he said quietly, his gaze looking over my shoulder. When I looked, however, I saw only shadow. Turning around quickly, I saw nothing except the flash of an owl's wing.

The comb's teeth ended in a two-story, A-frame house with no windows or doors that I could see, but Mátyás walked confidently up to it. "Normally, I can just walk in," he told me, "but I suppose I should knock."

A door materialized out of the darkness, and Marge opened the door. Or at least I thought it was Marge. She was young and muscular. Mátyás seemed nonplussed by the new Marge. "I'm only going to ask nicely once," he said with a smile that seemed more razors than teeth. "Where's my papa?"

The handsome gray-haired woman that was Marge shrugged. "Where the dead lie," and she shut the door.

Our grassy field became a graveyard.

I held on to the door handle with white knuckles as Mátyás's Jag raced across town at top speed. "I should have known," he said through clenched teeth. "He's only ever dreamed of Saint Sebastian when he's in torpor."

"She told us she worked at Sunset Memory Gardens too," I said. "It's the perfect place to hide a vampire."

The Jag skipped over an uneven patch of road. My stomach lurched. "Sure," Mátyás said, "*if* you drive a stake through his heart."

I looked over at the speedometer. The red line was well over a hundred. "Can't this thing go any faster?"

According to the sign, the cemetery didn't open until eight. The ten-foot wrought-iron gate was locked. The spikes on the top of each post looked like serious deterrents.

"Why do people do this?" I said, attempting to rattle one of the bars. It didn't even shake despite my best efforts.

Mátyás stabbed the shovel into the trimmed grass with a metallic, slicing sound. "To keep out people like us." He laced his fingers and hunched down. "I'll give you a boost."

I looked at the spikes.

"They transfixed him with something like that," Mátyás reminded me.

I damn near leaped into his arms.

Mátyás's boost got me onto the second rail, and I managed

to wedge myself over the top without jabbing myself too hard in the crotch. Getting my other leg over proved more difficult.

I landed on the other side with a bruising *thud*. When I saw him heaving the shovel over the gate, I had to scramble out of the way. The dew-covered grass was slick and the handle nearly whacked me in the head. Mátyás was pulling himself over when we heard a growl.

A mangy coyote strolled into the deserted street. Its lips were curled in a snarl. In the thin light of dawn I swore I could see a string of drool slide from between sharp canines.

Mátyás dropped back to the ground. "I'm going to be heroic now," he said. "So don't blow it."

"But he's a God," I said. "You don't have any magic."

"Not like yours, but I *am* my father's son," he said, and for a second in the half light I saw the hint of trench coat and hooded eyes. "Run," he commanded.

Coyote took a step closer.

Out of the corner of my eye, I saw Mátyás's shadow separate itself and slide along the street toward where we'd parked the Jag. The coyote's eyes were drawn to the shadow, and it whined. While it was distracted, Mátyás hauled ass over the fence.

"I thought I told you to run," he said, picking up the shovel. He gave my shoulder a slight push. I got the hint and started moving. "He's not going to be distracted by that for very long."

"You just did a Peter Pan," I told him, my mouth still slightly agape. We ran blindly into the graveyard and my toes kept catching on markers. Every time I tripped over one, I was very aware that I was standing on someone's grave. "Since when could you do stunts like that?"

"Since I read Jung," he said.

My foot snagged on another stone simply labeled "Mother." I had to spread out my hands to keep from falling on my face. "Are you talking about the psychologist? Seriously?"

"He did a lot of work with dreams and archetypes and it occurred to me that I can walk into people's subconscious when they dream. Once I read Jung, I realized just how much the subconscious operates in our conscious minds. If the light is right," he said, looking up at the dark rose-colored clouds visible through the tall pine trees, "I can play parlor tricks on the mind."

"That's more than just parlor tricks, if you can fool a God incarnate."

"Even Gods dream, apparently."

We'd reached an older section where the monuments became covered in moss and lichen. The stones were more ornate. Some of the fancier ones were even carved to represent extinguished torches or weeping cherubs.

"Any idea where we should be going?" Mátyás asked.

Speaking of dreams, I was pretty sure I'd seen this place before. A dog had been chasing me then too. What was that? Oh, the beer-and-pizza-inspired dream I'd had the night after I'd first tried to find Sebastian in the astral plane! I'd thought at the time that I was in Lakewood, but I was here. Where had I ended up? I could see a crow sitting on something, what had it been?

"The mausoleum," I said.

Luckily, there was only one. The shovel broke the lock with a dramatic spark. The sarcophagus was an entirely different problem. Mátyás hacked at the granite a few times with hollow, useless-sounding clangs. "Christ," he said, flexing his hands. "I felt that one all the way to my elbow. Did I even chip it?"

I inspected the box. "What we need is a sledgehammer."

Mátyás sat down dejectedly on the prayer bench. I sat opposite him, facing the open door. The sun rose, and golden slivers of light dappled the rosebush that nearly obscured the marker just outside the door.

"Maybe I could use Lilith," I suggested.

"Can you turn her off before she slaughters Sebastian and me?" Mátyás asked wryly.

I thought I probably could, though it was true that I found it a lot easier to bring her up than to put her back. There was another problem as well. With Coyote so close, would he try to steal her again when she was out in the open and vulnerable? I chewed at my lip and stared at the roses. They were picture-perfect, the way the dew rested on half-closed buds. I could just make out the first few letters of the name inscribed on the stone: Ster . . .

"Sterling," I said, jumping up. "The silver bullet. That's the key somehow. Maybe there's something that could help us over there."

"Let's hope it's a crowbar and a pneumatic drill hiding behind those bushes," Mátyás said.

Upon closer inspection, it was clear the rosebush was newly planted, as was the sod. Mátyás ran back to the mausoleum to fetch the shovel and started digging.

And digging, and digging, and digging.

We took turns shoveling. Thank Goddess the ground

had been recently disturbed or we'd still be there. Several times while I was resting I thought I saw Coyote dashing among the gravestones just beyond the hill, so I sent up wards of protection. Though I really wanted to infuse them with a blast of Lilith's power, I decided better of it. Lilith's energy just might draw Micah to the scent.

It was my shift when we hit something solid. My palms were covered with blisters and even though the temperatures were only in the sixties, I'd sweated through my clothes. My arms were covered in muddy streaks. At first, the feeling of something hard beneath the shovel made me thrilled. I'd imagined a coffin just lying there, like in the movies. Of course, what I hit was the concrete vault.

Mátyás, who had jumped down to help smooth away the dirt, hung his head in defeat. "We're back to square one. The cemetery will be open in less than an hour."

Was it nearly eight o'clock already? We'd been at this for almost three hours. No wonder my arms ached.

I heard a dog bark. Looking up from the bottom of our deep hole, I could see the gray muzzle of Coyote peering down at us. "I'll make this simple," he said. In a blink, he had become Micah kneeling at the edge of the grave. "Give me Lilith and I'll give you Sebastian."

Mátyás, apparently, was too tired to negotiate. In one smooth move, he stood up and whacked Micah with the broad head of the shovel. Being so far down, he mostly smacked Micah's knees, but Mátyás was already clambering up to continue the fight. I didn't need direction to know my job was to get Sebastian out now.

I dug my raw fingers into a corner of the vault. Even though I was standing on the lid, I gave my most mighty heave. Of course, my fingers slipped, scraped and bloody from the edges, and I fell on my ass. I could hear the sounds of fighting overhead, and though I had faith in Mátyás's desperation, Micah was a God. He had the home-court advantage.

I was going to have to use Lilith, even though I was certain that was precisely what Micah wanted. I started to call her. I felt the familiar fire race along my nerve endings as she surged upward. Reaching for the lid again, I readied myself for her full arrival. Just as her heat began to peak, something cold and sharp, like claws, scratched my back.

Coyote dug into me, sapping Lilith's strength. This time I was more aware of the sensations as he began to steal her. The knife points became needles drawing away her strength and power. My fingers slipped on the concrete.

Just then, I sensed a faint echo from inside the vault. The part of Lilith that had stayed with Sebastian was trying to answer my call for help. Even as Coyote pulled pieces of Lilith from me, I concentrated on connecting with the weak signal below. I heard a groan, and then a momentous snap as the vault lid came up. I gave the half in my hands a toss over my shoulder and was surprised to see it fly up out of the hole. I heard someone grunt in pain and prayed that I hadn't just crushed Mátyás.

Flee, I mentally sent to Lilith, though I had no reason to believe she'd listen or obey. She did, though. I nearly fell over when she snapped back inside me.

I heard the coyote howl.

I could see a steel coffin inside the vault. Sebastian was inside it, I was certain.

"Mátyás!" I called. "Are you okay?"

"Not really," he said. "But the coyote is gone. After you whacked him with the flying slab of concrete, he ran off with his tail between his legs." He looked down into the hole. "Jesus, Garnet. You ripped that concrete like it was paper."

I had. I was still standing on half of the vault. There was a jagged edge where Lilith peeled the vault top like it was a can of sardines. I would have been more impressed if we still didn't have to get the coffin out and somehow pry it open too.

I looked back up at Mátyás. His face was bruised and his right eye swollen. "Bright Goddess! Are you okay enough to help me get this out?"

"One way to find out."

Turns out neither of us had the strength or leverage to get the steel casket out, but we were able to pry up the remaining half of the vault lid so we could use the shovel to break the locks and pry open the casket. There wasn't a lot of room for us to maneuver, but we managed to only step on each other's toes a few times.

"Remind me to ask for a wooden box," Mátyás said, just before the lid came open with an ugly hiss.

Mátyás was right. They'd transfixed Sebastian by driving a stake through his heart, but they'd also turned him face-down. He'd scratched at the velvet lining quite a bit before slipping into torpor. I grabbed the stake and pulled. Given how hard we'd had to work to get this far, I was surprised when it popped easily into my hands. There hadn't been much to anchor it to, though it had been enough to immobilize Sebastian.

We rolled him over. He felt like deadweight. Sebastian's

eye sockets were sunken and his features were gaunt, ghastly. "Sebastian?"

No flicker of life.

They'd buried him in his street clothes, of course. It was kind of strange to see him lying there all dead looking in a T-shirt and jeans.

"How do we get him to wake up?"

"Blood would do it, I'd imagine." Mátyás was already rolling up his sleeve.

"No," I said. "It should be me. It's my fault he went off looking for a ghoul that morning." And what? Marge jumped him? "Anyway, I think it should be me."

For once, Mátyás didn't argue. He handed his pocketknife over silently.

You'd think given all the time I spend hanging around vampires and their sort, I'd be used to the whole stab-yourself-and-stick-it-in-someone's-mouth thing.

Still, Sebastian's life hung in the balance. It was do or die. With the knife poised over my wrist, I squeezed my eyes shut.

Mátyás grabbed the blade before it struck home. "Bullocks! Are you trying to kill yourself? Give that thing to me."

I expected him to plunge the knife into his own flesh, but instead he grabbed my wrist. Twisting my hand over, he made a shallow slash across the top of my forearm. "Ow!" I shouted, jerking it back. I cradled my arm against my chest. Blood oozed between my fingers. "You cut me!" I accused.

"Yes. Now don't waste it," he said. Then he gave me an evil little smile. "Plus, I've always wanted to do that."

I stuck my tongue out at him. He glanced meaningfully

at Sebastian and I got the hint. Still, I was nervous. I'd seen what Sebastian was like after only having been trans-fixed for a couple of hours. He'd nearly bled Feather dry. I could only imagine what his hunger would be like after several days of stake-induced torpor. My hand shook as I held my arm over Sebastian's prone body. Blood splattered everywhere.

Mátyás rolled his eyes at my ineptitude. I pushed my wound closer to Sebastian.

Nothing happened. I sat straddling Sebastian's chest, with my bleeding arm extended like bait, and waited. Sun slanted into the hole. Dust motes danced in the shaft of light. Somewhere a lawn mower started up.

I was just about to remark that I guessed the cemetery was open and that at any moment we'd be arrested for tres-passing and grave desecration when sharp pain seized my arm. Looking down, I saw Sebastian attached to me like I was a ham hock. I didn't mean to, but I screamed. I tried to pull my arm away, but he held tight, like a great white shark. I wondered if I bopped him in the nose if he'd let go. Not that I could have done anything so coherent when all my thoughts could be summed up with: "Ow, ow, let go!"

Mátyás leaned over my shoulder, patiently speaking into Sebastian's glazed eyes. "Father. Father, it's Mátyás and Garnet. Wake up."

I wanted to argue that Sebastian was clearly awake since he was sucking the life out of me, but again with the screaming and the desperate attempts to get away.

Lilith growled.

Everyone paused. Mátyás looked at me. Sebastian let go and blinked curiously at me. I stared at myself—well, I really kind of just looked at my chest, but, given how loud Lilith had been, I thought maybe I could have seen her sticking out somehow.

"I hate to be so cliché, but where am I?" Sebastian asked. Then he looked at the coffin, the broken vault, and the deep mound of dirt. "Oh," he said. "Ugh. Get me out of here."

Mátyás and I helped him out onto the grass. I looked around for any sign of Micah or the coyote. Though I didn't see anything, the hackles raised on my neck. I had a sense he was near. "We should get out of here," I said.

"I don't know if I can walk," Sebastian said. We'd propped him up against Sterling's marker. His hair, which I'd often teasingly complained was always more luxurious than mine, hung in limp, tangled strands. "I feel so heavy, so cold."

"You need more blood," Mátyás said.

Even though my arm pounded with each pulse, I steeled myself to offer more. My mouth was opening to volunteer when Mátyás stripped off his shirt. He crawled over to his father and curled himself into Sebastian's lap. His chin rested on Sebastian's shoulder. Sebastian's head fell forward. They looked like they were embracing tenderly, father and son.

I looked away, letting them have their moment privately. A guy on a riding mower zoomed past several rows down. He glanced up. Our eyes met briefly, and then I heard the engine choke. No doubt he was looking at the gigantic mounds of dirt spread around the grave and the shovel perched on top. My mud-streaked face and dusty clothes probably didn't help our case any either.

"Uh, guys, we need to scram," I said. "The caretaker has spotted us."

Sebastian let out a disappointed groan, but I expected he was going to need a lot of blood—more than Mátyás or I had to spare—before he made a complete recovery. They disengaged. Mátyás struggled to his feet a bit woozily, but we all got moving when we heard the caretaker shout, "Hey, you kids, what are you doing over there?"

We ran. In the daylight I had an easier time not tripping over all the sunken markers. But, between the blood loss and my muscles aching from hours of digging, my side quickly got a stitch in it. Puffing, I dragged myself along. Luckily, the caretaker continued to inspire me by shouting, "Oh my God! What have you done? I'm calling the police!"

It was a surprisingly excellent motivational speech. We managed to get out past the gates and into Mátyás's Jag before the caretaker thought to walkie-talkie for reinforcements. Some guys in a rattly pickup truck were just rounding the bend when Mátyás let out the clutch and the Jag's tires squealed with the stench of burning rubber.

"I hope they didn't get the license plate," I said from the backseat. Sebastian took shotgun and I wasn't about to argue, though I wished he were in the back with me. I hadn't gotten much of a chance to tell him how much I missed him.

"Let them call the cops. We're not the ones who buried someone alive," Mátyás said.

When Mátyás asked where we wanted to go, Sebastian and I exchanged a look. It was obvious we both agreed that, besides a bath, what we really wanted was some time together to reconnect—alone—so I told Mátyás to drop Sebastian and me back at my apartment. With Mátyás at his place, mine seemed the best, even given the circumstances.

Besides, if someone wanted either of us dead, it wasn't necessarily the first place they'd look for us.

That's right! I needed to catch Sebastian up on everything that had happened so far. So, as Mátyás drove, I explained everything from the magical attacks to Micah's capital-C Coyote.

"I've always hated dogs," Sebastian muttered. "Man, I can't get over it. Your apartment is gone? I love that place. Is Barney okay?"

"I love you so much."

Mátyás made a gagging sound. "We're here," he said, bumping the curb slightly as he pulled up. "I'll stop by the store and tell William what happened."

"Oh my Goddess," I breathed. "Mátyás, that would be so . . . sweet."

"Yeah, well, don't get used to it," Mátyás grumbled as he drove away.

Clambering under the caution tape, Sebastian and I tiptoed up the stairs. I didn't think the downstairs neighbors were awake, or even home, but coming here felt so illicit it seemed only right to try to be sneaky. It was after eight in the morning, but it was a Sunday. No contractors at work.

"It's like breaking into the old high school," I whispered to Sebastian.

He nodded, though I knew he had absolutely no reference for that. Did they even have secondary education when he was alive?

I had that strange sense of light-headedness as I passed

by the gaping hole in the living room. Sebastian, on the other hand, seemed almost drawn to it. "Whoa," he said, leaning over the flattened couch to look down at the lawn below. "Check it out."

"No, thanks," I said. I stayed back by the archway that separated the living room from the dining room and clutched the wall. Normally, I wasn't afraid of heights. What scared me wasn't the distance to the ground so much as a phantom sensation of what it would be like to jump. It was as if I couldn't trust myself not to leap to my doom if I let myself get too close. Even though this was only one story up, I could far too easily imagine breaking a leg or worse on impact.

While Sebastian continued to marvel at the damage the tree had caused in the physical plane, I decided that I should look at it in the magical realm. Something, I chided myself, I should have done right away. I opened up my magical senses.

The hole in the wall pulsed with darkness. Swirling around the edges were thousands of pencil-thin, black smoky worms. They slithered over bits of broken plaster and lath, disappearing into crevices, like a swarm of carpenter ants.

"Get away from there, Sebastian," I said, though they seemed completely oblivious to him. He had no aura, after all. No doubt he didn't register as living.

"There's something still here, isn't there?" he asked, coming off the couch slowly as if wary that the creatures might notice his movement and attack. "Some kind of ghost of the magic?"

I nodded. "Or something. I wish you could see them," I said.

"I can feel them," he said. "They're familiar somehow."

"Like the magic that KO'd you? Coyote's magic?"

He shook his head thoughtfully. "No, more intimate." He backed away. "Anyway, you should talk to the contractor."

I laughed. "About what? A magical infestation?"

"No, but I'd bet money they're going to have delays in reconstruction if you don't do some kind of cleansing. Whatever's left behind is sure to cause problems for the workers."

A bunch of bad-luck bugs causing nail guns to malfunction or accidents to occur. I shook my head; it was a hex—an insidious one at that. "Somebody really hates me."

Sebastian looked around at the ruined apartment. "But, speaking of all that, do you think we can be safe here? From what you told me whoever it is has attacked remotely before."

It was my turn to flash Sebastian a wicked grin. "I've been thinking about that," I said, leaning closer to run my fingernails down his chest. "We've always had very powerful sex magic."

"Hmm," he said, ducking down to capture my lips with his. "I do *so* love the way you think."

But first we needed to get clean. I was covered in mud and Sebastian . . . well, Sebastian smelled like a funeral home. I was pleased when the water came on in the bathroom, and I set it for filling the tub. I squirted in a large dollop of bubbles, figuring that the more I used up the less I'd have to move later. The steam smelled faintly of lavender.

Sebastian watched from the doorway with hungry eyes. Standing up slowly, I smiled seductively. I pulled my top

over my head, wiggling my hips in my best imitation of an
erotic dancer. I thought for sure Sebastian would laugh at
me, but instead he gave a low, appreciative rumble. Apparently, the sight of my sweat-slicked, mud-streaked, naked
breasts worked for him.

I shimmied out of the rest of my clothes. I kicked off my
shoes. Now I was completely bare. Even in the humid bathroom steam, I shivered a little with the sudden and complete exposure.

Sebastian continued to stare, unabashedly appreciative.
With his eyes on me, I leaned over the tub and turned the
faucets off.

After lingering in that position just a little longer than
necessary, I stepped closer to him and reached out to unbut-
ton his shirt. His palms rested on my shoulders, cool from
torpor. Slowly, he stroked along the contours of my back.
Cupping my buttocks, he pulled me against him. The fabric
of his clothes felt rough on my sensitive skin. My hands
were pinned between us. When I looked into his eyes, I felt
the heat of his need.

"You're beautiful," he said. I needed a bath. Still, I believed he meant it.

I wanted to tell him he still looked too pale and too thin,
but it seemed unkind. "I missed you so much," I said instead.

The bath in my apartment was one of those deep claw-
footed ones. Sebastian and I easily fit into it. We sat facing
each other at first, using my body scrub to softly wash
each other. I delighted in watching the water sluice down
the flat planes of Sebastian's chest, and he teased my
breasts with light, quick caresses.

To wash his hair I had Sebastian scoot around so that he

could lay his head in my lap. I rubbed his scalp with soap, until he had a bubble mane. I poured cup after cup of warm water through his hair. His eyes closed with satisfaction. I traced a finger along his jaw; he needed a shave.

We switched places and he did my hair. His gentle ministrations nearly lulled me to sleep. A sigh of absolute pleasure escaped my lips. Then some soap got on the cut on my arm and I hissed.

"Let me look at that," he said.

I offered up a soapy arm. Sebastian smoothed the bubbles away to look at the cut. As he held the wound close to his face, his body stiffened. His fangs descended.

"It's bleeding again," he managed to say. Then, I felt his lips lightly probe the gash. It was sexual the way Sebastian's tongue darted in and out of the folds of the injury, slightly spreading the edges.

"Oh," I managed to say, my mouth going dry, while another part grew wetter.

Pressing his mouth to my arm, he sucked. Tenderly, he lapped at the skin and torn flesh. In the water beneath my head, I felt his arousal stiffen.

I shifted slightly so that Sebastian could continue his exploration of my wound, and, though it was a bit awkward, I found a way to use my mouth and tongue in a similar fashion.

The water had gone cold and my fingers were pruned and wrinkled by the time we got out.

We adjourned to the bedroom after drying off. I just couldn't get enough of him; it was like we hadn't seen each other in a year. Slowly, Sebastian kissed my throat and shoulders. I let my hands find familiar curves along his back and arms.

I reveled in the strength of his muscles, taut and solid. Cupping my breasts in his hands, his mouth covered my nipple. He sucked and nipped, sending stabs of pleasure deep inside me. I arched into him. Grabbing fistfuls of his hair, I begged him not to stop. When he did pull away, he softly blew cool air over my aroused skin. I trembled with delicious stimulation.

Dropping all the way to the floor, he tugged at my robe. Needing no further encouragement, I slipped out of it, letting it drop to the floor.

"I lied when I said I'd never go on my knees for you," he said, pressing butterfly light kisses against my tummy and thighs. I bit my lip to hold back a moan as his mouth unhurriedly progressed toward the moist spot between my legs.

When Sebastian's tongue finally found the center of my pleasure, I couldn't stifle a whimper. He pressed deeper and I found I actually couldn't stand the intensifying stimulation and my knees literally buckled. I fell backward onto the bed with a squeal.

Sebastian looked startled to find me writhing alone on the bed, but then laughed. "I can't say I've ever gotten that reaction before."

"Oh, shut up and get over here," I begged.

Though it took less than a second for him to climb onto the bed, it felt like an eternity until my legs were wrapped around him and he was inside me.

Sensing my anxious need, his motions were leisurely. I moved frantically against him, urging him to faster speed.

To get my point across, I clutched at his back, letting my nails sink deeply into his flesh. "Oh," he growled into my ear. "You want to play rough, eh?"

I nipped his ear in response.

He ground himself into me. I gasped, but reciprocated. I was done with slow. I wanted him, all of him, now.

We set a pounding tempo and I could feel myself beginning to reach a crescendo, but there was one thing missing.

"Bite me," I demanded between breaths.

He almost faltered.

"Bite me, Sebastian, like you mean it. Please. Bite me."

I must have convinced him that I was serious because his fangs descended. A tremor of anticipation rolled through me in a wave. His teeth sank into my shoulder, and I screamed. A searing pain blinded me, but at the same moment I came, hard. A combination of hurt and arousal electrified every nerve ending. When he finished, I felt spent—more so than ever before. I lay panting and out of breath as he held me and stroked my hair.

"Are you all right?" he whispered softly.

"Oh my Goddess," I said. "Let's do that *again*."

And so we did, only with variations on the theme, until I finally remembered we were supposed to be doing protective magic. By that time, I was too physically exhausted to summon anything more than a loose circle around us. Sebastian's arms encircled me, however, and felt strong and safe, and so I snuggled closely in his embrace.

I woke up to pounding. At first I thought I was experi-encing some kind of wicked morning-after sex headache, until I realized the hammering was coming from my living room. The light that came in the window was muted, as though it were early evening.

The floorboard creaked. It sounded like someone wandering around. "Looters," I whispered to Sebastian, who had shot upright a second after I had.

Quickly, I grabbed clothes from my dresser. Underwear and socks, cutoff jeans, and a T-shirt that asked, "Got Magick?"

Sebastian raided his side of the closet for a fresh pair of jeans and a button-down. He left it undone as we snuck out into the living room to see who the intruder was.

We spotted him peering at the hole in the living room. He pulled at some of the loose boards experimentally. "Stop that," I shouted, thinking of the hex magic that still clung to the damage.

The intruder jumped and spun, holding the crowbar and flashlight in his hands like a weapon. In the twilight, he squinted at me. "Garnet, is that you?"

The voice sounded familiar, though for a moment I couldn't quite place it. Could it be my landlord? "Randy?"

Randy was in his sixties and had a full head of hair. Athletic and trim, he had intense green eyes and a handlebar mustache. With his sensible shoes and fashionable suit coat, Randy looked like a cross between an aging biker and gay guy. I always figured he might be both of those, in fact.

"Are you still living here?" he asked, sounding horrified. "And who's this? Is this someone I should add to your lease?"

I introduced Sebastian as my fiancé. They did the manly shaking of hands.

"Congratulations," Randy said. "I hope you two will be happy here after the remodeling."

I looked at Sebastian. Then, I took his hand in mine. "Actually, I'm moving in with Sebastian."

"We'll probably look for our own place," Sebastian said to me. Although his words were a statement, his eyebrows raised in question.

"Sure," I agreed, while giving Sebastian's hand that extra squeeze to tell him I'd come to a decision. "There's no hurry. It's very comfortable at the farm."

We walked over to Jensen's where Sebastian picked up his car. Our fingers entwined as we walked. The evening air was cool and smelled faintly of fish where it blew in across the lake. Nighthawks flashed through the air, gobbling mosquitoes as they flew. The car was parked in the alley behind the shop.

"So," I said, as I got into the passenger side. "There really was a Mustang?"

"Yeah," he said. "But I never even got in the door. Someone shot me with an arrow in the alley." He touched his chest as if still feeling phantom pain. "Once transfixed, I couldn't move. They—it was a man and a woman—hauled me into a Jeep and drove off to the cemetery. The grave was already dug. I think I heard the funeral before I drifted into torpor."

The thought of being buried alive made my skin crawl. At least Sebastian didn't need to breathe. "I saw where you scratched the coffin."

He nodded. "When they removed the arrow and replaced

it with the stake, I had a moment to try to escape. They were too fast. Supernaturally so."

"Yeah, Micah's a God."

"That would explain it," Sebastian said with a raised eyebrow. He started up the car. We drove for a while lost in our separate thoughts.

"I'd thought you were with Blythe. Or a ghoul," I said. "I'm sorry."

"It's okay. Once I fell asleep it wasn't so bad."

Micah was still out there somewhere too. I was surprised he hadn't made another move on me, actually. That thought made me nervous. He and Marge must be planning something.

"Maybe it's time to pay Marge a visit," I said.

I explained Marge's connection to Micah. Sebastian got out his cell and called William to ask him to look up Marge's address on the coven list. Mine had gotten lost with a lot of my loose papers when the tree attacked my house. Sebastian's copy was all the way back at his farm. "You have William on your speed dial?" I mouthed while Sebastian waited for William to find his copy.

Sebastian shrugged. "He's a good guy."

Did I detect a note of "and he's cute too" in Sebastian's voice? Sebastian had once tried to use his glamour on William. I'd had to break it up before Sebastian sunk his teeth into William's neck. "William had better not be in your little black book," I said.

"He's not; he's on speed dial," Sebastian said, his voice full of teasing.

I smacked him in the arm playfully.

"Driving," Sebastian reminded me.

A second later, we were on our way to Marge's house. Streetlights began flickering to life. Tree frogs chirped a chorus of good-nights. Soon we reached Marge's house. As we pulled up, I was surprised to find her sitting on a front porch swing, reading a book.

She had one of those grand, wraparound porches on a stately, though clearly in need of minor repairs, Victorian. Paint peeled and blistered on slats, and here and there shakes had worked loose on the roof. Still, there were pots filled with flowers on the stairs, a neat lawn, and a pleasant garden filled with cheerful black-eyed Susans. My first impression of her place was much the same as it had been of her person—a little dumpy, but extremely comfortable looking.

She looked up when the car door slammed shut. Clasping the book to her chest, Marge's eyes were wild with fear. She stood up as though looking for a place to run.

Sebastian did that creepy vampire thing and was at her side with his hands on her shoulders before I could say, "Stop her."

I blinked.

"Uh, good. Thanks, Sebastian," I said, as I made my way up the buckled wooden stairs.

"I'm sorry," Marge squealed. "It was wrong, I know that now, but . . . but it was like I was under some kind of spell. He's so handsome and so charming, and yeah, okay, I've never had that kind of power and it seemed so tempting . . ." She cowered deeper as I came face to face with her. She put the book up between us like a shield. "Just don't hurt me."

"You tried to kill me. You buried my boyfriend." Now didn't that sound strange out loud?

Marge glanced nervously up at Sebastian's impassive

face. He was doing his stony-faced, badass grimace. Marge shrank in his grip. "It wasn't me," she said.

"Try again," I said, poking a finger at her Hawaiian print. "I know you're working with Micah."

"That's the thing. He made me."

"He made you?" She looked so freaked out, part of me wanted to believe her. But I couldn't quite buy it. "I don't think so," I said, trying to sound like the "bad cop." "I think you panicked when I asked you if you knew where Sebastian was and you used your magic to try to strangle me."

"Okay, yeah, that's true," she admitted.

"And," I continued, "I think *you* suggested to Micah that your cemetery would be the perfect place to entomb a vampire. I'll bet you're hoping to get something out of it. You made some kind of deal with Micah. The question is, what for? Love?"

"Power!" Marge said, suddenly breaking free of Sebastian.

She launched herself forward as if trying to strangle me. I flung my hands up wildly to protect myself. I grabbed hold of something just as Sebastian came up from behind and pinned her arms. Marge jerked back wildly. I heard a snap. In my hands I held the broken remains Marge's dog pendant necklace.

Marge was still screaming heebie-jeebies and I thought she might be beginning to speak the words to a spell, so I reached for Sebastian. "Grab my hands, let's make a circle!"

He let go of Marge, who had been wiggling out of his grasp anyway, and clasped hands with mine. I shut my eyes to visualize a bubble of steel trapping Marge and her power inside. Sebastian's energy merged with mine with a sudden sizzling pop. I cracked an eye open to peek at him, and he flashed me a "yeah, wow!" smile. We hadn't had that kind of connection since the night we mingled our energy together to stop the Vatican witch hunters. My magical eye saw a quicksilver sphere completely encasing Marge. She railed against it like an insane mime.

Sebastian and I stepped back to admire our handiwork. Marge's voice even sounded muted as she continued to hurl insults at us and tell us how no force on earth could stop the ancient power of the Trickster. She pushed her arms out dramatically, like a child pretending to have superpowers, as though she was trying to funnel magic at us.

The bubble didn't even shimmer.

Sebastian rubbed his hands together. "You'd think she'd at least be making a dent. She used serious firepower to rip out of my grasp," he said.

I looked down at the broken necklace in my hand. "I wonder . . ."

But before I could finish my thought, the screen door opened. Max appeared with two glasses of iced tea on a tray. He had a paperback novel tucked under his arm. He stopped short when he saw Sebastian and me. After looking at Marge still doing the pantomime against the invisible bubble, he turned on his heels and went back inside without a word.

"You're not much help!" Marge screamed quietly.

I'd have to agree. I tossed the charm in my hand a few times, waiting for Marge to catch sight of it. When she saw the necklace, she halted her raving. "I don't think you're getting much help from any quarter right now," I pointed out.

Marge's face crumpled. "You mean the necklace was the source of my power? But . . . but Micah said I was his protégée. He said . . ."

"He lied," Sebastian pointed out. "You were tricked."

"That *dog*," Marge hissed.

"What do we do with her?" I asked Sebastian. "We can't keep the circle up forever, not at this strength, anyway. And without the charm, she's not much of a threat."

Sebastian considered for a moment. "Let's go," he said. "The circle will fade within a day. By then, hopefully, we'll have dealt with Micah too."

The things Marge called us as we left scorched my ears.

Once we got back to Sebastian's farm, I buried Micah's charm in the cornfield to negate its energy. After I fed Barney, Sebastian treated Mátyás and me to his famous homemade stuffed peppers. As father and son had a heart-to-heart, I snuck upstairs for a long, hot shower. Exhausted, I fell into Sebastian's bed and slept.

I woke up to the sensation of lips nibbling at my earlobes. "Hmmm," I muttered sleepily, and it changed to an "Oooh!" when Sebastian's hand cupped my breast. I pushed him away reluctantly. "Mátyás is downstairs."

"Actually, he's been out all night. I guess he has a new friend from that coffee shop next to your store."

Oh my God, Izzy's getting lucky! I rolled over and tipped Sebastian's mouth to mine. Well then, I thought, I might as well join her.

* * *

Since there were still a few hours until I had to open up the store, Sebastian and I decided to stop at our favorite breakfast place: Ella's Deli. Ella's Deli is probably most notable for the large carousel out front, but inside is even stranger. It's filled with crazy things. There are toy trains that move overhead, weird animated jugglers, and things that pop out at you when you least expect it. It's a bit like having a kosher-style breakfast at a funhouse.

It was early enough that we had the pick of the place. I chose my favorite table, the one that showed a display of Pez dispensers under the glass top. As we pored over the menu, Sebastian's foot slid up and down my leg. I think he just wanted a physical reminder of my presence.

After the waitress took our order, I asked, "Are you okay? Really?"

"Torpor normally revitalizes me, but I'm not usually staked through the heart."

It was hard to believe that was only yesterday. Blood, sex, and several hours of natural sleep had brought back Sebastian's preternatural "togetherness." I should be so lucky. I had bed head, resistant dirt under my broken fingernails, and blisters on my palms. My throat was still raw from the attack and the bruises on my knees from my bicycle accident still ached.

I looked up from my menu. Sebastian looked flushed and happy. He'd taken a bit more blood from me this morning, but I knew he'd have to find a more steady supply soon. "Hey," I asked him. "Why didn't you tell me you were breaking up with your ghouls?"

"Who told you that?" Sebastian sounded affronted. Of

course, that's when the waiter brought us our plates. I had eggs, hash browns, and toast. Sebastian got a pile of pancakes.

Once we'd unrolled our silverware, I said, "Alison. Oh, and can you please explain your choice there? Please tell me she's got AB negative or whatever the heck, because talk about high maintenance."

Sebastian snorted around a mouthful of buckwheat and maple syrup. "I prefer O positive, the universal donor, but I don't pick them for their personalities." He chewed a bit more while staring at his plate. "How on earth did you get Alison's name? She didn't contact you, did she? I mean, I knew she was upset, but I thought all of that vowing to kill you stuff was just hot air."

I smacked my forehead so hard I think I left a welt. "You never thought to tell me someone wanted me dead?"

"Alison is such a nonthreat, darling. Anyway, all the ghouls were pretty upset. I didn't think anything of it."

"Well, guess what? Someone's been trying to kill me."

"Yes, but magically. That can't be a ghoul. Magical practice is expressly forbidden among ghouls."

What was it Mátyás had said? *Someone's a little rule breaker.* I had felt a shock when Alison and I first shook hands. Could she have powerful enough magic? Her aura *had* seemed almost hobbled by something. Now my money was on Alison. But it could be anyone, really. "Did all the ghouls have the same reaction?"

Sebastian poked his fork through the syrup on his plate, then glanced up at me. "Pretty much, yeah."

"How many ghouls do you have?"

"None currently," he said. "But I had seven."

One for every day in the week. "Do you really need that much blood? How are you going to cope if you need some every day? I can't do that. I mean, I *would*, but I'd be anemic in a month."

"I'll cope. Are you saying you think one of my ghouls has been trying to kill you?"

"Well, it's pretty clear that there's another attacker besides Micah and Marge. They were both there when someone tried to scorch your roof."

Sebastian nearly snorted coffee out his nose. "My roof?"

"Didn't I mention that?" I hadn't thought to check for damage either. "I think it's okay. You should probably . . . your house was kind of hit by lightning. Several times."

"But no one was hurt, right?"

"Right," I said.

"Still," he said, taking a big bite of pancake, "I'd sincerely like to kill the responsible party."

I rubbed my neck. The near-fatal attack was likely done by Marge, so actually, other than property damage, whoever this second attacker was, s/he wasn't bloodthirsty. Or, maybe s/he just had terrible aim. "It's possible the damage has all been accidental. Maybe more proof that this is someone who's a rank amateur when it comes to magic."

"Hmmm," he grumbled. "Then maybe I'm just hungry."

Even though I suggested Sebastian should go home and check on his roof and generally put his affairs in order, he insisted he come with me to the store. "I don't want you out of my sight until we figure out who's after you."

"Fine," I said, turning my key in the lock. "But stay out of the way. No distracting me while I work."

Sebastian gave me a wicked grin. "No promises."

In fact, it turned out the storeroom was an excellent place for a quickie. But despite that, we managed to open right on time. Fresh cup of coffee in hand, I stood at the ready behind the counter.

Not a soul came in all morning.

The midafternoon shift was just as dead. I sent William to nap in the back, blushing at the thought of what I'd been doing back there. But when I checked in on him, I found William with his feet propped up on some boxes and his head nestled against a pile of yoga mats. I sat up front with my head in my hands. Sebastian curled up in the "book nook" reading something about politics and witchcraft. His eyelids drooped, and I thought I heard soft huffs of snores. Watching the door with half-closed eyes, I struggled to keep conscious.

The sound of the fire alarm jolted me upright. I smelled smoke, and my eyes burned. Instinctively, I grabbed the fire extinguisher from behind the counter. I struggled with the pin, but managed to get it out. Then, I rushed through the aisles trying to locate the flames. A smarter woman would have gone out the door to safety, but my only thought was that if the sprinkler system kicked in, like it was supposed to any minute, all the books would be completely ruined and I'd be out of business before I even started.

Sebastian was right on my heels.

In the witchcraft section, I found that a circle in the middle of the wood floor was on fire. The flames seemed concentrated in the center of the aisle, and somehow, they had not reached any of the much more flammable books yet. I let loose a stream of white goop just like the fire marshal taught me during the safety training seminar. Splatters of gunk flew everywhere, not only covering the fire but also splashing the bottom row of books. Still, I told myself, it had to be better than an entirely soaked store, although I wondered if my concerns were moot given the stench of smoke in the air.

William ran past us in the next aisle with a wet rag over his mouth. I heard the bells over the door chime as he threw the door open and escaped onto the street. Two seconds later, I heard the door bang again. "Garnet, are you in there? Sebastian?"

"I'm okay! The fire is out," I yelled over my shoulder. The alarms had stopped their clamor, but I could hear the sounds of sirens approaching. I was just about to join William outside when I felt something, like a hand, on my shoulder. I turned, expecting to see someone standing there. Instead, I saw a slither of black smoke. As tall as I was, it hung there in the air, not dissipating, just undulating slowly, like a snake.

"Sebastian," I said, "do you see that?"

Then, it attacked.

The smoke snake dived toward my stomach, and I felt its teeth tear at my flesh.

When I doubled over, I felt Sebastian's arm around me. The instant our bodies touched the silver cord between us sparked.

As if in response, the smoke creature reared up, as though disgusted or alarmed. It hissed. Although, really the sound was more of an insect's dry rattle, reminding me of the magical bugs that I'd seen crawling in the ruins of my apartment. "Alison?"

Behind me, I felt Sebastian go taut with anger. "It is her?" he snarled. "Damn it, Alison. Is that you?"

As if sensing Sebastian's rage, the smoke creature fled, disappearing through a vent in the ceiling. With magical sight, I looked for traces of a signature power. There were bits of energy scattered about, swirling aimlessly like confetti.

I didn't know for certain that it was Alison, but it certainly was the same power that attacked my house. I didn't have much of a chance to ponder its significance because the next thing I knew, a bevy of firefighters came bursting through the front door. Just as suddenly, I found myself outside, breathing into an oxygen mask. Sebastian stood guard over me. Everyone wanted to know what had happened. How could I tell them the truth? It was a magical attack, Officer, honest. I couldn't even offer an explanation that sounded remotely plausible. So, I tried to answer their questions as honestly as I could. "It just looked like the floor was on fire," I said.

"The floor," the firefighter repeated skeptically. He was an impressively large black man, who looked striking in the bright, fluorescent yellow of the uniform. "When there was all that paper everywhere?"

His deep, disapproving frown made me suggest another option. "Maybe there was some spilled wax there or something?"

"How did it start?"

I shook my head mutely. "I don't know. One minute I was sitting there"—albeit half asleep—"and the next, the alarms were going off."

"Did you see anyone come in?"

I couldn't lie to that formidable stare. "I had a late night last night," I said. "I can't honestly be sure." Of course, given the long-distance magical attacks that had happened before, I highly doubted that the culprit needed to be anywhere nearby to start that fire.

"Are you hungover?"

"What kind of question is that?" Sebastian snapped.

I felt like I was being quizzed by my father, only *my* father was never so stern, and I could probably tell my hippie dad about the magic. "No," I said. "Just tired. I didn't get any sleep." And, to be fair, it'd been several nights of little or no rest and then, ehm, a whole lot of physical activity. I blushed again. "I might have dozed."

Even though I gave him a weak, friendly smile, I got a sense that the firefighter wasn't terribly impressed with what he saw. "You're lucky. It's a good thing you had that fire extinguisher close at hand." Then he turned to matters of business and I was kept busy filling out forms for insurance claims.

So, it was two hours later that Sebastian, William, and I finally got around to cleaning up the mess. The entire bottom shelf of books was going to have to be thrown out, and when I wiped up the floor, I discovered the attacker had permanently scorched the hardwood.

Sure, just when I was going to buy the place.

I scrubbed angrily at it for several minutes while tears rolled off my face. I'd had enough. This person had gone after my place, Sebastian's house, and now my store. It was time to take the fight to her.

12.

Eris

KEYWORDS:

Strife and Discord

I did something I never do; I closed the store early. It felt so wrong to flip that sign over, but the place smelled of smoke. I might even have to keep it closed a few days while it aired out.

We all stood out on the sidewalk under the awning. I stared angrily at the darkened interior.

"Do you really think it was Alison?" Sebastian asked.

"Alison? Totally," William said, from where he sat on a bench tossing the remains of his whole wheat and tuna sandwich to the pigeons. "She has spent some serious time trashing both of you on LJ."

"What has she said?" I asked. At the same time, Sebastian asked, "What's LJ?"

"It's an Internet community," William told Sebastian. "And, as for what she said, it's totally not worth repeating.

It's just all a big rant about how Garnet is a psychic vampire who is enslaving you, Sebastian."

"See," I said to Sebastian. "It's got to be her."

"Just because she hates you doesn't mean she's broken the code and started using magic. It could just be coincidence."

"Except the part where she's calling for revolution," William noted.

We both looked at him. He'd gotten the attention of an entire flock of pigeons, who were bobbing and pecking on the ground at his feet, despite the fact that he'd run out of bread crumbs minutes ago. They all scattered with coos and a rush of wings when a bicyclist came past.

"She wrote this whole screed," William said, "about how the vampire masters are keeping true magic from the suppliers. She had this whole pseudo-historical argument that the first ghouls were Witches and the whole concept of Witches inviting the devil into their coven was really about how they used to be ghoul harems for vampires."

I was deeply offended by the idea. "Are you serious?"

"Oh, believe me, she got flamed for that," William noted.

Sebastian was silent. He was the only one of us that was old enough to truly dispute Alison's claim. I gave him an elbow. "That's not true, is it, Sebastian?"

"No, of course not," he said. "Ghouls were most often slaves or indentured servants."

The social, economic, and political ramifications of that made my head hurt.

Sebastian must have notice my look because he shrugged guiltily. "It was a different time."

"I think it's time to pay a visit to Alison," I said.

"You're right," Sebastian said.

After dropping William off at his apartment, we drove for several blocks before I realized we weren't headed anywhere I recognized. Sebastian's car was an antique and didn't have air-conditioning. My window was cranked all the way down. Sunlight glinted painfully off passing cars.

Sebastian's phone rested in his cup holder. Grabbing it suddenly, he began to dial. "Alison," he said into the receiver. His tone was gruff and curt. "It's me. We need to meet. Now." There was a pause then, with a brief sideways glance at me. "Yes, in the usual place."

He snapped the phone shut. We turned onto the Beltway. Sebastian frowned forbiddingly at the morning rush-hour traffic. A million and one questions raced through my head, but I leaned my arm out the window and let the wind buffet my skin.

We pulled off onto a highly industrial boulevard. Modern glass-and-steel office buildings stood a short distance from the road. A strip of perfectly maintained green grass led to sandstone gravel and scrub bushes. Sebastian pulled into a reserved space in the parking lot and turned off the engine.

After a few moments of dark silence, Sebastian said, "I don't like ghouls knowing where I live."

I glanced at the office building. "So you have an office?"

"Not exactly," he said. "I don't want other people knowing where to find me either."

Now I was officially confused.

"I own a business real estate company," he explained, un-buckling to turn to face me on the bench seat. Our knees touched, but our eyes met only sparingly. Sebastian spoke evenly, but he was clearly uncomfortable explaining all this to me. "We lease space to companies all over the metro area. All sorts of businesses come and go, so there's always empty office space—though rarely the same ones for very long."

I glanced again at the building with its straight lines and rows of bluish reflective windows. "You meet in empty offices? Isn't that kind of . . . impersonal?"

Sebastian cracked a slight smile—the first since we started discussing this subject. "That's kind of the point, Garnet."

I couldn't even begin to picture Sebastian's rendezvous, so I just gaped at him mutely.

His eyes slid away again. "I try to keep things as busi-nesslike as possible. Even so, it's not easy."

No, I thought, my hand rubbing the sore spot on my shoulder, you have to put your mouth on them. It's personal.

Sebastian clicked open his door. "Let's go. We don't want to be sitting here when she comes."

"Yeah," I said, following him out. "What is our plan, exactly?"

"Kill her and bury the body where no one will find it," Sebastian said grimly.

I glanced at his face to make sure he was kidding. The deep frown scared me. "You're not serious."

"How many times has she tried to kill you?"

"Three, but that's assuming they all were her. We don't know for sure it's Alison, do we? What if it's not?" I'd stopped moving.

Seeing the cornered expression on my face, Sebastian

took my hand. The heat carried the smell of chemical fertilizer from the grass. "Then we leave in peace. But, if it's her that's behind these attacks, I need you because she's clearly got some kind of astronomically powerful magic. Lilith needs to hold that at bay."

Sebastian glanced over my shoulder at the parking lot. "Let's discuss this inside. Alison can't know you're here. It would destroy any element of surprise we might have."

Numbly, I followed Sebastian through large glass doors. A security guard glanced up at Sebastian briefly, eyes widening momentarily in recognition, and then she feigned a sudden overwhelming interest in a pile of papers on her desk. She was still rearranging them frantically as we stood in front of a burnished chrome elevator. Sebastian stabbed the up arrow. A man in a suit and tie joined us. After checking his expensive watch impatiently, the suit leaned over to press the button himself, as if Sebastian's move hadn't been sufficient. It seemed like an eternity until the soft chime of the elevator greeted us. The three of us got on. Sebastian pushed the button for the tenth floor; suit for the sixth. In typical midwestern fashion, no one said a word; we just stared pointedly at the red digital display that counted the floors for us. Suit snuck a couple of curious glances at me. I'd opted for comfort again today, so I wore a bloodred halter top, a black mini, and combat boots. My hair was still mussed from the fire, and I hadn't really had time to freshen my makeup. Goddess only knew what the guy thought of me, but his step was rather quick when the bell chimed and the doors swooshed open on his floor.

Sebastian chuckled. "I wonder what he'd think if he knew I owned the whole building and twelve more like it."

I smiled and squeezed his hand. "We can't kill her. Not really, you know," I said.

"I know," Sebastian said. "There's no practical way to get a body out of here undetected. Not during daylight, anyway."

I'd been hoping to convince him of the immorality of the idea, but if pragmatism worked . . . I shrugged. "What do you want to do?"

"We're still going to have to neutralize her power somehow."

"I've been considering that," I said, as the elevator let us know that we'd reached our destination. We stepped out into a darkened hallway. There was a strong smell of new carpet and fresh paint.

Sebastian strode confidently through the darkness. I stumbled hesitantly, gripping his hand tighter. He stopped and flicked a row of switches. Muted fluorescent squares shone across the ceiling.

"So, what have you been thinking?" he asked. We stopped in front of a wooden door with a frosted glass window. Pulling a card from his wallet, he swiped it through a key reader, like the kind you see in hotels. A thin, green rectangle lit up with a sharp series of beeps. He pushed the door open. Despite sunlight streaming in from large windows, I tripped on the plastic drop cloth on the floor.

When my eyes adjusted, I noticed cans of paint and ladders strewn about, though the walls looked all one color. Once again I tried to picture the scene: Sebastian waiting here for Alison—maybe leaning there, against the shallow windowsill. Then what? Did they speak? Exchange pleasantries about the weather? Did he ask her to get comfortable, maybe sit on the floor, or did he just throw her up against the wall and bite?

"Your plan, Garnet?" Sebastian asked, wedging himself into the corner of the windowsill, much as I'd imagined, looking a bit like a spider in a web.

"Uh, it's not so much a plan as an idea," I admitted, shaking my head to try to stay focused. "Ever since the attack on my apartment, I've been trying to figure out how anyone could have so much magic at their disposal. I keep coming up with one answer: a Goddess. I think Alison has a Goddess the same way I have Lilith. Except I think maybe she has this Goddess more like how Coyote has Micah—by force, by bondage."

"So, you want to try to free this Goddess?"

Perching on the edge of a cloth-covered desk, I faced him. "It's risky. Maybe that's not how Alison operates at all. Maybe she's just a really powerful Witch."

"All of a sudden? I doubt it," Sebastian said. "Your theory makes sense. But if you can't break the chains, can you forge some?"

"I don't know. Honestly, I've never tried to do either." Plus, there was the added consideration: would Lilith willingly help me enslave another Goddess?

Sebastian chewed his lip. Then he perked up, as though he heard something I hadn't. "Well, it's what we've got. Worst-case scenario, we go back to my plan. She's coming down the hall now."

With a glance, Sebastian indicated I should hide behind the desk. I scooted onto the floor and ducked under the sheet.

The plastic underneath crinkled noisily, and I cringed. Holding my breath, I heard the latch of door click open.

I strained to hear what was going on. I heard footsteps rustle on the drop cloths and then what seemed to be the weight of someone sitting on the desk I was under. No one said a word. Then, I heard a sudden intake of breath, a gasp.

Sebastian was biting Alison. Right over my head.

I'd expected angry words of confrontation or accusation—some kind of cue for when I was supposed to leap out and say, "The jig is up!" or something else equally dramatic. Instead, Sebastian was just going about his usual thing. Maybe he planned to drain her to weakness and then question her? Or perhaps I was supposed to strike now, while she was distracted?

We should've had a clearer plan.

I decided that I'd better get into magical mode regardless. If he needed me now or later, I didn't want to be caught more unprepared than I already was. Reaching down, I slowly woke Lilith from her slumber. She rose like thunder. Hot spikes of pleasure shot through my veins. My fingers itched and tingled, as though my nerves were awakening after a long sleep.

Above me, Alison's gasps became rasps of ragged breath. She grunted and moaned to the envy of any porn star. My own jealousy spiked, but I had to hold it in check. Lilith could subsume me and kill them both in a rage.

Opening my magical eye, I scanned the office space for a Goddess or other hidden power. Sebastian was a void, so dead and not-there to almost be a presence in its own right, the way a black hole is visible in comparison to the matter around it. Alison pulsed red, like blood, hot and aroused. On the surface, she seemed like a normal human; not even the glimmer of witchcraft showed in her aura.

Then I saw it—a flash, like the sparkle of a diamond's facet. It was buried deep inside her heart chakra. It looked unnatural, as though it were a piece of shrapnel trying to work its way through flesh and bone. With magical fingers I began to pry at it, slowly teasing it toward the surface . . .

The desk moved as the weight above me shifted suddenly. "You bastard," I heard Alison shout. "Where is she?"

This was the moment I'd been waiting for to reveal myself as the cavalry charging over the hill, except I was on my knees under a desk. There was no graceful way to extricate myself. If I were Wonder Woman, I could lift the desk up over my head and send it crashing across the room. As it was, I scuffled out and awkwardly sprawled on my butt. Plastic ripped and the heel of my boot dragged the sheet that had covered the desk onto the floor with me. Even so, I pulled myself upright as quickly as I could with fists raised.

And no one even noticed me.

Alison had her hands around Sebastian's throat and was squeezing with all her might. She apparently had *not* gotten the memo that vampires don't need to breathe. Still, it looked like whatever she was doing pained Sebastian, so I figured I should get on with the big rescue.

I suspected Sebastian would be able to subdue her—she was half his size and thin as a rail to boot—as long as nothing else was going on in the magical realm. So, I opened my magical eyes completely.

And looked into the face of Hel.

Yes, Hel, the Norse Goddess of the Underworld. I recognized Her because half of Her face was a rotting corpse, and the other was, well, blue—okay, actually kind of navy, really, or possibly even indigo. I suppose I should have been more mesmerized by the pale half, what with strings of shredded flesh hanging from milk-white bones, and maggots dripping from open sores, but I'd never seen anyone with truly blue skin before. The skin of Her full, sensual lips was a slightly darker shade of blue, and Her eyelashes were the color of lapis lazuli. I thought I could detect a deep navy tint in the waves of black hair that fell past rounded shoulders in thick braids.

Plus, She looked noticeably bored. When the Goddess noticed me gaping at Her, She gave a little roll of Her eyes as if to say, "Can you believe I'm stuck doing this lame job?" Of course, I might have felt more at ease if one of Her corneas wasn't bugging out of an open socket.

I also noticed the slight glint of sliver at Hel's wrists—a symbolic chain that held the Goddess to Alison?

"Do you want to be free?" I asked Hel, using mine and Lilith's voice.

Hel's lips parted to reveal a truly ghastly smile, filled with rotten and missing teeth. "Oh yes," she hissed.

I let Lilith rise. There was an explosion that sounded like a gunshot, and then my worldview shifted.

I was no longer in the office building, but somewhere else. Everything was a grainy white and there was no discernible horizon line. "I'm calling you out, Sister," I heard a voice that was mine, but not-mine say.

Hel stepped out from the grayness. Her blue-black hair flowed luxuriantly in a nonexistent wind and maggots crawled visibly in a hole in her cheek. I only hoped Lilith looked this frightening. Hel bowed her head slightly, in the international "let's do this thing" gesture.

I felt myself lunge forward, a fist raised to strike. Hel

countered. An unstoppable force met an unmovable object. I could feel a shockwave that should have shattered worlds, but neither Goddess seemed affected.

Then they laughed.

"Thank you," said Hel, as she began to fade into the grayness that surrounded us. Through Lilith, I understood that the fight had been for show. The tremor caused by their one-punch battle had shaken Hel loose from her bondage.

Grayness turned to black.

I woke up to Sebastian standing over me. "Well," he said, "that was a little like using a nuclear bomb to swat a fly."

The room actually smelled a little scorched. I rubbed my eyes and looked around. Alison lay on the floor, her eyes shut. Plastic had melted around her in the shape of a Nordic rune. "Is she dead?"

"No," he said. "But probably stunned. I mean, seriously, Garnet, did you have to let Lilith out? Do you even know what that's like?"

I had no idea, actually. I went away and Lilith came. It was our arrangement. "But, but," I stammered stupidly. "She had Hel."

"Hell?" Sebastian shook his head, looking down at Alison's crumpled form. "Yeah, that's what you gave her all right."

"No, I mean the Norse Goddess Hel. She had her in bondage." I frowned. "How are we going to keep her from doing it again?"

Sebastian chuckled darkly. "Lilith took care of that, I think."

"She did?"

He nodded. "Alison's magical connections are fried. I'm not sure what she did, exactly, but if I had to guess Hel and Lilith ganged up on Alison and gave her a kind of magical feedback loop. Wasted the 'circuit' as it were."

Ouch. Now I understood what Sebastian meant by going nuclear when a flyswatter might have been better. "What are you going to do about her? I mean, is she still going to be your ghoul? Anyone's ghoul?"

"She's not mine anymore," Sebastian said with a slight lift of his shoulders. "What she does with herself now is none of my concern."

Cold. Well, it wasn't like they were lovers, or even friends from the sounds of things. They didn't talk at all before he bit her. He really did just use them for their blood.

Sebastian noticed my expression and said, "Too harsh?" He shook his head. "There really is no pleasing you in this matter, is there?"

"What do you mean?"

"You're looking at all this"—he raised his arms to indicate the empty office space—"and you're thinking that I'm too impersonal, too severe. Yet, if Alison and I were friends you wouldn't believe we weren't lovers. If we were lovers, you'd never trust that I loved you best."

"You're probably right," I said. Sitting back down on the now-exposed desktop, I sighed. "But I do trust you more than you think, Sebastian. I have Alison to thank for that, actually."

We both looked at Alison, who rolled onto her side with a groan. "Really?" he asked. "How's that?"

"I found out from her you that were cutting off ties with all of them in preparation for the wedding." I caught his glance and held it. "That's sweet, Sebastian, but fool-ish. I can't be your only supply of blood. Your need would kill me."

"I know. But . . . but I thought that we could start fresh after the wedding. You could, I don't know, take part in the selection of the ghouls? Help me make the rules? Whatever will help you feel more secure."

I wasn't sure I wanted that much information about or control over Sebastian's ghouls, but it was nice of him to offer. "We can talk about that later," I said. "What are we going to do with her?"

Sebastian grimaced. "She's out. I think other than a seri-ous case of magical posttraumatic stress, she's probably fine. We could leave her."

Normally I would have disagreed, but Alison really did look like she was snoozing quite peacefully. "You're sure she's okay?"

Very carefully, Sebastian knelt down beside Alison and checked her pulse and her breathing. "She didn't concuss. Her eyes just rolled up into her head and she fell over."

"Still, I'd feel better if we called an ambulance for her. What if all that scorchy smell is, like, her brain matter?"

"It's plastic, and only if you want to spend time in jail."

"Why would we go to jail? I didn't even assault her," I said.

Sebastian pointed to his teeth. "I did."

Ah, good point, and what a media circus that would be. "What are we going to do with her?"

He pulled out his phone. "I have an idea. I hate to do this, but the suppliers have their own system for dealing with these sorts of things. I'll make some calls."

Sebastian called what sounded like some kind of bureaucratic council in charge of ghouls, which, apparently, promised to take care of Alison.

"So what just happened?" I asked.

"Censure," he said.

I looked over at Alison. She looked almost peaceful, except for the drool pooling on the plastic. "What's censure?"

"She'll be bound magically so she can't practice witchcraft again and shunned by the community."

Could be worse, I thought. "Can we go home?" I asked, trying to keep the whine out of my voice. "I just want to sleep, and . . . sleep in."

He smiled. "You're insatiable. Let's go."

I felt kind of relieved, like my worries were over, when a coyote stepped out into the middle of the highway. The brakes screeched and Sebastian yanked at the steering wheel. Being a vampire with preternatural strength and hyped-up reaction speed is normally an advantage bar none. But when traveling at sixty miles an hour, suddenly turning your wheels at a ninety-degree angle is not, shall we say, a factory-recommended move.

The car flipped.

Time compressed, and it seemed like I had hours to reflect on what might have caused us to become airborne. I also watched with horrified fascination as the ground rose up to meet us. I had two instincts that I acted on without conscious thought.

One, cover my face.

Two, call up Lilith.

My guts dropped out as we hit the ground and began to bounce. Metal rent. Glass burst with a shattering pop. All around me the car exploded into pieces. But other than the nauseating sensation of being on a badly managed roller-coaster ride, I felt nothing. I cracked open my magical eye to see Sebastian and me enveloped in a dark static cloud—a kind of Dark Goddess airbag.

When the car finally stopped, we sat in the demolished frame, which was still miraculously completely intact. That was one thing about old, solid cars, they hung together well. However, we wouldn't even have had seat belts if Sebastian hadn't installed them himself.

Meanwhile the steering wheel was crushed beneath Sebastian's knuckle-white grip. His eyes were squeezed shut. I had curled into a fetal ball around my seat belt, from which I slowly started to unwind. The car landed in the grassy median between the two sections of highway. Traffic around us skidded to a halt, but no one else seemed to have gotten in an accident.

"Sebastian?" I said.

The stench of burned rubber and overheated engine filled my nostrils. Slowly, he cracked open an eye. He stared grief-stricken at the remains of the car all around us, then looked at me. "Are you okay?"

I started to say yes when I noticed a sudden and profound emptiness deep in my belly. I unbuckled my seat belt and scrambled out of the car.

"Where are you going?" Sebastian shouted.

"Micah!" I shouted at the stalled, gawking traffic. My eyes scanned the landscape, frantically searching for any sign of him. "You tricky bastard! Give Her back!"

I struggled up the weed-tangled embankment. Once up the slope, long black skid marks pointed me to the direction we last saw Micah. Sebastian appeared beside me and grabbed my hand as I started to try to cross the highway. "Wait," he said. "Tell me what's going on."

"I can't believe he'd pull a stunt like that," I said, holding back a sob. "I could have been killed. You could have been killed. Any one of these people . . ." With Sebastian in tow, I dashed through the slowly moving vehicles, despite yells of "Are you people crazy?" and "Do you need an ambulance?"

"You'll never catch him on foot," Sebastian said.

I gave him a startled glance. "Are you about to tell me you can fly?"

"No, but I can move a lot faster than you can." He started to break from me, but I squeezed his hand in restraint.

"Don't go alone. He wants us apart. That's why he buried you," I said with sudden clarity. We slid down the ditch together on the other side of the road. Tall, thick stands of ferns and grasses scratched my bare legs. We stumbled over scraggly mounds of yellow-flowered crown vetch.

"We should try to head him off in the astral plane," Sebastian said.

My toe caught on a chunk of sandstone rock, nearly sending me to my knees. A low, barbed-wire fence stood between us and a pasture filled with grazing Holsteins. Near the horizon, I could just make out a black-tipped tail darting through a stand of willow growing along a shallow creek. My shoulders drooped in defeat. "But I've lost Her, Sebastian. How can I?"

"You are a powerful Witch, Garnet, with or without Lilith. Besides, like you said, we should do it together."

I tried to squeeze myself through the gap in the fence only to come away scratched and frustrated. "Okay," I said, though I really wanted to keep moving. I couldn't see Micah at all, only the sway and ripple of movement through the underbrush.

"Look into my eyes," Sebastian said.

Pulling my gaze away from the retreating form of the coyote, I reluctantly did as he asked. When our eyes met, I was instantly drawn in. Power pulsated in the golden streaks that encircled his pupils. I felt it flow into me, through me, awaking something buried, old, and unused.

"You, my darling, have forgotten that *you* are a Goddess," he said. Then, he kissed me, strong and hard. His urgent touch sent an awakening tremor through my body— sexual, but also something more. I felt a call ring deep into my soul, fanning embers nearly extinguished from neglect.

Suddenly, I remembered.

Raw strength—my own—drew power from the alfalfa-scented air, up from the sunbaked grass, from the tinkling of the nearby creek, from the blazing heat, and from . . . here. Me. The center of it all.

The grass rustled, and a coyote bounded over the barbed wire. Seeing Sebastian and me, it did a very human double take and sat down hard on its haunches. It looked behind it and then back at us. Shaking its ruff, it glanced behind again.

"Neat trick," Micah said, standing beside us without a visible transformation. "But, it won't do you any good. I'm keeping Her this time."

"Against Her will?" I asked, turning from Sebastian to face him. "Are you sure you want to do that?"

Micah's smirk crumpled slightly, but he recovered quickly. "You're just a mortal now," he reminded me. "You're out of your league."

"Maybe," I said. "But stealing fire gets you burned."

"Ha!" he laughed, and a flock of crows that burst from the field echoed his cry as they soared overhead.

Approaching sirens wailed in the distance. All too soon, the real world would intrude. I decided to make my move. Without warning, I leaped at Micah, hitting him squarely in the chest with my head and shoulders. We tumbled backward into the tall grass.

It was the same tactic he'd used on me, after all—catch him off guard and strike while his defenses were down. I wrapped my arms around his chest and squeezed in two places at once, here and in the spiritual realm.

I could feel Micah begin to resist. I didn't have much time before he would overpower me physically and spiritually. Letting my spirit seek out Sebastian's, I held on to the magical bond we'd formed and, with our joint strength, I opened my heart.

With my heart bared open, I made an offer. *Lilith,* I sent, *if you want me as your vessel, I am yours.* In a heartfelt whisper, I added, "If not, I bless you, thank you, and release you. I remain your loyal devotee."

Thing was, as I lay there on top of Micah, smelling the rich scent of grass and baking earth, I meant it. Sebastian had reminded me that I didn't need Lilith to be strong. I had my own magic. And, regardless of what happened at this moment, I would nurture it again, as I had in the days before Lilith. I felt a strange peace settle over me.

Coyote howled.

That's when I knew She would return. Seconds later, I felt it, the electricity searing through my veins. Normally, when Lilith entered me, it hurt. This time, though, sparks of purplish light danced along my skin, I felt something completely different. Something shifted across my chest, painful, but not unbearably so. Where normally Lilith burned me, heat slowly began to spread along my limbs, almost like warm water or a massage.

Just then, Micah rolled us over. My head bounced on the grass and my back slammed into the ground with a painful slap. Micah grabbed my shoulders and started to shake me. Sebastian throttled him around the throat. I started kicking.

But, like it or not, Micah was a God.

Thrashing against him in the physical world wasn't doing much damage. In the other realm, I could feel his weight pressing against me, like a vise, squeezing the life from me. I gasped for air, though it wasn't breath that failed me.

Floundering, I clutched for any kind of magical purchase. Lilith hadn't completely reentered me, and I sensed her straddled between this world and that. Sebastian must have sensed Micah and me grappling in more than one way because, suddenly, I felt Sebastian's strength flowing along the old blood-bond connection. I knew then that the three of us—Sebastian, Lilith, and me—could defeat Micah together.

I stopped pushing against Micah. I went completely limp and allowed myself to completely surrender, to be a conduit.

Lilith rose.

But this time, instead of blacking out, I merged with Her. We were Goddess incarnate. Sensing the change, Micah's hold loosened. Fear flickered through his eyes. A wicked grin spread across my face. Time, I thought, to separate the God from the man. We reached up a hand and plunged it into Micah's heart.

He screamed. I could feel the heart of chaos, of Coyote, slither in my grasp. Slowly, I began to draw my hand out. "If you love something, set it free," I murmured.

"No." Micah gasped, his face graying. "You'll kill me."

At first, I/Lilith thought Micah's panic was a clever ploy to invoke our sympathy, causing us to weaken our hold on him. But, the pain in his eyes seemed real. I paused, my fist inches from open air.

"I am Coyote," Micah said. "We're one. He and I merged hundreds of years ago. If you tear him from me, we'll both cease to exist."

Should I buy it? I squeezed my fingers tighter, eliciting a gasp from him. "But I saw you in the ritual," I said. "You were separated there to no ill effect."

"Only for a second," he rasped. "Like you, I've become a hybrid. Man-God."

I released Coyote back into Micah and removed my hand gently. "I believe you. But you leave me with a problem," I said, my hand resting lightly on his chest. "How can I trust you not to try to steal me again?"

"How about a peace treaty?" Micah said with a gruff laugh.

"Doesn't seem right, somehow," I said with a smile. Bees buzzed on a tuft of nearby clover.

Removing my hand from Micah's chest, I pressed it

against my own heart. Pantomiming turning a key in my fingers, I locked my own heart. "There," I said. "That should do it. Now I'm bound just like you."

"Uh," Sebastian said from where he knelt. "Garnet? Was that smart?"

"*I* think so," I said with a little smirk, and Lilith disappeared quickly inside me like the fall of a curtain at the end of a show. "Oh, Goddess, what did I just do?"

"You and Lilith are really one being now," Micah said. "Forever."

Micah let me go, and I struggled into a seated position. He bowed his head. "It's over for me."

"No, it's not," I said, holding out my hand. "I would have given you what you needed, if you had just asked."

"Why would you give anything to me?"

I shrugged. If Lilith and I were really going to live forever now, I might find myself in Micah's very position some day. "I might call in a return favor in a couple hundred years," I said, laughing at how preposterous that sounded.

Micah nodded seriously. "Done." Micah's hand grasped mine. I reached my other out to Sebastian. We formed a circle of three in the grass. "He needs to remember his own inner God," I explained. "He needs an energy boost to stay alive."

A simple, quiet transmission passed between us. I drew a bit from Lilith, but also, as I had before, I used the energy of the earth, air, sun, and water to fill Coyote. He drank it in slowly, as though savoring a fine wine.

We sat there in the grass like that until the emergency vehicles arrived. As the first police officer walked toward us, I let Micah's hand go, confident the magic had worked. He nodded at me in acknowledgment and gratitude. Then, he stood up and walked into a tangled patch of buckthorn. A coyote came out the other side. Sebastian and I spent the next hour filling out accident reports and trying to convince the police that we were serious that we didn't need to go to the hospital.

My hand rested against my belly, but I no longer felt Lilith there. She was everywhere in my body now, like she had stepped into my very skin. While cops and emergency personnel filed around me, I kept returning to what Micah had said—*forever*. How long had Coyote and Micah shared the same body? How long did I have now? And what of me—my sense of self? Coyote seemed to imply that Micah and he shared a merged personality; would I become more like Lilith as time passed?

Finally, they let Sebastian and me go. Staring at the pasture before taking a seat inside the squad car that had offered us a ride home, I wondered if I would ever see Micah again.

When the cop car pulled up to Sebastian's farm, Má-tyás met us at the end of the drive. Wordlessly, he embraced his father. Sebastian returned the hug warmly. "I'm so glad you're okay," Mátyás said once they separated.

"We've been through a lot," Sebastian admitted tiredly. Then, as if it only just now occurred to him, he added, "My car is totaled."

"Not the roadster!" Mátyás gasped.

Sebastian nodded sadly. They lamented the loss of a fine vehicle as they moved up the drive toward the house. I lagged behind, giving them some room to bond.

On the wind, I heard the lonely call of a coyote.

Epilogue

I never thought of sitting in an accountant's office as particularly romantic, but after the seventeenth time Walter asked Sebastian, "Are you *sure* about this?" the more Sebastian's calm, insistent response sounded like, "I do."

"Okay," said Walter with a melodramatic sigh. "Sign here."

Sebastian did.

Then it was my turn. Walter didn't even meet my gaze he was so furious at Sebastian for "merging assets." Larry, however, who sat at a nearby computer terminal, ostensibly doing office work, gave me a broad wink and a big smile. I signed on the dotted line.

"Well," Walter sneered. "That's that, I guess."

Sebastian, who sat next to me in a hard wooden office chair, reached a hand to my chin and gently turned me to face him. He leaned over to kiss me softly, but intentionally, as though sealing a deal—or pronouncing us man and wife.

A tear welled in my eye.

"That's so beautiful," Larry said. Walter grunted something unkind.

"I'm thinking about a December wedding," Sebastian said. "What do you say?"

"Yes," I said. "I do."